9/2015

ALL THIS LIFE

ALL

A NOVEL

THIS

LIFE

JOSHUA MOHR

COUNTERPOINT | BERKELEY, CALIFORNIA

LIBRARY OF CONGRESS CATALOGING-IN-PUBLICATION DATA
Mohr, Joshua.
All this life : a novel / Joshua Mohr.
pages ; cm
ISBN 978-1-59376-603-0 (hardcover : acid-free paper)
1. Internet—Social aspects—Fiction. 2. Interpersonal relations—Fiction.
3. Digital media—Fiction. I. Title.
PS3613.O379A79 2015
813'.6—dc23
2015005117

Interior design by Elyse Strongin, Neuwirth & Associates, Inc.
Cover design by Debbie Berne

Soft Skull Press
An Imprint of COUNTERPOINT
2560 Ninth Street, Suite 318
Berkeley, CA 94710
www.softskull.com

Printed in the United States of America
Distributed by Publishers Group West

10 9 8 7 8 6 5 4 3 2 1

Can you feel my heartbeat?

—NICK CAVE

ALL THIS LIFE

The thing you need to realize about my equation $E=mc^{despaired}$ is that no one has ever thought about psychology and thermodynamics and existentialism as they relate to mathematics before. Not even you, Albert, though I know technically you were a physicist, and I'm saying all this with the utmost respect to you and your work. For without you as my predecessor, I wouldn't have been able to take your research to the next level. I never would have developed existential mathematics, which is really what my century needs. See, you were a product of your time, as we all are. Your $E=mc^2$ brought us to nuclear fusion, which is the greatest and most treacherous advancement of your century. Back then, the world was only concerned with science and science and science. Modernity. Technology. Urbanization. And now my generation is paying the price for all that. You should see us now, aspiring to be computers. Machines are man's best friend. You led us down a lonely road, one you wouldn't have been able to foresee, but trust me, it's bad here. It's burning. We are all about to burn. And the question is: Why are we burning? Why is the earth heating up? Maybe it's all the fossil fuels, the greenhouse gases. Cow farts are killing us. The methane. None of those are my areas of expertise, and I'm not invalidating those things as contributing forces. What I'm saying is those aren't the ONLY factors. There's one gigantic cause that no one talks about, and it's the foundation of my equation, my $E=mc^{despaired}$: Human sadness is what's heating up the earth. We are so somber, Albert, our lives are squared by despair and thus we all emit such a sad heat that our planet will torch unless we get it under control. Everything adds up. Pretty soon bodies will turn to ash and scribble the sky and mix with other people's ashes and mix with other *people's and still mix with others, but what if there is a solution, a way to put off our doomsday, a way to repair our sadness? Wouldn't that be a lovely fate? So I thought of you, thought that if you were to come back, we could work together. As equals. As colleagues. As heroes. I am conjuring you, Albert. This communication proves our minds are connected. I've been training for this. I am focused on bringing you back, sending this signal out to find you. I've liberated all my neurotransmitters from any societal incarcerations, and I can safely say that I am the only one on the planet capable of seeing this thing through. We need you more than ever. We need your expertise. Otherwise, I fear the worst. I am dedicated to our cause and need only a signal from you, a sign that will alert me to our work. I am blessed with fortitude. Lots of people have convictions yet most lack the resilience to face consequences. I will risk everything, Albert. I will bleed to keep this world uncremated.*

PART 1

INSIDE
THE
SEARCH
ENGINE

1.

It's another brittle day, all of them inching over the Golden Gate Bridge into San Francisco, their typical trek to cluttered desks, schlepping with their hangovers, their NPR, carpools and podcasts, prescription pills and nicotine patches, their high-def depressions, Lasik so they can see all their designer disaffections, lipstick smeared on bleached teeth, bags under their eyes or Botox time machines, bald spots or slick dye jobs, bellies wedged in pants or carved Pilates bodies, their urges to call in sick, their woulda coulda shouldas.

More rationalizations and regrets running through the air than cell signals.

No one wants to get to work. Even those claiming to enjoy their jobs still bristle at the idea of oozing into ergonomic chairs, reviving computer screens, feeling the day's flickering chaos erupt on their faces.

A couple extra hours of sleep. A half-day. Telecommuting. Something other than the full slog. The particulars of their jobs don't even matter because all the variables lead to one delicate plea: Please give us a day off. A day to ourselves. A day to feel free. To be alive.

But this is a morning without such clemency and so there they sit, in their Hybrids and leased sports cars and family sedans, eeking a couple toes on the accelerator before hitting the brake again.

Bumper to bumper.

A Bluetooth chain gang.

The weather is perfect. No wind. No fog. Well, there is fog hanging out over the Pacific, but it hasn't pushed in yet. The sun's out, shining off the bridge's bright orange paint.

The posted speed limit is 45, which is a brutal joke at this time of day.

It should say *4* or *5*.

Someone needs to fix that conjunction-less sign.

Not only does the speed limit tease, so does the traffic zooming out of San Francisco, motoring next to them, by them, zipping along right at the 45-miles-per-hour clip. That drew some sighs from our commuters, pining for U-turns and quick getaways and sordid adventures.

The bridge is one level, laid out in such a way that the traffic lanes are flanked by walkways teeming with tourists snapping selfies, joggers in fluorescent kicks, bicyclists in outfits that look like sausage casings. Buses dump out their international passengers so they can run out to the middle of the bridge, *ooh*ing and *aah*ing at Alcatraz and Angel Island, the 360° view, the ocean gleaming on one side, the Marin headlands looking lush from the north, San Francisco sparkling, immaculate, vibrant.

It's always hectic here on the bridge, always full, always rushing, even in traffic. Because these days you don't just work at work. Technology, that noose. Everyone is reachable *all the time*. Including traffic jams. Devices bring emails and conference calls and video chats in an uninterruptable river.

A peek in the window of some cars shows mouths screaming into headsets, forlorn expressions on faces as to-do lists multiply, workdays grow into evenings into all-nighters, weeks into weekends. Life its own traffic jam.

A white Prius houses a father and his fourteen-year-old son. They keep away from each other in the morning. Or Jake keeps away from his dad, his surly chauffeur. Jake knows the sad hierarchy: A Google search of his father's favorite things would not return the boy as a page one result. Jake has never understood what makes him so moody as they drive in together, and yet there's really no way his father could explain it. No way for the father to unpack adult disappointment. It's impossible for the father to convey that he'd expected his life to amount to more than some middling stake in a PR firm, and it's too late to fix.

How can he tell his only child that commuting is a kind of daily desolation, his mind always flapping to the past even when it's the last thing he wants to remember? Being young: when he released his potential and passions and possibilities up into the air, freeing them like doves, his whole life ahead to watch all his dreams come true. How can he tell his son that becoming an adult is learning to live with your failures, learning to dodge these dying birds as they thump back to earth?

How do you say that to your boy?

You don't. You commute. You make your boss happy. You collect those paychecks and keep your eyes peeled for dead doves.

The father turns the volume up on an AM sports talk show, the next caller saying, "I'd like to discuss how our quarterback is an effin' moron," and the father settles into another unfulfilling distraction.

Jake, never trying to disrupt their frail truce, spends his time filming things out the window with his iPhone. Stealing frames from people's lives. Poaching and posting them online, his pieces of property. Yesterday, he captured a woman flossing her teeth while steering with her elbows, the day before a guy with little scissors trimming his moustache like a bonsai tree.

So far, today's material has been a bunch of stinkers. The highlight has been an old lady fighting with a fast food wrapper, frustrated with how it constricts her breakfast sandwich. Jake's even stooped to trailing some seagulls bouncing along the bridge's railing, and he hates those nature shots, thinks they're for old people, the Discovery Channel backwash his mom's always watching, when she's in town.

Jake likes capturing real human life, snatching seconds away from those who don't suspect an audience. The other day, for example, he captured a guy's catastrophic ponytail waving in a breeze, looking like a windsock; Jake immediately set it to music, Dylan's "Blowin' in the Wind," then uploaded it to YouTube.

309 views so far.

Not bad.

But today's turning around for Jake.

Because right as he's bemoaning all his benign options—the fast food wrapper, the boring gulls pooping and perching on the rail— that's when he sees the band.

They're just coming onto the bridge's walkway on the San Francisco side, by the tollbooths; they're moving toward Jake. Playing their instruments, forming a roaming pack. Jake counts twelve of them, three trumpet players, two saxophonists, two clarinets, two trombones, a snare drum, a bass drum, and a tuba player.

They're all done up in wild outfits, clothed in mismatched prints and patterns and clashing colors.

Are they clowns? he wonders. No, their faces aren't painted. They just have no fashion sense.

He hits record, holding his phone up toward them, zooming in.

The brass band is too far away for Jake to make out their music, but they are all playing. Sort of dancing, shuffling along, moving their instruments back and forth in time with the song. They seem to be all ages, all ethnicities. White, black, and brown. He spots one bald man and two women with gray hair, the rest looking in their thirties or forties. Wait. He spies one girl who doesn't look that much older than Jake. She's tall and skinny, wearing purple striped pants with a paisley shirt, a butterfly collar. She's playing the clarinet.

The most predominant noise comes from two men banging on the drums, one beating out a quick pattern on a snare, the other producing a slow rumble on a bass drum connected to his chest. It's the size of a tractor tire, and his mallets hit either side of this musical wheel, deep thunderous booms that remind Jake of dinosaurs walking in the movies.

There are also certain loud notes exploding from the horns—the trumpets—little staccato bursts, punctuating something, but he can't tell what they're playing, what all the instruments' contributions add up to yet, too far away to hear a melody.

Soon, though.

In anticipation, he says, "Turn down the radio, Dad," kneeing the back of the driver's seat.

The father, engrossed in a discussion of the 49ers pass defense, just grunts.

"There's a band out there," says Jake.

"Not now."

"I need to hear them."

"Later."

At that, the boy loses interest in luring his father into this strange display on the bridge. Jake is a banner ad that the father won't click. He's a pop-up. He's something equally as annoying: He's a son in the backseat of his father's car, talking.

Jake rolls down the back window, stretching his arm out, hoping he'll be able to hear the brass band's music and not the steady chug of traffic. But he can't hear them yet, still about forty feet away. He frames the band as they bop and weave with their instruments, the sun glaring off of the horns, refracting little rainbows.

The band stays huddled together, forming an oval, like a lung turned on its side. They take synchronized steps, marching like soldiers, dressed like hipster gypsies. Jake can't believe his luck finding this, filming this. An emoji of his face would convey an overjoyed anxiety, with the head gritting his teeth with a furrowed brow and flames burning in each eye socket.

Jake's father lurches the car in small chunks every thirty seconds or so, the bridge even more gridlocked than normal. A couple hours ago, somebody ran out of gas, and the morning commute never recovered; he learned this from a traffic update during a commercial break from his sports talk. The empty car sat there for half an hour until Caltrans removed it, traffic trying to spread around the stalled vehicle like water around a rock. But it really screwed things up. His dad actually admires the stuck car, this idea of stopping, of quitting.

Jake fidgets in his seat.

His arm reaches as far as it can out the window, limb extending his iPhone, trying to get as close as he can.

The outline, the shadow, wisps of the brass band's music finally reach him. It's a fast song, something peppy and vivacious. The kind you might hear a marching band play. All major chords with a dance beat.

But it's the way they move that fascinates Jake. Their oval, their lung. As they get closer, he notices that they move like a breathing entity, a subtlety he couldn't make out before. They position themselves right next to one another in the oval and then they move away a few steps, the lung expanding, swelling. Then they come together into a mass again and this continues, in and out, this breathing. The brass band does this and still keeps making forward progress.

"What the hell?" his dad says, finally taking notice.

"What song is that they're playing?"

His dad turns down the sports talk. "Roll up your window."

Jake pulls his arm in, cranks the window up halfway. Knows better than to tussle with his father so early in the morning. But he keeps filming.

The brass band plays its song and moves in its inhaling and exhaling choreography, and one of the trumpet players, a man, breaks free from the formation, moving over to the bridge's orange railing.

Throwing his trumpet over the side.

Climbing the rail.

Folding his hands in prayer.

Leaping toward the ocean.

Jake watches and records, records and watches, and it's not really happening, there's no way this is really happening, so he keeps filming. The brass band stops its forward progress. Jake has to crane his head backward to watch it through the car's back window because his father's ride inches toward the toll plaza.

The brass band staying huddled, keeping its music going.

Then another runs from the pack. The paisley shirt, the butterfly collar, throwing her clarinet and heaving her body over the side.

Then another trumpet player jumps.

Then one of the saxophonists.

Then a trombonist.

"They're jumping, Dad," says Jake.

The father adjusts the rearview and side mirrors to get a look at the scene. He takes in the huddle. Sees one of them break away, lob a trombone over the railing, following it quickly.

The father stops the car, opens his door in the middle of traffic. He is the first person to do this, standing and gawking. He is the empty car; he is out of gas. He holds everyone up as he hunts his head for an interpretation, a way to understand what he's witnessing. He twists all these things he's seeing up into various balloon animals, attempting to form a shape that makes sense.

Two people behind him honk. He doesn't acknowledge their protests, only stares at the remaining members of the brass band. A few other honks come and he points toward the musicians, a gesture meaning *Are you seeing what I'm seeing and why is this happening and what does it mean?*

Other people exit their cars, too, facing the brass band, standing like zombies in the road. The people who had been on the walkway, joggers and bicyclists and tour bus explorers, all stop and give the band a wide berth.

Shouldn't there be a good Samaritan among them?

Shouldn't there be at least one hero on the bridge?

But *should* has no place in a moment like this.

Better reactions don't matter.

There's only what happens, what these people do. And the watching.

Nobody feels a calling brought on by adrenaline, by belief, by programming, by fear, compelling them into action.

The bridge still, except for the band.

Another woman tosses her trumpet over the side and follows.

"Are they dying?" Jake says from the backseat.

"Close your eyes," his dad says.

Several more witnesses hop out of their vehicles. All standing in the middle of the bridge, watching while another band member hoists his tuba, climbs the rail, and springs off backward.

The other clarinet launches like a spear. Its player also, falling headfirst toward the Pacific.

There are only three musicians left—one saxophonist, the snare and bass drum players. They keep performing, though their sound is so thin. Their lung almost empty.

Almost all of the commuters are out of their cars, standing transfixed, some still holding travel mugs or half-eaten bagels, some making phone calls to 911.

The person playing the snare drum lets it fly over the railing. It looks like a hatbox.

A man yells out, "Don't do it."

The drummer doesn't answer, follows shortly behind his instrument.

The saxophone flies off the bridge, spinning like a boomerang, but instead of coming back, it arcs down to the sea. So does its player.

The last one left plays the bass drum, the tractor tire; he smacks it a few more times on both sides, beat slowing and finally stopping. Dropping the mallets on the walkway. Disconnecting the drum from his person. Carrying it over to the railing and letting it tumble from his arms.

"Please, don't," a woman calls to him, a jogger locked in place about fifteen feet away.

"This is a celebration of life," he says.

"Stay alive," a commuter shouts from her stopped vehicle.

"I will be alive even after I do this," he says, climbing the railing, standing on top of it. He has a good sense of balance and stays there, perched on the rounded guardrail for about seven seconds.

Then he folds his hands in prayer, pushes off with his feet, falling toward his band.

Jake gets out of the car and stands next to his father, who's crying. The boy has never seen his dad weep, and it almost makes him start, too, which surprises Jake because he doesn't understand what he'd even be crying about.

"What do we do now, Dad?" he asks.

The father doesn't answer. There are no words to make sense of any of this. He wants to call the whole scene surreal, but does that work? Is this surreal? Standing there on the bridge, it seems to the father that it's exactly the opposite. It's real, painfully real, painfully human. Thinking, *We're the only species capable of doing something like this.* The father wipes his face, imagines another one of his dead dreams landing at his feet.

Some people get back in their vehicles, sitting with their hands on steering wheels, no idea what to do next.

Others climb over the short fence between the road and the walkway to peep over the edge and stare at the ocean. Are they hoping to see the band swimming there? Hoping the members of the brass band have all survived and after retrieving their instruments pick up the song where they left off? Hoping for a happy ending?

"What do we do now, Dad?" Jake says again.

"We go," he says.

"Can I look over the edge, too?"

The sirens of cop cars and ambulances in the distance.

"No."

"I want to see."

"You've seen enough," says the father.

"I want to see over the edge."

"You have," the father says.

He ushers the boy into the car's backseat, trying to sequester his child away from this disaster, but he doesn't know that the suicides exist in the car, too. Jake fires up his phone and watches the clip again.

Traffic isn't moving.

Getting out of there is impossible.

Everything is blocked off until the authorities ascertain what happened.

The father calls his office and tries to explain all this to his assistant, though he's talking to himself mostly, fumbling for a pat interpretation, hoping one might flutter into his mind like a flake of ash.

Jake sits in the backseat. His new emoji would be a head with a can opener spinning around its crown and peeling up the skull and plucking out that brain and whirling it around on an index finger like a basketball.

He keeps reliving the moment, watching his phone as the band slowly travels toward him, serenading the world before leaping off. Once the video ends he starts back at the beginning. Looping. Jake running on this clip like it's a treadmill. Dying to get this to

YouTube, but unable to disconnect his consciousness from it long enough to post.

Start to finish.

Start to finish.

Start.

2.

Already 99° and not even 10 AM. Another pointless scorcher in the Nevada desert. Another day for Sara to gaze out the window of her cinderblock bedroom, in her cinderblock house, in her cinderblock life. Sara looks out the window and wonders how these people found such a vulgar conviction, marching to the middle of the Golden Gate Bridge and killing themselves.

This morning, Sara is like everyone else learning about the brass band. It's all any of the news hubs talk about. She opens CNN's app on her burner and watches clips, experts retching cranky speculations about what triggered this public display of violence; all these know-it-alls trying to construct psychologies that offer context and meaning, making crazy leaps in logic but none of the talking heads call them on it.

She wishes someone had the brazenness to tell the truth, not just about the brass band, their "reasons" for jumping, etc., but the truth about everything: We'll never know. So stop asking. There are no answers.

Things. Just. Happen.

It all makes Sara laugh a bit. Not at the people who jumped. No way. Sara understands that impulse to explore—the what-if seductions of what may or may not be waiting for us after we die. It's normal to flirt with these things, she thinks, but you never act on it. You don't mortgage tomorrow because today is streaked in shit.

She learned too young how unfair the world can be. How you should under no circumstances wonder if life can get any worse, because it always can. There's no such thing as the bottom. Not really. You might not be able to sink any deeper but you can sprawl down there, exist horizontally.

That's what happened to Sara. First, her junior high school boyfriend, Rodney, her perfect Rodney, lost in a ridiculous mishap. They had been inseparable, kindred spirits, who couldn't stop kissing, couldn't stop laughing and stargazing, sleepovers in a tent outside Sara's house, roughing it on the tough desert floor. But one afternoon in the park changed all that, an accident turning Rodney into someone else, barely able to talk. Sara can remember crying to her parents, using the real F-word, FAIR. Saying to them, "It's not fair! It's not fair!" and they consoled their child, cooed platitudes at her and tried to help her heal, to move on, you can still be his friend, they said, he's still alive. Mother and father tried to help her until they couldn't. Until it was they who weren't alive. A car accident. Both gone. Just like that.

Sara was fifteen when they died, three years ago. Fair had nothing to do with it. Fair has nothing to do with anything. Things happen. Period. And you careen from one event to the next.

These are things you know with certainty when your parents die. When they're taken away and you're fifteen and the courts, in all their voluminous, wide wisdom, give your older brother custody, just because he's eighteen years old. Hank, who's never met a steroid he won't shoot and a fight he won't delight in winning, and he's in charge. Are you absolutely sure that's a good idea?

They were sure. Good enough for the courts, so it had to be good enough for Sara.

So she wouldn't have jumped off the Golden Gate today, but she empathizes with the instinct, that itch to wonder whether things might be better; and if that possibility, no matter how remote, offers a kind of sanctuary you can't crawl inside here, Sara says *So be it, jump.*

She keeps scrolling around CNN, clicking links, following paths. This latest article produces a detail that surprises her:

SAN FRANCISCO (AP)—The morning commute turned tragic earlier today when several people jumped off the Golden Gate Bridge. Multiple witnesses confirmed that twelve people playing musical instruments walked to the middle of the bridge and took turns leaping over the railing.

"They threw their instruments over the side and jumped," an eyewitness said.

The Coast Guard responded to the scene and found one survivor in the ocean. She is in critical condition at a local hospital.

"She's one of the lucky ones," a spokesperson said. "Not many people survive that fall."

The woman's identity has not yet been released.

There have been over 1,500 documented suicides from the Golden Gate Bridge since its opening in 1937.

Sara shakes her head, trying to fathom surviving something like that. You think you're going to some place better. You think your days of being trapped are done. You think you'll come to feel inspired and free and pure. Maybe you do, maybe you don't. But you expect to at least *go* on the journey. This poor jumper has to awaken back here, in this life she tried so desperately to abandon.

No beautiful getaway.

Just things happening.

Sara needs a break from all these doomsday proclamations, so she puts her phone down on the bed next to her, peeks out the window at the desert's long shadows, the sun still making its way to high noon to release its rays in full hellish glory. Sara sees all the scrawny leafless trees, the mesquite, the acacia, sticking out of burned earth. For years, she'd stare at these sad, stuck things and it was obvious that Sara would escape this place; she wasn't going to spend her whole life cooking in Traurig. No way. All she had to do was turn eighteen and she was out, but here's the rub: That eighteenth birthday came and went six months ago, so what's she doing here? Why is Sara still planted here?

She can tell herself next week, next month, can tell herself she's saving up money. And those can all have merit. But this can be equally true: She can wake up and be fifty years old, divorced—at least once—with a child—at least one—still waiting tables, still hoping to flee her cinderblock life but doing nothing to dilute that dream into her reality.

But that jumper—she can't shake that jumper—waking up, thinking she's somewhere fantastic, some place erased of all pain. She comes to, enthralled to understand the complexities of this new reality, but there are restraints on her wrists. There's a nurse in the room. There's a doctor. There's a psych eval. There's a prescription. There's a therapist. There's a battery of consequences for her recklessness. There's a new reality, sure, but not the one she yearned for.

Sara keeps chewing on this, masticating away but not making much progress.

Sara having no idea what a luxury it is to chomp on the story from a safe remove, until that distance dissipated.

Until she's the thing being devoured.

Sara suddenly getting all these texts.

The first one is from her friend Kristine and says: *Um . . . hey, slut?*

It's not unheard of for Kristine to call her such names in raunchy camaraderie, so Sara texts back, *Who gave you a UTI this time?*

Did you make a sexy vid with Nat?

Why?

Ask the Internet.

Oh shit.

If there were a customer service center that regulated the whole information superhighway, she would have dialed it immediately. But it's the Wild West. Utter anarchy. No one's really in charge, so long as you're not trying to coerce a kid into bed or buying weapons. No one would help her track down a measly sex tape unless she were famous with mountains of money, lawyers with lockjaw. And without any help hunting the clip down and snatching it away, Sara's helpless. The sex tape rushes and ricochets around, completely out of control.

Their movie is already moving like water, washing over the world. On one site for a few seconds and someone else sharing it, then it's onto another, momentum building between mouse clicks and posts, skywriting Sara's naked body across an online horizon, one that everyone can marvel at simultaneously. No countries. No continents. No time zones. The zeroes and ones of the sex tape coursing through the earth's circulatory system.

The texts keep pouring in:

Sara, what are you doing?

Are you okay, Sara?

Are you crazy, Sara?

What are you thinking, Sara?

What if Hank sees this?

Did you know Nat made this tape of you?

How will you live with this, Sara?

They were asking questions and so was Sara. Why Nat would do this to her, *Why would he hurt me, weren't we falling in love?*

And if love is a bit of an overstatement, didn't these types of tapes find their way online only after a couple breaks up? Some sexual retaliation? As far as Sara knows, they're still dating, or had been until he first sent the clip out into the wild.

Because last time she checked, this isn't how love works—or almost-love. Call her a stickler, but she doesn't think it functions on dupes and deceptions. Its engine won't even turn over with only lies in the tank.

But apparently Nat has his own definition of almost-love, and it includes dubious ingredients like malice, selfishness, abject cruelty. That's the only explanation for why he'd post their sex tape. At least he could have asked. And is this his way of breaking up with her?

Sara snatches her cell and asks Nat, *Why?*

She stares at it and stares at it.

Nothing coming back.

This is a savage violation, one that Sara should have seen coming: This is what happens when she starts believing in someone. It all turns out to be so much worse than she ever thought possible. And she's right. What Nat did is digital rape, sharing their sex without permission, making it public consumption.

Sara wishes she could claim she had no idea about it. A hidden camera, maybe, the tape made without her knowledge, but those would be hollow claims. She was into it. They were into it. They'd watch it together and have even more amazing sex and what was the harm in that? They were eighteen, their bodies looked the best they'll ever be and, fine, she'll say it: Making the tape turned her on. Granted, one of the major liquors in this aphrodisiac was consent. It was theirs, they owned it, and they shared it, only with each other.

More texts pour in, some people even traveling back to the twentieth century and calling Sara. The point is that people knew about it. People she knew *knew* about it. The whole town of Traurig, every cinderblocked rectangle of it had access to seeing Sara screw, and word of the sex tape spread like a common cold.

She can't say she wasn't warned. Nat liked to phone flirt from the get-go. He was tall and skinny and pale, and Kristine, one of her friends from work, called him Frankenstein. As in, "Are you sexting with Frankenstein's monster again?"

"I think it's hot," said Sara.

"Are you sending him pics?"

"Only when he sends them first."

"Dirty ones?"

Sara shot her a look like *Duh, what kind of pictures do you think we'd send each other?*

"Sexting with monsters is dangerous," the friend said.

Which at the time seemed funny to Sara. A joke. Some sexual gallows humor—they were young and being controversial and loved every minute of it, consequences seeming too remote to even entertain their fallacies.

The critical problem, at least in terms of chronology, is Sara needs to be at work in half an hour. The job that's already in precarious standing. Her manager, Moses, has said, "I have a three-strike policy and you're on your twelfth. But what can I do? When you're on, you are my best server. It's that other Sara who shows up every once in a while that I don't like."

That other Sara.

So one solution is to call in sick, roll the dice again hoping Moses is of the mind for strike thirteen. That's risky, though. Jobs don't grow on trees. Hell, nothing grows on trees in Traurig.

But okay, what if only some pervs saw the sex tape? What if guys like Moses, upstanding citizens and whatnot, probably too old for porn anyway, had no idea about it? What if going to work will not only give her a pocketful of tips but a few hours' asylum from bridge jumpers and betrayals?

Sara is not high-strung, not prone to panic, but damn if she doesn't feel weird getting ready for work. Damn if there's not some odd energy emanating from her chest, her heart, and spreading through her limbs, a low hum in her hands and feet, a few watts making them all sweaty. She's anxious to get to work and it's the last place she wants to end up, and her breath is bad, for some reason, despite the fact she just brushed her teeth. So she brushes them again, scrubs that tongue. It's hard to think of anything other than Nat, still not answering her text, still out there, her unexplained mystery.

Things happen, she tells herself, heartbeat cranking, the hum in her hands getting more volts running into them.

She puts on her uniform. She can't be late, otherwise why not call in sick? Moses will be equally pissed, late or a no-show.

She gets in her car and motors down the cul-de-sac; it's not a dirt road, but its pavement has seen better days, charred by the sun and badly creviced. There are about twenty houses, all cinderblock palaces, topped with metal roofs. Front yards are mixtures of scrub brush and cacti, sand and dirt and rocks. The occasional yucca stands up above the rest like a celebrity.

She speeds down the block, notices a couple hillbillies sitting in their yard, tying lures on their fishing poles. She has her music pinned and is driving a little fast and her heart should really slow down, yes, it doesn't need to beat so many times a minute, please calm down.

She pulls into the diner's parking lot. She sits there. She notices that she's breathing, which is something everybody does all the time but you don't necessarily realize you're doing it, you breathe—that's what you do—that's how people stay alive, and what the hell is she going to tell her brother, Hank, about the sex tape and why the hell did Nat do this in the first place and she should have listened to Kristine's public service announcement, sexting with monsters is dangerous. Sexting with monsters can kill you.

Her palms pour sweat and she wipes them on her black pants and hears something coming from outside the car. It's knocking. Someone is knocking on her window, and someone is knocking on her hands from the inside, a tiny little pirate trapped in there looking for treasure.

Sara looks up and sees Moses standing by the driver's side, pantomiming for her to roll down the window.

In her purse, her phone vibrates and vibrates and vibrates, and actually that's what her hands and feet feel like, cells set to vibrate.

Every new message about Nat, the sex tape.

Every new message about the end of her life.

She obliges Moses, cranks the window down.

"I don't need you today," he says.

"I'm on the schedule."

"I have to suspend you."

She shields her eyes and looks up at him for the first time: "You can't."

"I can do whatever I want."

"Isn't that discrimination?"

"Call the ACLU."

"When can I come back?"

"This is a small town, Sara. Let's let this blow over a bit."

Her phone vibrates again. So do her hands and feet.

"I need tips," says Sara.

"I'll call when we're clear."

"That doesn't help me with money."

"I'm not firing you," Moses says, walking away, ending the conversation whether Sara has more to add or not.

She speeds off toward home. Cranks the stereo. Driving way too fast. For the first time since she found out about the sex tape, she cries. She's stupid, so predictably stupid, and what's she supposed to do with this anguish barreling through her?

Twitching, malicious thoughts race around Sara, and an unequaled loneliness swells and crests and crashes, crushing her down. She's hyperventilating. She needs to get home. She needs to be alone. She might be dying. This might be a heart attack, an aneurysm, a stroke. She needs to be in her room with its cinderblocks.

She turns onto her street. So close. So almost there. Still speeding. Still crying. Still listening to rock and roll at the top of the stereo's lungs.

She'd seen a couple of her neighbors tying lures on before, but now one's in the road, practicing fly-fishing casts, whipping arm sends his line bouncing on the damaged asphalt. Sara slams on the brakes, barely misses hitting him. Here he comes up to her window and kicks her car, the side mirror flying off.

Of course this is happening, she thinks.

Things keep happening.

It's not even noon and now she must indulge in one more meanness.

The sun is almost to its apex, baking the street, the town.

Sara gets out of the car.

3.

Everybody calls him Balloon Boy. Started calling him that once he fell from the skies. Once he went thump-splat ouch. From that moment on, his real name Rodney was retired, and Balloon Boy was born. Or that's how he thinks of it, there being two of him: In his head, all the words compose themselves like a hip-hop MC delighting audiences with a nimble tongue, wild rhyming schemes. Maybe a TV minister auctioning off salvation at mach speed. But when Rodney's perfectly composed thoughts try to cross that threshold and make it out of his mouth, things malfunction. Reduced to speaking in monosyllables.

Reduced to being Balloon Boy.

Today is his eighteenth birthday, and he wakes up feeling ripe for adventure and for a few minutes it feels possible. Somebody like him can be summoned to greatness. Someone like Balloon Boy can do something extraordinary! Just because of his accident, just because he's lost that connection between the life transpiring in his head—one crackling with consonants, one unctuous with chewy vowels—it doesn't have to be a death sentence. It doesn't have to be poor Balloon Boy *being* his condition. That's not all he is. Because if in fact he's poised, ready to be summoned to greatness, that won't happen if he's feeling sorry for himself, if he's mired in a poor-me soup, swimming in it. No, this is a time to feel optimistic, to charge into his adulthood. There will always be a harsh disconnect between what people see—Balloon Boy, the name he detests—and the inner life of Rodney, the diatribes and monologues lobbed eloquently around his skull. It's like a crowded theater in his head and he stands alone on stage, reciting Shakespeare, getting all the accents and rhythms right. He might not be able to articulate this, might falter trying to share with someone how he's giving a topnotch soliloquy in the amphitheatre of his consciousness, so don't go thinking that because his actual out-loud talking is garbled there's only mud thrumming in his mind.

He's eighteen now and can join the military, can go anywhere without needing any consent except his own. He is his destiny and nothing as silly as a broken mouth will stop him.

He stokes these calls to arms, these fantasies with his eyes closed, lounging in bed, imagining distant lands filled with beautiful women who actually like listening to him speak, who think it's sexy how he takes his time delivering every sound. They don't get frustrated with him. They don't badger him.

All these possibilities disappear when a booming knock smacks through his plywood door, these declarations and illusions that had thrived in his solitude now scatter like bugs, once Uncle Felix shakes the meager door with his anger and enthusiasm, saying, "Hey, it's fish o'clock."

"No," Balloon Boy says, and six seconds later adds, "thanks."

With open eyes and a gruff uncle making too much noise, the reality of Traurig hits him like the heat outside.

Rodney sighs deeply, wipes his eyes. Each day always starts with the same action: looking at the picture on his bedside table, the shot of him and his mom on horseback, taken when he was ten years old, before the thump-splat ouch, before she ran away. The shot is taken head-on: Rodney sitting in front of his mother, all of their faces lined up in a row—horse, boy, mother.

The day she left for good, she tucked this picture under his pillow, and he's come to think of it as a love letter, a last letter, an explanation, her way of saying she's sorry and she still cares for him, even in her absence. Yes, sometimes letters don't have words; sometimes the image tells you everything.

Yet some do have words: There is one other picture that Rodney has from his mom, a postcard. He keeps it tucked between his box spring and mattress. He had received it a few weeks after she left. It's of the Golden Gate Bridge on a sunny day. On it, his mom has written, "Some day, I will tell you everything." He likes reading the message, but what he adores examining is the return address, chiseled into his memory. He has no idea if she's still there but at least it's a way to start.

More knocking from Felix, the plywood barely standing up to his knuckles.

"You can't skip, not even on your birthday. I let you sleep in," says his uncle, "but fish wait for no man."

"Five," says Rodney, "more, min, utes."

"No more minutes. Fish beckon us. They challenge us. There's a fight to be had, and we will not lose."

"Oh," Rodney says, "kay."

Balloon Boy knows it's not worth pointing out that there aren't any fish waiting outside, not even a body of water by their house, doesn't feel compelled to point out that they're going to cast their lines in the street. But the facts won't help him win. Nothing can. Uncle Felix will not accept any excuses, any logic, and so Rodney sighs and rises, bemoaning this beginning to his birthday. It's not as though he was expecting anyone to deliver an ice cream cake to his room, leave him with a spoon to gulp down the whole thing in peace. It's not as though his dad and uncle are the kinds of people to barge in his room with a pitch pipe, get that perfect starting note and regale him with a harmonized version of "Happy Birthday" while wearing those little coned hats, blowing into kazoos as the song concluded, but did his first day as an adult have to start with *fish o'clock*?

"Today we may catch Moby-Dick," says Felix, pounding a couple last times before walking away, calling to his nephew while marching down the hall. "Let's snare the white whale!"

Rodney gets out of bed, stumbles over to his dresser. Damn does he wish for central air conditioning. They do have a swamp cooler, but it only pumps its chilly air into the living room. The bedrooms, mere cinderblock squares, are like jail cells. That's another reminder of his mom in his room—the way they painted the cinderblock walls like a chessboard, alternating black and white. "Let's make your room look like Alice in Wonderland," his mom had said, and they spent a weekend taping each cinderblock off, making sure they did an impeccable job.

Now, though, some of the black paint has peeled off; he'll find chips of it on his concrete floor, withered by the sun, the flecks looking like dead flies.

Rodney dresses, shorts and a tank top, no shoes, and starts walking toward the front yard, to watch the catch and release of the street fish.

He stops in the front yard, which is only sand and dirt and scrub brush, a little dune in the middle where his dad, Larry, stands, king of his sad hill. Rodney climbs the two-step dune and says, "Hi."

Larry, clutching a whiskey bottle, says, "How are you?"

How am I?, thinks Balloon Boy. *I'm a year older. I'm ready to celebrate. Ready to break out.*

But what he says is "Fine."

"You wanna cast after Felix?" asks Larry, pointing at his brother. Uncle Felix is in the middle of the street, like he's knee deep in a stream, expecting a trout to nibble any second.

"Asphalt practice is better than nothing," says Uncle Felix, but it's unclear who he's talking to.

"Want a plug, son?" says Rodney's dad, shaking the whiskey bottle.

"No," he says.

"Not even on your birthday?"

Oh, so he does remember.

"No," Rodney says again.

"More for me," his dad says, getting a good buzz on top of his tiny dune.

"And me," Uncle Felix says, tossing another cast. "Fishermen have an unquenchable thirst."

Larry admires the cast with a whistle, then says, "Gotta pay our respects to the brass band," taking an honoring sip.

"Don't distract me talking about them crazies," Uncle Felix says. "A fisherman needs to keep his focus. He has to keep his mind submerged under the water trailing all those schools of fish."

Sara comes speeding up the road, all vengeance and vinegar. From where Larry and Rodney stand, she misses Uncle Felix by a few feet, her car skidding to a stop.

Balloon Boy wants to say something to Sara, ask if she's okay because she looks distressed. But he thinks better of it. Seeing Sara is hard. Reminds him of all he lost after the thump-splat ouch. They used to be best friends, Sara and Rodney, kissing sweethearts from back in eighth grade. Back before the balloon went up with him as a stowaway. After his accident, Sara stopped coming around much, which makes Rodney wonder if he's wrong—maybe there's not two of him, his true self surrounded by a shell of Balloon Boy. No, he might simply be the one the world interacts with, might simply endure a life trapped away from all he loves. It's like living behind a window that's been painted shut. No one can hear his true self from the outside. The Shakespeare actor, the MC, the minister, the boy on the horse. Nobody knows that there's more in him, that there's honor and the ability to love and thrive. But how can he help strangers see these things when he can't even talk?

Uncle Felix storms toward Sara's car, lifting his boot and kicking her side mirror, which goes flying, and he says, "Are you crazy, driving like that?"

Balloon Boy and his dad walk down the dune, across the dirt to the edge of the curb. "Your girlfriend really did it this time," Larry says, guzzling from the whiskey bottle.

"Be," Balloon Boy calls to Uncle Felix, knowing the rest of his thought but waiting for his mouth to catch up, "nice."

"Huh?" his uncle asks.

"Be. Nice."

"Stay out of this," says Felix.

The music blares from Sara's car, a rock and roll song with the singer rapping over the electric guitars. Balloon Boy wants to hear the whole song, wants to soak up the way the rapper deflects all those quick syllables off of one another. That's what he wants for his birthday: words coming fast and agile from his mouth.

"Don't hurt my car," Sara says to Felix while flinging her door open and standing up like she wants to fight. Balloon Boy used to joke that she's so small because someone shoved her in the dryer without reading the tag first.

"You almost killed me," Uncle Felix says. "Why can't you drive like a normal person?"

"What do you know about normal?" she says. "You're fishing in the road! Hank's going to kick your ass for busting up my car." She hops back in the driver's seat, tearing up the street something jugular.

Uncle Felix picks up her side mirror, shaking his head, and says, "She sure made some choppy waves on our calm waters, right boys?" and Larry agrees, tilting the bottle again. They go back to what these three remaining members of the Curtis clan had been doing in the first place, two enjoying some time practicing their fly fishing, while one imagines a life outside the concrete river of Traurig.

Before long, Sara's car comes screeching back toward them, bolting from the cul-de-sac and barreling their way. Past a yard

ALL THIS LIFE

with an aboveground pool out front, surrounded by an army of tri-cycles. Past the house with all the wind chimes hanging out front. Past the cactus decorated to look like the Incredible Hulk. No one else is outside their house, late morning, too hot, too stifling, and yet this is the specific time that Rodney's dad and uncle like to road fish: They've told Balloon Boy many times that they thrive in extreme conditions, drawing a comparison between their noon sessions and boxers who train in the mountains, at extreme eleva-tions, so when they go back and fight at sea level, they're in supe-rior cardiovascular shape. Does the analogy hold up? Not really, but Rodney would nod at them, *Yup, you guys are like professional boxers, uh-huh, no doubt.*

Once he sees the car coming, Uncle Felix steps into the middle of the road again. Pulls his arm back for another cast when the car hits the brakes and Sara's brother, Hank, rockets out. He's gowned in muscles like an old-fashioned gladiator.

"You kick her car, Felix?"

"Ease up now, Hank."

"Did you?"

"I did."

"It was me," says Larry.

"Me," Balloon Boy says for the sake of solidarity. He doesn't want to get involved, but that's what the remaining members of the Curtis clan do, stick together no matter what. Unlike some other Curtises, a gone mom who fled to California after the thump-splat ouch.

Hank points a paw right at Rodney and says, "Stay out of this, Balloon Boy." Then he snaps at Uncle Felix, "She's only eighteen. What kind of man scares a little girl?"

Felix throws his fishing pole down on the grass, saying, "The kind who almost gets made road kill."

"Give me her mirror," Hank says.

"That's my mirror now," says Uncle Felix.

"It's mine," Larry says.

"Mine," Balloon Boy says, fearing the worst.

The Curtis boys and their skyscraping loyalty, unlike some Curtises who need fair weather all the time. Whenever Rodney asks where his mom went, Larry says, "It never rains in California so she went there," and Balloon Boy wants so badly to ask more questions—why in California, why not here with me, is she still at that old return address? But it would take him too long to gut out those inquiries and he knows his dad won't tell him much.

Hank spots Sara's side mirror lying snapped and jagged on the lawn and moves toward it.

"Don't touch that," Uncle Felix says.

But Hank picks it up and threatens each witness from the Curtis clan: "Don't treat my sister like that again or else." He goes back across the lawn and steps on and cracks in two Felix's fishing pole.

"Three of us against one of you!" Uncle Felix says, incensed.

"You've gotta be kidding," Hank says.

Felix lunges toward Hank, who cocks his fist, the one holding Sara's side mirror, and hits Uncle Felix with it. Felix falls, bleeding from the temple. Larry tries to tackle Hank but gets fixed in some vicious headlock and tumbles down after one hit in the kidney.

Hank looks at Balloon Boy. "You wanna dance, too?"

He doesn't, of course. Doesn't even want to be outside, in this sweltering pointless situation. Doesn't want to road fish or watch them drink whiskey anymore. Doesn't want to be here in this disconnected head, the muscles in his mouth not responding to any cues from his brain. Rodney doesn't want to be stuck away from all the good stuff, the real stuff, doesn't want to feel this cruel division between himself and all the other humans, those people with their own baggage and yet solely because his words are slow, he's ostracized.

He doesn't want to watch anything bad happen to Sara, and especially doesn't want to fight Hank, who will no doubt beat him into a coma.

These are all the things he doesn't want, things he never asked for, and yet he possesses all of them. These are his birthday gifts. These are his future.

He yearns to be back in bed, where there are fantasies and possibilities that today will turn out to be the one he's been waiting for, the one to launch him on a splendid adventure, his hopes taking flight.

And that word—*flight*—is what lured him onto the weather balloon that day. The idea of an effortless voyage. At the time he wanted Sara to get on the balloon with him, but thankfully she refused, watched him drift up until he crashed back down, thump-splat ouch.

The importance of flight has only flown higher itself, gaining more altitude over the years. Back on the day of his accident, Rodney was merely a boy showing off for his girl, being silly, with no concept of anything like consequences or injuries. But since his mom left and his talking left and Sara left, Rodney's yearning for flight has been profound. If there is a quest awaiting his arrival, it has to be soon.

Yet before any grandiose adventures can crack open, there is the issue of Hank, steroided Hank, standing and frothing in front of him. The last thing Rodney wants to do is lose a fight, but unfortunately that's what's going to happen. He's going to defend his stupid uncle and his liquored-up dad because they are his family. They stayed. They've taken care of him, as best they can, and he's going to get his ass kicked for solidarity.

4.

Kathleen is a caricaturist. One of those entertainers and hustlers and performers down by Fisherman's Wharf—the part of San Francisco reserved for tourists. It's all shops and restaurants and trinkets. All cioppino and cracked crabs. Clam chowder served in sourdough bread bowls. Ferries to Alcatraz. Carousel rides. Saltwater taffy stands. Sea lions barking on K-Dock, bellowing like drunkards. Gulls, those winged mercenaries, trailing children for lost pieces of corn dog bun. The whole bay can be seen from the end of Pier 39. Sailboats and tankers and the Golden Gate Bridge. The fog creeping in from the Pacific.

She sets up her easel on the Embarcadero, almost skipped work today because of what the brass band did earlier that morning. Traffic still hasn't recovered. News vans cluster at each end of the bridge, various channels' anchors hiking out into the middle to make their own melodramatic reporting. Helicopters hovering in the sky above, offering their viewers an aerial shot. A letter has surfaced, a kind of suicide note, found on the kitchen table of one of the jumpers' apartments: a manifesto, saying that they are all musical notes in a melody, a tune that would carry them away to paradise. Now they'd live a life unburdened by human frailties. "A note in a melody," said the letter, "doesn't have any concerns. A note is a note."

So that created a whole new batch of talking points for the news hubs, gossiping with new guests and experts who spin context, analysis, condemnation. They demonize despite the fact they don't really know what happened. Or why.

But the way Kat figured it, if tourists have spent money to fly here, they aren't wallowing in hotel rooms, pondering the significance of this tragedy. If this is your vacation, you explore. So she sits next to her easel, waiting for her first customer.

There are other caricaturists out and about, too, though not as gifted as she. Kat can draw wonderfully, and for five dollars people go home with a solid souvenir. She was one of those kids always doodling on something or other and that habit carried her into the world. She didn't have to work when she was married. Her husband had a good union gig so she stayed home with her young son. Once he started kindergarten she'd watercolor and sometimes oil paint. But her first love was drawing portraits, headshots. There's something special about constructing your version of someone else.

And with caricatures, it should have a bit of funhouse mirror to it, which is a freedom she loves taking advantage of. You have buckteeth? Well, now they're going to jet out of your mouth looking like water slides. Eyes close together? She'll only draw one eye, right in the middle of your face. Big ears? See how they look like open car doors.

She does this with a smile on her face, which translates to her clientele, most of them taking her facial remixes in stride, giggling and shaking their heads. Sure, occasionally some sulk seeing their "worst" features exaggerated, branding them in idiosyncrasy. But to Kathleen that's the way life works: We are defined by our worst features. We are those mistakes. We are defined by the discrepancy between the life we think we have versus the one everyone else sees.

We have a collection of mistakes and failures, stacked up like those sea lions on the docks, a pile of all the things we've flubbed. Our mistakes barking into the air.

She sets up her chair, another for her clients. Gets out her pens, pencils, and erasers. Sometimes, she'll simply sketch a bit, whatever's on her mind, let tourists walk close and inspect her talent before committing to a purchase. More often than not, in these instances, she'll draw her own caricature. Let the general public see that she can laugh at herself. She'll show Kathleen in the foreground, her son in the back. She'll show her walking away from him. Her face will be a trash can of self-sympathy, true torment in the eyes, mouth agape, mounds of brunette teased out and up, looking like an appalling hat, one of those Russian jobs, an ushanka. Sometimes she's armed with a suitcase, motion lines showing she's running away from the boy in the background. Or she'll sketch a large hot air balloon with teeth near the basket or snakes dropping to the ground in place of ropes. She knows the tourists can't tell the drawing's significance.

She's also been known to draw pictures of her boy. When she does this, these portraits are flawless, so lifelike. She exaggerates nothing. And he looks perfect and some day she hopes to have him model for her in person.

Kathleen does one of those now. Re-creating an old picture of the two of them, though Kat deletes herself in this rendition, lets the boy be the star. It's a photo she's drawn many times since leaving—it's the one she left by his bed before bolting: a shot of mother and son on a horse together, and the boy has dazzle and awe plastered on his face. It was his first time riding a horse.

"What will it cost us?" a couple asks, sneaking up behind her.

Kathleen crumples up the portrait of her son. "What did you say?"

They walk around her and sit on the chair. They are both young, in their mid-twenties. Younger even? Kathleen hopes not.

Because the girl has a black eye.

The guy does not.

And the girl is pregnant.

"What will it cost us?" the girl with the black eye says again.

Kathleen stares at the young man with her. Looks about the age when her husband turned violent—he was a good husband up until her son's accident, and after that every one of them had closed head injuries, not only the boy. Their beautiful boy who for whatever reason climbed on that weather balloon, floated thirty feet up in the air, and was dumped onto the concrete. He survived, which was a miracle, but his brain was never the same. It wasn't only him, though. Every one of them was rewired.

"Only five dollars," Kathleen says.

"Can we do it, Tyler?" the girl with the black eye says.

"Fine."

"Don't make me look fat," the girl says to Kathleen.

"You're not at all fat, sweetie."

"Dude, you should see her naked," the guy says, nudging the girl and laughing. She hits him playfully on the arm and says, "Shut up, Tyler."

He apologizes, though it's obviously insincere. Kathleen gets the sense that if these two were home alone, barricaded in some trashed apartment, Tyler wouldn't be saying sorry for anything, but slugging beer from a can, a dune of tobacco bulging from his bottom lip and making the girl with the black eye wait on him like an indentured servant.

"Better suck in your gut," Tyler says and pats the girl on the stomach.

"That isn't a gut, asshole. That's your baby."

"What kind of background do you want for the picture?" says Kathleen.

"It can be anything?" the girl with the black eye asks.

Kathleen nods.

"Where should we go?" the girl says to Tyler.

"I don't care," he says, and Kathleen watches him check out another girl's butt as she passes by. Then he looks at Kathleen, shrugs.

"Paris," the girl says to Kathleen. "Can you draw us in front of the Eiffel Tower?"

"Sure."

"Pack your bags," the girl says to Tyler. "We're on our way to Paris."

Kathleen prepares to draw the girl with the black eye first. Normally, she captures her subjects mostly from the neck up or with tiny bodies, but she doesn't want to this time. No, she wants to make sure and capture this pregnant young woman whole.

There's life in her.

There's hope.

There's hope until there's not.

Kathleen can see their future so clearly because it's identical to her past.

And since today is her son's eighteenth birthday, she's feeling both nostalgic and cruel. These emotions knotting around her neck. These emotions leaving her no choice but to lash out at this innocent couple because she's tired of lashing out at herself.

She draws the girl's black eye first. Swollen hues puffing under it. The black eye is huge. It's going to be a monument for every woman's eye that has ever felt a man's knuckle. Tyler has to be able to decipher his own violence.

"Are we in Paris yet?" the girl with the black eye says. "I'm in the mood for a chocolate croissant."

"We've started our final descent," Kathleen says.

"Good. I'm starved."

"There's a shocker," Tyler says.

"Should I deprive your baby of sustenance?"

"Our baby is going to be fine."

Kathleen cringes at the use of the word *fine*. An impossibility. She draws the girl with the black eye's stomach much larger than it actually is, a huge belly and a big baby visible through her skin, and she draws a black eye on the baby too because it's a lesson every mother needs to learn. Disaster is inevitable. Disaster comes disguised in all kinds of gentle ubiquities, such as your son going to the park. Trying to ride a weather balloon. Trying to live.

This girl has to know what her child is in for, what they're all in for: that their child won't evade the world's wrath because nobody does. Maybe it's as simple as Tyler drinking too much and beating them up. Or there might be a car wreck, a lightning strike, any of a million iterations of violence too asinine to be true until they warp your world into pulp.

Kathleen runs her pen in circle after circle around the baby's black eye. Defacing the baby. She makes the baby frown and tears run down its face and splotches from her red pen on the cheeks. The girl with the black eye and the baby with the black eye, and it's time to draw Tyler.

"Have we landed in Paris?" the girl with the black eye asks.

Kathleen can't stop this tentacle of anger slapping and convulsing around inside of her. It's empowered by everything she left behind in Traurig. Feeling the high-octane angst of someone who has done something unforgiveable. It will burn forever, this fire. Never needing to be stoked.

"I'm doing my best," Kathleen says, drawing Tyler's face snarling and beads of sweat collecting and trickling from his forehead and his right hand knotted into a fist, scars across his knuckles, and his left hand has the girl with the black eye by the hair and there's a conversation bubble coming from Tyler's mouth that says, "Life beats babies!" and Kathleen hasn't drawn the Eiffel Tower behind them because she doesn't want to take them anywhere. Forget Paris. She wants them to remain here, with their baby's bruised face and life's unruly way of torturing everybody and the way that her husband turned on her after their son's accident, the way they turned on each other. They always drank too much, sure, but now it was different. Screaming blackouts and hangovers and trying to adjust to their new damaged son and then the same the next day and the next. A recurring day. An outlandish hallucination. All this life, a punishment repeating until the end of time. Rolling that boulder up a hill but never reaching the top. Having your liver pecked out by an eagle every day. No parole or pardon or hope. Punishment until the world ends.

So she traded in that shared punishment for a new one. Not really an escape, because once she fled Traurig and got sober it was worse. Once her head cleared, she had her consciousness back. Her conscience. To relive her decision. To ponder every day what she did and why and maybe she had her reasons and maybe they were cogent reasons—at least understandable ones—but maybe they were not.

Three years living sober has taught her one malicious lesson: She made it worse once her head dried out. That's when she was assigned her official boulder, her hill. That's when the eagle got her address.

"I think I'm finished," Kathleen says and turns the portrait around for them to see.

Their faces are astonished as they take in all the caricature's details, the detritus of violence, the line of dialogue: "Life beats babies!"

No one says anything for about ten seconds, and finally Tyler stands up and says, "What's wrong with you?" and Kathleen doesn't say anything, and he says, "Lady, you can't do that!" and then he knocks over the easel, and Kathleen keeps holding up the picture and the girl with the black eye sits there speechless and Tyler rips the portrait from Kathleen's hand and crumples it and tosses it on the sidewalk and Kathleen falls down, too, landing next to her easel and caricature, while the girl with the black eye walks away, Tyler consoling her with each step they take.

Kathleen sits alone on the street, snatches the portrait, smoothes it out, looks at what she's done.

The anger tentacle goes dormant inside her as she caresses the picture, feeling tenderness, an empathy she wishes she could've shown the girl with the black eye and Tyler and their baby, but it's over now. All she has is this picture, this memory, and so she rubs it on her face, snuggling, smelling it, wishing it had the wonderful scent of her son's scalp after he was born.

And she allows herself to do something forbidden. Something she doesn't regularly indulge in, something off-limits and toxic and tough.

Kat imagines a portrait of her own hopeful family. One before Rodney set foot on that weather balloon. One before their mythological punishment. Kathleen, Larry, and Rodney all smile in this picture. They are together, and they have no idea what awaits them.

5.

It's been two days since the incident on the bridge, and Jake and his father are both at Paul's home, both glued to their respective computers. The boy in his room upstairs. The father at the kitchen table, drinking a beer; he scours the Internet, learning everything he can about fantasy football. Sports have never been something that interested him, not playing them in real life and certainly not playing pretend ones online. But the guys at work have a fantasy league and extended Paul an invitation to join. That was what made him want to do this: the invitation itself. An act of inclusion.

In ten minutes, at 7 PM, the league is set to have its draft, divvying up players on various rosters. Paul has a sip of his beer and frantically Googles things about fantasy football, about real football, anything to help him make sense of what he's supposed to do once the draft kicks off. He has a nominal sense of the game, its rules and best-known players, what he's gleaned from all the AM talk radio, but hopefully this crash course deepens his understanding. Hopefully, he can fool these guys at work into thinking he's one of them.

Paul sighs at the thought, feels stupid about trying to impress his subordinates. He's even being fraudulent with this, faking his way through fantasy football. Pathetic. Paul has another pull off the beer.

He doesn't want to be a phony. Doesn't want to be posing as something he's not, but he doesn't exactly have a full social schedule. He doesn't want to scare these guys off because maybe it starts with fantasy football and soon there are drinks after work, happy hours, greasy appetizers. Maybe one of them has a girlfriend who has the perfect woman for Paul, and they all go out together.

He needs to have sex. Soon. It's been over a year. He has to stop masturbating into his socks. Paul, ever a convenience freak, noticed that an argyle could make the cleanup easy, but from an emotional angle, there was nothing sadder than a grown man jerking off into a sock, day after day, and that's not to mention the shame he felt catching his reflection off the computer's screen, a sock on his softening penis.

So sure, this is only a fantasy football draft, but what if it's the proverbial first step? What if this is the beginning of Paul being a little bit less alone?

Fantasy football is a subterfuge, a way for Paul to spend time with his new friends and simultaneously put off the rate at which they realize how boring he is. They work in the same office, but three out of four of them report to Paul, so it's not like they include him or know him in any capacity other than that guy who sends too many emails and micro-manages, the miser who should order them catered lunches more often.

Or they haven't included him until now. Now, he's being initiated. Now, he can become one of the guys.

Paul sighs again, wants to believe this, and yet it sounds so far-fetched. It's impossible to give himself the benefit of the doubt. Too much self-loathing: It takes every cell in his body to be average.

Paul slakes for a clean slate, no dependent, no ex. Don't get him wrong, he loves his son, but ever since Jake entered their lives all those years ago the enjoyment got ground up, splintered—Paul too busy being a parent and a husband and an employee to focus any time on himself, his needs, his wants. Back then, he never made it to the bottom of a daily to-do list, which only made tomorrow's longer and the next one stretch until he couldn't even see the goddamn end of it, and weeks and months and years vanished until he looked up at that beleaguered, middle-aged stranger in the mirror and thought, *Now who the hell are you?*

Football, fantasy football, he knows this is dumb and yet it matters. It has to matter. It matters because of what it represents. Of what it can mean moving forward. It matters because it will give Paul something to do.

That's what makes all this so tragic: Even Paul doesn't buy his story, his yarn of a life wasted providing for his family. It sounds great, don't get him wrong, but isn't that giving him too much credit?

Of course, there was time.

Time for Paul to spend on himself.

Time for him to pursue these mysterious interests—mysterious because even he doesn't know what they are.

Sure, the first couple years of being a parent are a fugue state, tunnel vision, a staggering lurch forward with blinkers blocking your periphery, but once Jake started school, there was time for Paul to dote on himself. Problem is, he didn't know what to do with his free time. So he spent it working. He spent it puttering on their house. He spent it with Jake. He spent it with his ex, when she wasn't yet his ex.

Naomi, what to say about her? For years, Paul considered them to be in a state of pre-divorce. No one left but neither of them was happy. Paul thought they'd slog on into retirement, take cruises and ignore each other, embrace every devastating cliché.

It was Naomi, god bless her soul, who saved them from that slow ruin. They were both asleep one night, and out of nowhere she sat up in bed, saying, "I'm being eaten alive here."

"What?" said a groggy Paul, an Ambien swimming in his blood-stream.

"A mosquito."

"Huh?"

"I'm almost sucked dry, Paul," she said. "Do something."

The light was switched on. A magazine was folded in half and poor Paul danced around the room, trying to smear the bloated mosquito's corpse all over the cover of *The New Yorker*, but he couldn't catch him, the mosquito veering, zigzagging, Paul hopelessly late with every Ambien-slowed swing.

"It's up by the light," she said.

"I see it."

"So hit it."

"I'm trying."

Whiff. Whiff.

Paul, embarrassingly, was out of breath.

"When?" she said.

"Do you want to?" he asked.

She nodded and stood up on the bed. He handed her the magazine. Paul lay down on his side and watched her stalk the insect. It took a matter of ten seconds for her to hit it with the magazine, the mosquito landing on their comforter, stunned, still trying to fly. Naomi, careful not to squash it on their duvet, picked the mosquito up and put it inside the magazine, then smushed the pages together.

"Do you want to see?" she said.

She opened the magazine up, showing the bloody smudge over a skyscraper of text.

"I hadn't finished reading that one," said Paul.

"You can still read it," Naomi said.

There was something in that moment, an inherent conversation, scripted lines they were supposed to say. Maybe it's only Paul's memory plumping it up, but he swears there was an electricity, the two of them sitting on the bed with the blood smear on the page.

He sat there for what felt like a hundred hours until Naomi said, "We need to make a change."

"Okay."

"We forgot how to be married."

"What?"

"When we had Jake," she said. "We became parents and stopped being married."

It was true: The family took on an exclusionary geometry. It had shapes to it: Paul and Jake, Naomi and Jake, Paul and Naomi and Jake. But there was never any time when Paul and Naomi were together, and if they were it was only to discuss logistics, practicalities. They never had *fun*.

"What can we do about it?" he asked.

But all Naomi did was shake her head.

Paul can still see her so vividly, the finality in her movement. It must have taken her years to work up the courage to quit their marriage, and it was right there in her swiveling face, left to right, right to left, *We are through*.

The overhead light was turned off; the bloodied copy of *The New Yorker* was recycled.

That was ten months ago. Now Paul lives in a condo, a sad stucco orphanage for wayward men, shamed divorcés. It's only a couple miles from his former residence, where Jake lives with his mom. Normally, they share custody, but she's in Bali for a few weeks with a new boyfriend, some tan asshole with an accent that sends Paul into a murderous rage every time he calls him *mate*. A murderous rage he'll, of course, never act on. Unless there's a fantasy murder league.

Paul has six minutes before the fantasy draft kicks off and keeps Googling, sifting through various strategies, players to target. He has six minutes and there's another pale ale in the fridge, and for a few seconds he feels like he's forging these new friendships already—Paul and his pals—just by preparing himself to be an active member of their league, and all of this makes him feel hopeful.

He clicks on a link that says "The perfect plan (for your draft)" and has another sip of beer. He's not drafting pretend players; he's drafting real friends.

Paul smiles.

That's when he hears some strange thumping noises coming from upstairs, from Jake's room.

SOMETIMES HIS MOM—when she's actually in town and not traveling with her new boyfriend—says that the world is an oyster. But that's a stupid expression. That's the kind of thing that maybe applied back in 1981 or something. Not now. No, oysters have nothing to do with the current state of things, and Jake knows exactly what the world is:

The world is a search engine.

Jake can type anything into the world's search bar and scroll through pages of results. Limitless returns. Adventures coming in every denomination, every fetish. Any whim he can whip up.

There's no other conclusion for him to draw. Especially now. Right now. Jake clicks refresh compulsively, watching the views and comments multiply on his video's YouTube page, all these citizens of the world coming to him. 827,148 people have viewed it already. And that's not even mentioning how many times Jake personally has replayed it. Maybe he's watched the brass band 827,148 times, too.

So when he's not clicking refresh, he clicks replay.

And when he isn't clicking replay, he simply stares at the scene, reliving it, time-traveling back to that morning on the bridge.

Refresh . . . refresh . . .

827,176.

There are other posted videos of the disaster, but no one captured its entirety. Jake got the brass band's approach, their shuffling along the walkway, their song; he got every person going over the edge. The other clips of it start when one or two of the brass band have already jumped. These are getting hits, too, but nowhere near as many as Jake's.

He's a disaster shepherd, and this YouTube page and its contents are his flock. He nurtures them all. He owns this disaster, as any shepherd owns his sheep. Their deaths are his property.

Refresh.

827,192.

The thing that's happened to him today is that he's building a personal ranking system of their jumps. He didn't start off doing this on purpose, but slowly, view after view after view, he found himself looking forward to certain deaths more than others. Found himself being drawn to certain styles of going over the edge. For example, he cherished the saxophonist who launched his instrument like a boomerang, the gold thing shimmering off the bridge and slowly disappearing down, then its player following it.

His favorite, though, is the tall, skinny woman, the one wearing the purple striped pants, the paisley shirt with a butterfly collar. How she hoists her clarinet like a javelin and stands admiring her toss before going after it.

He wouldn't tell anybody. About his ranking system. About how he's built a hierarchy of suicides. No one would understand, or maybe they would but Jake won't share it. He can't. He's learned not to open himself up to anybody at school. They already have plenty of ammo to heave at him because he's always—as his mom says—"acting out." He's not, though. He's not acting; he's not out. He's only being himself.

Mom in Bali with Simon, and they probably don't even know about the brass band. They don't even know that Jake has captured these suicides, or maybe they're a couple of his viewers. Maybe they watch it and wonder if the poster, username TheGreatJake, is the great Jake that they know.

Or they're snorkeling.

Or they're enjoying some time away from him.

That's what it feels like since his parents split up, that his parents don't want him around, even though they show it differently. His mom always going on trips, weekends here, full weeks there, with Simon. Always trips only for adults, his mom says. "Us, honey. Simon and I."

And his dad, distracted, grunting, moping around, always ordering pizza; Jake is the only teenager in all the Bay Area tired of pizza. His dad is taking the divorce like somebody bucked off a bull, limping to get out of the way before the animal's horns hit him.

Whatever.

Parents all have horns, he guesses.

It's nice to see how many people want to interact with him online. Refresh the page.

827,211.

With new comments.

Most of these comments aren't directed at him, per se. They're reactions to seeing the suicides. Some are mean-spirited. Some are religious, supportive, tolerant. Some have nothing to do with the video, trolls posting things like "Meet sexy singles in your area."

But one of the new comments is directed straight at TheGreatJake:

```
All comments (9,293)
Noah911
I feel SAD for whoever posted this.
```

This is the one he fixates on. In the thousands of comments on his page—and Jake has read through them all many times—he can't remember one that incites such an immediate reaction within him. There are others about ethics, about the moral decision to post the video in the first place, but these don't burrow under Jake's skin. They are only opinions and he shrugs them off and gets back to his flock.

But *I feel sad for whoever posted this* is demeaning, like getting made fun of in the hall at school by a couple dudes and everyone else hears them and now the whole crowd is involved and laughing, except here the hallway is the whole Internet and Jake is getting mocked in Ecuador and Madagascar and Morocco and it's not fair of Noah911 to do that.

But this *I feel sad for whoever posted this* isn't going away. It isn't the usual Internet white noise. Jake feeling impaled by the word *sad*. People have called him much worse in the comments section, and yet all their pejoratives and hyperboles invalidated them, made them radio static. The simplicity of *I feel sad* tunnels through his defenses and cuts him, sadness mutating into ire. The boy feeling publicly humiliated, which will no doubt lead to more people disappearing from his life. His parents split up, and his mom's always off with Simon and his dad is downstairs but there's no connection between them, he could be down in Mexico and it would feel the same to Jake, and the kids at school don't care about him and now Noah911 is turning his own flock against him, hitting him in a space that should be all his own, an online world where he is important and happy, this one portal to escape the puckered maw of reality.

An emoji of Jake's face would be a serrated saw hacking off his scalp and someone jamming a lit candle inside his head so he blazes like a jack-o-lantern.

He wants to break something, which of course he's going to do, which of course is how these things work when the urge to break something comes on so flagrantly. You do it. You take the nearest weapon (a baseball bat in the corner behind his bedroom door) and you hit the nearest thing (an empty pint glass sitting next to his computer) and sometimes one pint glass is enough to quench the thirst of these violent feelings and sometimes it isn't and this happens to be one of those non-quenching times and so he swings the bat again, coming down on top of his printer and still it is not enough and Jake finds another target, killing his alarm clock, composing comments back to Noah911 in his head, *I'm not so sad, but what makes you think I'm so sad, you have no right to talk to me that way because I'm not so sad, okay!!!*

Jake wonders why he has stopped smashing stuff so he sucks up more voltage from the feelings inside him and picks up the bat again, hunting for a target and finding the thing in his room that represents the great disconnect between him and his parents, preparing to swing the bat at a plant his parents had given him the day they told him they were getting divorced.

They had taken Jake into San Francisco that afternoon, into Golden Gate Park. There was someone selling succulents out front of the conservatory of flowers, and they walked past her table with pots of aloe, cacti, agave, yucca. Jake's mom paid the entrance fee for the conservatory and said, "Back here," and led the three of them to a room, an indoor butterfly garden, hundreds of butterflies moving through the space.

There were only two other people in there, a young couple, kissing and holding their palms out, coaxing butterflies to land.

Most of the walls were made of windows, and sunlight filled the indoor garden.

"Your dad and I have to make a change, sweetie," said his mom, and then outlined the separation, the divorce, their plan to split custody. "It has nothing to do with you," she said. "Right, Paul?"

"It's between your mom and me," he said, a butterfly landing on his dad's chest before he brushed it away.

"Do you have any questions for us?" his mom asked.

"Not yet," he said.

There was a pause in the conversation while all three of them watched the young couple make out, butterflies swirling around their bodies.

The family left, and once outside the conservatory his mom said, "Let's get you a plant."

They walked up to the table of succulents.

"Do you even want a plant?" Paul said to his son.

"We're buying him a plant!" she said.

"But what if he doesn't care?"

"He cares."

Jake said nothing.

"Pick one," she said.

Jake surveyed the table, all the plants, pointed at a small pot with a cactus in it.

"They don't need much water," his mother said, "so it's easy to keep them alive."

"Okay," Jake said, holding the plant up.

"It's for you to take care of."

"Why?"

"Good question," said his father.

"You do a good job taking care of the plant and we'll get a dog when life normalizes again," his mom said.

A dog?

What, was he eight years old?

Didn't they know anything about him?

So the cactus is an easy item for Jake to target, and in fact the plant should have been the first thing he smashed, though it doesn't have great placement in his room, in a corner on a chair with dirty clothes around it, but now he remembers it and now would be the perfect moment to show his parents he doesn't want to do a decent job of caring for anything and he doesn't want a dog and he doesn't care about their divorce and he's not so sad and he swings the bat at the cactus and dirt ricochets all over the place and he keeps hammering it with the bat until he's out of breath.

"What are you doing?" the boy now hears from his doorway, turning and seeing his dad.

No answer from Jake, though he does have the craving to click refresh.

"Jake, what's going on?" Paul says, looking at the smashed cactus.

"No dog, I guess," Jake says, moving toward his computer, sitting down in front of it.

"What the hell are you doing?" Paul says, still in the doorway, surveying all the damage.

Jake finally clicking refresh and seeing a gleaming new number. 827,238.

"Look at all of them," says Jake.

"Are you okay?" Paul says stupidly. He knows that what he's walked in on isn't normal, isn't healthy. He's tried to be there the best he could the last couple days. He's been working from home, allowing Jake to play hooky from school. They've watched movies together, eaten pizzas. He's asked Jake countless times if he wanted to talk about the brass band, but the boy never did. Paul has heard "I'm fine" enough to make it hard to keep asking, figured his son would reach out to him when he was ready.

Paul could hear Naomi, all the way from Bali, say to him, "It doesn't matter if he answers us, we have to keep asking. We are the adults and always have to check in with him."

Paul shakes her know-it-all timbre out of his head; it's so easy for her to pop up with aphorisms between trips with Simon, when Paul was doing the heavy lifting of being the day-to-day, default parent right now. It's like she's been on spring break since the divorce, parading and partying, sowing her paroled oats, while Paul is still locked up, left to deal with all this.

In fact, the night after the band died, Paul had sent her an elaborate email of what Jake had seen on the bridge and all he got back from her was this one measly line: "Can you handle it?"

His response: "I'll try."

Those sorts of interactions made him remember the mosquito's blood smudged on the magazine's page.

But had he been trying as best he could? Paul wasn't sure.

The boy staring straight ahead at his laptop.

Paul only seeing the back of his head, a haze of blue computer life haloed around it.

"Jake, tell me what you're doing," he says.

Paul walks across the room, standing directly behind his son, caressing the nape of Jake's neck, both of them staring at the boy's computer screen.

"What is that?" asks Paul.

"It's mine."

"What is?"

Paul scours the screen. He notes the URL, then the imbedded video. Holy shit. Paul pieces the chain of events together, and his boy's refrain of "I'm fine" sounds different now. Jake isn't slowly processing and soon, once he understands his emotions, they'll have a heart-to-heart. No, Jake has already processed the event without him; he doesn't need his father. He has his computer and the video he's shot on his phone. He has his grieving process shared online, and Paul, poor pathetic Paul, downstairs with his fantasy football draft. He should've been up here. He should've been up here the whole time.

"You posted that?" Paul asks his son.

"I'm in charge of it."

"Play it."

"You were there."

"Click play."

Jake starts the video and Paul can't keep his head right, can't keep his head here, watching this clip because it's reminding him of the days after the September attacks, years ago, when he watched those planes destroy the country time and again. There was a kind of pornography to it, a surreptitious yearning to see something vulgar. He knew other people were watching those planes, too, probably at the exact time he was, but he hoarded his viewings.

Paul hates the thought that Jake is doing the same thing now.

The brass band walking toward them. Again.

Playing.

Dancing.

Stopping.

Over the edge.

One at a time.

Father and son not saying a word.

Again.

"Why did you post this?" Paul asks.

"I never wanted to get a dog," Jake says.

"Let's get you out of here," says Paul, tugging on Jake's shoulders. He has to get his boy out of there now, right now. Jake's too young to understand self-preservation, to value sparing yourself from seeing things you don't have to endure. Paul should have been more present at the moment on the bridge, should have told his son to put down his phone. Don't film this. Don't capture any of this.

And it's inexcusable that Paul is only finding out now that Jake posted it. He should have known right away. He should have stood guard outside his door, poked his head in every five minutes, if only to say to his son, "I'm here. I'm right here if you need me."

There's no need for fantasy sports when the real competition had been going on upstairs, Jake versus his own confusion, his naïveté, his limited understanding of consequences. Paul has let down Jake, and that stops now.

"I don't know why you thought I wanted a dog in the first place," Jake says.

"Are you hungry?"

"This is my favorite," says Jake, pointing to the screen, the tall woman in the purple pants throwing her clarinet then leaping.

"Come on," Paul says, "we need to go."

"Did you see how she holds her nose right before she jumps? Isn't that strange?" asks Jake.

"How about some pizza?"

"I like how she holds her nose like that."

"Pizza?"

"No."

"Macaroni and cheese?"

"Okay."

"Go downstairs and put on a pot of water. I'll be down as soon as I clean this up."

But the boy simply sits there, awash in the computer's light.

"Jake, move it."

Finally, he gets up and slinks out of the room.

Paul fishes his cell phone from his pocket, calling to set up an appointment with a psychologist. No one answers and he listens to the long litany of various instructions. He leaves a detailed voicemail, asking for an appointment in the next couple days.

He assesses the damage, begins cleaning things up.

He starts with the printer, unplugging it and collecting the scattered pieces of plastic. Paul goes to the hall closet and gets a vacuum, sucking up all the dirt. He puts the pieces of the alarm clock on top of the printer. The terra-cotta shards from the succulent's pot are the last thing he collects. Loads it all into a garbage bag. Remembering all those butterflies whirling around the garden as they dismembered their family.

He's finished tidying the room and walks to the door, turning off the light, which only amplifies the presence of Jake's computer. It is glowing. Paul stomps over to it in a huff, as if it's that very dog that Naomi had dumbly promised Jake and it had pissed all over the floor, Paul ready to shame the pet, rub its nose in the mess.

This is the computer's fault, not his boy's.

No way is it his boy's.

No way can his boy be blamed.

Paul sits down in front of the computer, lured closer to watch the clip again, but instead he scrolls down a bit.

He can see the comment. He can see, "I feel sad for whoever posted this."

And Paul bursts into tears. He crumbles under the mass of his own ignorance. Having a kid is the ultimate risk. It creates such a limited perspective. A tube of love. And your vision can be so obscured that you do not understand the dangers on the periphery. You want nothing else but to adore and train and watch them prosper, but the world will have its way with them. Protection is a wicked illusion.

Paul cannot keep Jake safe, even if he spends the rest of his days guarding the boy's room. He has to let him out. He has to teach his son to fend for himself, and that's the great paradox of being a parent: He doesn't want to teach him everything, wants to hold back just enough that Jake needs him. Paul wants to always be needed by his boy, but that greedy motive might prevent Jake from having access to all the tools needed to survive.

Even if you do give them every tool, it's like indoor rock climbing, Paul's main source of exercise. You can have everything you need, make it to the top, but what if you're scaling the wrong wall? Paul himself had all the tools, supportive parents that stayed together, a Stanford education, a trough of options, and yet he still found an existence that perpetually disappoints him.

That's what he'll try and focus on, making sure Jake mounts the right wall.

If Paul's parents were here they'd say, *Pay attention.* They'd say, *It will be the hardest thing you ever accept but you can't protect him. Teach him to scale the right wall and hope for the best.*

The final thing Paul does before going downstairs is close his son's computer. He unplugs it and carries it away.

6.

Before it became *that* morning, it was any other, yesterday rehydrated. Noah sat at his desk in his office on Montgomery Street, in San Francisco's financial district. It was a ghost town at 3 AM and Noah had been alone in his walk into the office. There was a street sweeper going by, newspapers being disseminated to various boxes and stands, sidewalks hosed down before the swarm, the explosion when the rest of the working stiffs showed up, pounding the pavement, flooding various cafés for caffeine and carbs.

Like clockwork, Noah arrived at this ungodly hour, putting everyone else in his firm to shame with his hawkish commitment to the details. This was what you have to do to be the best, and Noah was committed to storming the highest echelon. He'd been the best Ugly Duckling his first-grade class had ever seen, a lacrosse midfielder who would take your head off, and he was on his way to being the best futures trader at the firm.

There was something about futures that made sense to Noah. He had an instinct for both short- and long-term commodity trading. He approached the whole thing like an athlete, with the simple philosophy that it took diligent hard work every day. He never rested on one single laurel, but saw every futures contract that paid out—that he *won*—an opportunity to learn from and be even better for the next. There was no celebrating, no grandstanding, no days off. If you weren't pushing yourself to improve, then you were getting worse.

A lot of traders used futures to hedge their bets, reducing the overall risk of their clients' portfolios. But what made Noah so good at it was that he never approached futures in this condescending way. They were the closest thing to an actual competition in the market. Futures contracts either paid out or busted. Win or lose. Period. Noah flourished on the risk.

He cracked open a protein shake and peeked at the clock, 3:48. He could hear his sister, Tracey, ragging him about his early approach to his job: "You're the oldest thirty-five-year-old in the world," she'd say. "You're still pretty young! Go out and have fun!"

"I'm thirty-four, Trace."

"You're focusing on the wrong thing," she'd say, ten years his junior. "Why not enjoy yourself?"

"Did it ever occur to you that I might actually like working?"

"If you could see what I see," she said, shaking her head. Here was his sister with that knowing smile of hers, exposing crooked bottom teeth. She had eyes the color of cucumber peel and she loved to rag her brother. He loved it, too. This was a shtick they'd been perfecting for years, his over-concern, her under-concern. They balanced each other out.

Noah was always the greedy go-getter, a hardwired Type A pit bull. Tracey was flighty, wonderfully flighty—it was one of the things her older brother loved about her so much, all the whimsy she saw in the world, all the life, all the hope. How she could actually enjoy where she was without ruining it with superimpositions about the future.

Noah's therapist once told him that the difference between depression and anxiety was which way you were looking: to your past or to your future. People who were depressed fixated on the past, while their anxious counterpoints couldn't stop worrying about what was coming next week, next month, next year. A future that might not ever happen.

Noah was staunchly restless, fearful, the future this supernova waiting to blow. He'd always lived that way. And he always won. Captain of the lacrosse team, valedictorian, at the top of his MBA class. Life wasn't a game, per se, but if there were gods out there keeping score, Noah was winning.

Tracey was neither depressed nor anxious. She was there, floating from moment to moment, a leaf on a river.

"You're my Forrest Gump," Noah joked.

"You laugh, but Forrest had a ton of Buddhist wisdom."

"I think he was retarded, Trace."

When he left her that morning, she was asleep on their couch. Noah halved a pink grapefruit and spread hummus on a piece of toast, leaving them on the coffee table in front of her with a note that said, *Make sure my sister eats this, okay?*

He kissed her on the forehead and remembers so clearly thinking that she looked happy. She was flat on her back, drooling a little. The blanket was spilling onto the floor and so he fixed it, covering her up.

The expression on her face was pure—that was the word he always thought of when he saw her sleep. *Pure.* He leaned down and kissed her forehead, smelled the lilac from her shampoo.

The sun wasn't even thinking about coming up yet, and in the darkness of the room he paused to watch her breathe. This was a tradition that dated back to her being born; Noah was astounded by her tiny body in her crib. It was hard for him to tell if she was breathing back then or not, and he'd get scared, tell his mom about it. The two of them would sneak back into Tracey's room together, and their mother would put Noah's hand lightly on the baby's back, so he could feel her move with every swell from her lungs.

Noah could see her clearly breathing on the couch. Her nose whistled with every breath.

They'd moved to San Francisco together thirteen months ago. He was taking a new job, a huge promotion, and was excited to relocate to such a beautiful city, a nice pardon from their childhood in the Deep South. It had never occurred to Noah that Tracey would want to move with him. It didn't seem possible that anybody made such a huge life decision on a whim.

"Really?" he said. "You'll leave?"

"Why not?"

"If it was anyone else, I'd have serious questions. What will you do?"

"I'll figure it out."

"How much does that pay?"

"It's pro bono."

"So I pay."

"You pay the rent," she said, "and I pay with elbow grease, taking care of you."

They got an apartment in the Mission District, Noah immediately pouring himself into his new gig, excited to prove that he was the best hire they ever made. Tracey was living on the exact opposite schedule, staying up late, sleeping in, exploring. But she did keep her promise of taking care of their place. She didn't seem to know how to do her own laundry, and yet she made sure their common rooms were spotless, the fridge stocked with food.

They'd go out to dinners a few nights a week and she'd tell him all about her adventures. Spoken word shows. Warehouse parties. Underground circus performances. A punk rock squat doing illegal literary readings in a condemned apartment building.

"Where do you even find out about these things?" Noah said, while they were out at Pho, bowls of soup in front of them, the smell of basil and lime ripe in the air. The front windows of the shop were steamy from the bogs of broth. "Is there a website called 'Things That Might Get Me Arrested'?"

"I find out about them the old-fashioned way," Tracey said. "I talk to people. Do you remember talking to people?"

"We're talking right now."

"Not people you know already. Opening yourself up to the experiences a stranger might offer you."

"That idea makes my palms sweaty," he said.

"If I can give you some advice . . ."

"Oh, I can't wait for this."

Tracey used her chopsticks, pointing them at her brother and clamping them together periodically, like jaws, to punctuate her thought. "My advice would be to follow your sweaty palms. See what happens if you live a life that makes your palms sweat all the time. See what wonders await you."

"Did Forrest Gump say that?"

"Poor Noah," said Tracey, pouting, then sticking her chopsticks back in the soup and coming up with a bushel of noodles.

About six months ago, his sister ran into the apartment, tousled and screaming his name. He was at the kitchen table, spreadsheets all around him, a prison of columns and rows. The S&P had dipped eleven points and he was preparing to deal with spooked clients. Tracey kept calling his name from the hallway. He heard her throw down her keys, set what sounded like a weighty duffel in the hall, and finally scramble into the kitchen with something behind her back, blurting out, "Haven't you always pictured me playing music because I totally have?"

"Where have you been?"

"At Ivan's."

"Is that a new guy you're dating?"

"No, silly," she said, revealing the clarinet she'd been concealing, "I joined a band."

"You don't know how to play that, Trace."

"You don't have to know. He teaches you."

"So I guess you guys aren't very good," said Noah.

"Off to hone my craft, skeptic," she said, going to her room, screeching awful birdcalls on the clarinet all night.

History had taught him that Tracey would be excited about the clarinet for a few months until she lost interest and the next shiny idea infiltrated her life. That was the pattern, and Noah had seen it many times: jewelry making, culinary school, photography, poetry. Tracey tried a bite and moved on.

Now she was learning the clarinet and joining a band. So what? Should he have known simply from that what was going to happen? Was this a sign?

That was the horrible thing about signs: Often they were only legible once the outcome was clear. Reverse engineer from conclusions, work back and spot the initial germs. With that appalling hindsight, Noah could comb the preceding months like his spreadsheets and easily identify his sister first being seduced, recruited, ingratiated. Could see her spending more and more of her time at band practice.

"You should totally join," Tracey said.

This was weeks later. Maybe months. His sister coming home less and less, and even when she did make a cameo, all she did was shower and change clothes, then leave again. Her promise to pay her share of the rent with elbow grease long abandoned. It didn't really bother Noah; he didn't expect her to keep it up that long. He did, however, miss seeing her regularly. She was the only person that he talked to, besides work colleagues. Emails were his preferred method of communication for everyone, even their parents. Tracey was the only actual company he looked forward to, sought out, and missed now that she was out so often.

"We're getting ready to play a show," she said.

"Where's the concert?"

"We're still learning the song."

And she was off again, closing the front door and leaving Noah in solitary confinement with his spreadsheets. Shaking his head a bit at Tracey, actually sort of jealous: She seemed inspired by something. Noah liked his job, liked feeling a sense of winning, beating his fellow traders, beating the market, owning the futures, a steady stream of atta-boys from his higher-ups; promises of increased responsibilities meant that everyone already relied on him and saw a growing role for him. But it would be a stretch to say he derived pleasure from his job, not in the same way Tracey talked about her new band. Noah loved the competition. Tracey had a passion.

But on that day, on that morning, Noah alone at the office from 3:00 to 4:30 when coworkers started trickling in before the NYSE opened, after he left Tracey the halved grapefruit and toast smeared with hummus and the note, after he'd already prepped both the meetings he was to lead later, after he did three sets of bicep curls with the forty-pound dumbbell he stashed under his desk, after he ate two hardboiled egg whites and organic blueberries, drank a kale smoothie, after he chastised his young assistant for what he characterized as a "latent undergraduate slack ethic," after she sat looking at him as he bullied her with his idiotic words, after he watched her leave his office and commended himself at his deft handling of the situation, knowing he was helping her rise to his expectations, to be the best worker she could, mentoring her so she could thrive in this environment the same way Noah did, doling out this bit of tough love for her own good, her own career; after all this, Noah was alone for about three minutes with nothing much to do, and he considered another couple sets of bicep curls when his phone rang, and he yelled to his assistant stationed right outside, "I'm not here," and she didn't say anything back to him but he heard her greet the caller, and Noah retrieved the dumbbell from under his desk and started hoisting the thing and silently saying to himself, *One, two, three, four*, counting reps and feeling strong, feeling ripped, feeling like a champion, when he saw his assistant standing in the doorway.

"What?" he said.

"You need to take this."

The weight hanging limply in his dangling arm, and he said it again, "What?"

She stood there.

"Who is it?" he asked.

"The police."

The officer's voice was male, low and raspy, like someone with a cold. Someone barely able to choke out the words he had to say.

Noah held the phone with one hand and still had the dumb-bell dangling in his other and the officer gave him a cold, objective report of the facts that were known so far: A brass band jumped off of the Golden Gate Bridge about ninety minutes ago. They all had their driver's licenses in their pockets, and he was alerting family members of what had happened.

"Is she okay?" Noah asked.

"I'm sorry."

"Is she alive?"

"I'm sorry," said the cop.

Noah hung up. He didn't remember if the conversation was over or not. He felt an urge to wash his hands so he floated down the hallway with the weight still in his hand. Thankfully no one else was in the men's room. Noah set the dumbbell on the counter, him at the faucet with a pond of soap in both his palms, rubbing them together for what felt like the entire workday and letting the lather and water wash over each finger, each nail, each freckle and hair and scar, and he cranked the water temperature up as far as it would go and kept his hands moving underneath it, the backs of his hands turning the color of cooked salmon and throbbing and did that one cop have to call all the bereaved families himself, or did they spread the agony around the station, each officer taking one or two? Finally the heat was too much to take, and Noah held them at eye level, watching every drop jump off his hands into the sink. His sister was dead. He had been told that Tracey was dead. His hands hurt now, drying them on his pants and walking out and leaving the water rushing, the dumbbell perched on the counter.

Back to his office, Noah needed to compartmentalize, to paste on his face a convincing façade. There was nothing he could do to alter the day's events, so why indulge his emotions? It was like playing in a lacrosse tournament in college when he had a torn meniscus in his knee, not smart, not pragmatic, fucking painful, risking more damage, but he wouldn't hear his coach's pleas to step aside, to pro-tect himself—he was going to fight to the end and he was going to win and no one could stop him, nobody.

So Noah didn't tell anyone at work what had happened. He stayed and emailed and trouble-shot a client package with a col-league and led those two meetings with his team and ate a Cobb salad and even remembered leaving his dumbbell in the men's room and got it and stowed it back under his desk.

Compartmentalize and conquer. Get through this. Don't buckle. He was keeping the world at bay until he went into the kitchen for a bottled water and saw someone's half-eaten toast on the counter, and his feet tingled and his heart sped up and he saw tie-dyed things in his periphery and he lost track of how long he stood and stared at the toast till another trader said, "What are you looking at?" and Noah said, "What?" and the guy said, "You're just standing there," and Noah said, "Oh."

His hands ached all day from the scalding water. Tracey was gone. He had to tell their parents, but he was unsure what to tell them. How to tell them. He wondered if he should be like that cop and simply assault them with apologies. *I'm sorry, I'm sorry, I'm sorry.* Would that work? Maybe with their mom but certainly not with their father. No, he would not hang up on Noah. He would do the opposite. He'd bully, scold, blame. He'd hide his grief in anger and gift it to his son.

Noah owed them a phone call and one would come, but first, he and his aching hands sat behind his desk. The workday was over. The office empty again. But Noah did not know where to go—how the hell could he go home? To their house? To their house without her?

He wished he had a toothbrush, an acrid taste in his mouth, like getting off a fifteen-hour flight, that hangover of recycled air and germs and dehydration. Like the time his whole family went to New Zealand, Noah nineteen, Tracey nine, and once arrived, they both bought Cokes in the airport and raced to see who could finish the fastest, laughing at how many times Tracey had to stop and burp, her eyes watering from all the carbonation. Noah held his empty can and watched her try to finish hers.

He Googled "brass band+golden gate."

One news story he stumbled on had a hyperlink to a YouTube page, TheGreatJake's. That was how he found it. Creating a new account, settling on the username Noah911 because that was who he was now: He was Noah soldered to emergency. He was the guy with a new limb, a new life. He was the guy with a ghost attached to his person. There was no Noah without Tracey's tragedy.

This was his new identity.

This was him.

It was almost like the day she was born, a new addition, the quick change to his identity. One minute, he had a new baby sister. One minute, the nurse asked Noah if he wanted to hold her tiny body and he was too scared to stand up with her, fretting a botched handoff and dropping her, hurting her, so he sat in a chair and the nurse handed him the swaddled baby, a beanie on her head, her eyes closed and making a moaning, then a gurgling noise.

"I'm Noah," he said, "your brother."

He stared down at her shut eyes and asked their mom, "When will she get hair?"

She was in her hospital bed, exhausted, still doped up on an epidural. "You didn't have any hair when you were born, either."

"Really?"

"Nope."

"So she'll get lots like me?"

"Yes."

He stared back at her sleeping form.

"Are you going to be a strong brother for her?" said his mom.

"Yes."

"Promise?"

He'd hold her dead body right now, if they gave it to him. He'd sit in a chair to protect her from being dropped. He'd rock her. He'd say, "I'm Noah, your brother."

He viewed the clip many times in his office. How he hated and loved it. Easily spotting his sister. Tracey was tall. She wore purple pants, a shirt with a gargantuan collar. She had her clarinet. She threw it off the bridge like a pitcher's fast ball. She held her nose before jumping, the same gesture her brother had seen her do countless times off of high dives.

Yes, this was who he was now, Noah911.

And he didn't need to create the username to watch the video, but he did need to register an account to leave a comment. It took him almost an hour to figure out what to say. His ideas shot the gamut from pure vitriol at the person who could post this, indictments of his scruples, TheGreatJake's adoration of carnage trumping the feelings of the loved ones left behind, the clip besmirching them with every subsequent view. Noah would break the guy's nose. He'd hurt him much more than that. He'd make TheGreatJake his own emergency, soldered to whoever loved him the way that Noah911 loved Tracey.

He finally settled on the comment "I feel sad for whoever posted this," because he thought that maybe that message had the potential to reach TheGreatJake. If he cyber-screamed at him, Noah would be dismissed as another troll, another lunatic empowered by the Internet. But if he focused on his own sadness, thrusting it at the poster, if he made a simple and clean statement about the callused nature of sharing the video with the world, maybe TheGreatJake would hear him.

Or maybe he wanted somebody else to hear him because he couldn't say what he really wanted to say, what he felt in the deepest part of himself: It was his fault she died. His fault for not watching after her diligently enough. His fault for trusting her, or for trusting the world with her. He was the practically minded one; she needed his guidance. He helped her remember all sorts of things. In fact, the only thing he didn't help her remember to do was practice the clarinet. Noah911 actually thought that maybe the band was teaching her responsibility. He encouraged her music, her involvement. She was growing up, finding her voice. Tracey was changing for the better.

The memory of that tarred and feathered his heart.

And he deserved every daub of hot tar for not taking care of her.

Could he email his parents about Tracey? Was that allowed?

It wasn't; he knew that. Knew that but he thought that maybe it was okay, too. He typed in his father's email, his mother's.

The subject was simply: *Tracey.*

He stared at the blank body of the message, having no idea what to say. Should he imbed a link to the video? Should they get to see it for themselves, salvage the opportunity to witness her final minutes, or would that be too much for them? Noah didn't want to hurt them, didn't know what would help and what would throb with misery so he sat there.

Cursor flashing.

Stomach growling.

He wanted to get drunk.

His hands were feeling better.

He changed the subject to this: *I'm sorry.*

But he never typed text in the body.

There would be a phone call but not till later. He needed to find a way to peel himself from this desk, needed to summon the strength to go home. To walk in there. To be there.

He took a taxi home, the driver wanting to chat but Noah not really participating. The driver's eyes darted from road to rearview mirror. Noah asked the driver to let him off at the liquor store a block from the apartment. He bought a bottle of vodka and thought of it as a futures commodity that he'd never traded before. Numbness. This was what his future was going to need, and he'd pay anything for it.

Noah needed to be anesthetized before he saw reminders of her scattered everywhere, too many to tally. He had two long pulls off the vodka bottle and climbed the front stairs.

The sound his key made opening up the front door was horrid and loud. He could feel each scrape as the key hit the tumbler. He turned the knob and stood there, in the doorway, and didn't move.

He walked to where he saw her last, sleeping on the couch, where he saw her chest move with every breath. The spilling blanket. He saw the grapefruit, uneaten. He saw the toast, the hummus hardened into a brown meringue. There was one bite taken out of it. He could see her teeth marks. Even in the dark, Noah911 would swear that he could see each individual contour on the bread left by every sovereign tooth. He could see her so clearly.

He could also see the note he left her, *Make sure my sister eats this, okay?*

He opened up the vodka bottle and had a huge swig.

He fished his laptop from his bag and lay down on the couch. In her spot.

He watched the video clip many times. It's all that he had left.

Noah911 made another hurtful and necessary click on replay. Taking it all in another time.

As the video started, Noah didn't see anything treacherous. They were normal people playing instruments.

Until the moment they weren't.

7.

Sara would be lying if she didn't acknowledge a certain pleasure in Hank's impulsive and violent reaction to Felix kicking her car. It was beautiful medicine, watching her brother being protective of her. Especially after the sex tape. Especially after being suspended from the restaurant. Especially after hearing Felix cussing and screaming at her and bringing a boot to her car. She needed to know there was someone alive who would defend her, someone who cared for Sara even when she couldn't fathom caring about herself.

That was Hank. Her brother was stunning in his simplicity. He had no mind to do anything he didn't feel like. Hank would hit the gym religiously. He'd go to work when he had to. Besides those actions, he sat around watching MMA clips and drinking beer and doing pushups and playing darts in his room. A sound that Sara associated with a cruel lullaby. She tried to sleep through it nightly, each dart's *thwunk* into the board, the rip as Hank pulled it back out. So often she lay there staring at the cinderblocks, counting *thwunk*s and rips, *thwunk*s and rips.

Yet Hank could get his ire up fast. So when she came in the house four minutes ago and found him at the kitchen table cutting his fingernails, he looked up and witnessed the emergency on her face, the wide-eyed panic, and Hank said, "What happened?" and she leaked the whole story out. Well, not the whole tale exactly. Omitted were some need-to-know details. Redacted were the juiciest morsels. Hank had no investment, Sara figured, in the beginning of her day. His question, "What happened?" really meant *Tell me why you seem so upset this instant?* and thus she snipped the account to what she deemed the meat of the story, cleaving the fat to the butcher's floor.

The sex tape, the work suspension, even the fact she sped up the street and almost hit Felix—these were amputated particulars.

Sara's story was remixed in a way that emphasized the vulgar and unprovoked malice of the road fisherman, Felix going batshit for no reason and Sara scared that he was going to hit her in the face and he kicked her car, Hank, he ruined her mirror, Hank, he damn near took a swing.

"He almost clocked you, huh?" Hank said.

"He lost it."

"Did he now."

"I've always hated him."

"Keys," said Hank.

"Huh?"

"Give me your keys."

She handed them over and Hank sprinted out, peeled out, and Sara was alone in the kitchen. She is alone now, fixating on the twigs of fingernails on the table. The rusty little clippers next to them. The fingernails in a pile, like dried-out snakes.

Sara experienced what might be considered remorse. Because it wasn't only Felix down there. Rodney was in the front yard. The last thing she wanted was for him to get hurt.

They'd been so close before his accident. He was her first kiss, her first love. It wasn't fairy tale romantic or anything, that first time they felt each other's lips behind 7-Eleven, next to a dumpster.

They'd bought Slurpees and were playing pinball and Rodney's lips were purple from his grape Slurpee, which he refused to drink with a straw, a detail that Sara found wildly strange and endearing. Everyone drank Slurpees with straws, but not Rodney, putting his lips on the cup and taking small sips like it was coffee.

It looked to Sara like purple lipstick. She remembers thinking that: Rodney's wearing lipstick.

He was so into the game that he made contorted faces, puckering his purple lips as he manned the machine, about to get multiball when for the first time ever Sara got turned on—or at least the first time she could remember. She needed to kiss him. She had a craving for a kiss that had to happen right that second, no matter the setting or their sugared breath or how unreal the temperature was outside, pushing 110°.

"Come here," she said, dragging him from the machine.

"Wait, I've almost got—"

"Do you want to kiss me?"

His hands immediately fell from the machine, leaving it beeping and chirping and gloating as the silver ball drained down the middle, and Rodney's purple lips trailed Sara outside the 7-Eleven, into the side alley, with its smell of humid old hot dogs. They stood right by a dumpster teeming with processed foods and right on top was a cardboard cutout of a Nascar driver holding a glistening bottle of beer with a caption that said, "The one and only."

None of these details derailed Sara's titanium impulse. She would have this kiss and it would be amazing. She could sense it.

She could also, though, sense that Rodney was nervous, eyes darting all around, fidgeting from foot to foot. He pointed at the cardboard driver and said, "Did you know *racecar* is a palindrome?"

"What's a palindrome?"

"Something that's spelled the same way backward."

Sara tried spelling racecar the other way in her head, but didn't care enough to get past the first C, and she said to Rodney, "Kiss me."

And he did. He put his purple lips on hers. His mouth was cold. She could not only smell grape but chocolate, left over from a donut they split. The kiss lasted about twenty seconds. Then they pulled back and stared at each other.

"Wow," he said.

"Again," she said.

They didn't leave the alley for fifteen more minutes. That Nascar driver watched the whole show.

Which now that Sara thinks about it is a merciless foreshadowing. Because every perv in the world is kicking back with a cold one and watching her sex tape. Every creep on the planet knows that Sara is the one and only girl in the video.

She pulls out her phone and sends Nat this text: *Why?*

She tries to block out images of Hank pummeling Rodney.

It's possible that her brother wouldn't harm him. Hank knows their history. Knows how close they once were.

But when his temper cranks up, Hank isn't thinking about anything rational.

The feeling in her hands is back. The feeling that she has hands. That she's aware of having hands. With the sex tape and the suspension and Nat being a total asshole and Felix being mean, Sara's hands get the vibrating cell phone feeling again; however, it's worse this time. They feel heavy, like twenty pounds each.

Nat's not going to answer her text. It's over. This is his way of breaking up. That's who she should sic Hank on, her attack dog and protector. At least, Hank has her back. He'll always defend her. Without her brother looking out, Sara would have no one knocking the monsters away. She's lucky to have him, even when he frustrates her so much, even when it's hours of *thwunk* and rip.

She should make Nat explain it to her, decrypt the teasing why of it. Hank can hold him down and Sara can interrogate. Make her understand precisely why he treated her this way.

There's no reason not to clip her own fingernails, sitting at the kitchen table. She picks the clippers and only does the pinkie and then she feels a swelling in her hand, like it's about to burst.

Deep breaths, Sara. Don't flip out. Don't lose it. He's fine. Hank won't hurt him. He's only getting even with Felix.

Sara puts the nail clippers down and decides to use her phone as a diversion, catch up on her celebrity gossip, but everyone's still talking about the brass band from earlier in the day—the image on MSN's homepage is the Golden Gate Bridge with a saxophone superimposed on top of it. Caption reading, MURDER MUSIC.

So much for distraction.

She sends another note to Nat: *Didn't you like me?*

She paces, worrying about Rodney, wondering why Nat won't text her back. Paces and almost cries and there's no way to escape this new life—the one she never asked for—her life with a conjoined twin.

She realizes she'll never be able to separate herself from digital Sara, nude and pixilated. Perfectly preserved. Frozen for all time. Sex tape as fossil. Her twin will never age and will always be there. Her twin feels to her like a wholesale tragedy, and from here on out, Sara will never be alone again, always dragging this twin through their life.

And the mere presence of that thought in her head, the fact that it shuttles around within her, makes Sara hyperventilate, rest her head on the kitchen table, the Formica a bit sticky from one of Hank's pancake stacks. It's all a bit sticky. The whole room, the whole house. They should have moved after their parents died. They should have redecorated. They should've tried to make it less their parents' place, but neither of them really wanted to do that. It's a way of preserving the extravagances of memory, living in the house long after their parents have gone.

Take this kitchen. Take the linoleum floor that's white, yellow, and green, pocked by the jagged bottoms of the chairs, little potholes. Take the sun-bleached curtain over the sink. It used to be lavender, then gray, and now it's stark white, the wan light growing in intensity every day. Take the fridge, the wheezing fridge, its compressor barely holding on, emitting rumbles and snorts. Take the stove with three burners broken. The countertop with its stains and mildewed edges. The leaky faucet making its own muted *thwunk* with every drip.

These are things that should be fixed or changed. A lot of them easily remedied. Buy another curtain; they're cheap and easy. But nothing is cheap and easy about transcending grief, especially when it hasn't been given its proper due. Sara realizes that the grieving process in this house has been incomplete, was never really begun.

Sara could never clean up their house, after their deaths. It was the leftovers in the fridge that paralyzed her. After the funeral, Sara saw a quarter pan of lasagna, the last home-cooked meal that her mom prepared. Sara doesn't count Hank heating up turkey chili, or Sara reheating whatever the restaurant served for staff meal. No, that lasagna was the end of a family sitting down together.

After the funeral, Sara ate all that lasagna in one sitting; it was enough to serve four or five people, but Sara's grief was famished. Her mom had once told her that some brides kept their leftover wedding cake in the freezer and ate a piece to cheer themselves up over the years during trying times. Sara couldn't pace herself, though, her fork ferociously stabbing at the cold, congealed mess, choking on the dried noodles and cheese and over-baked sauce. Sara didn't taste anything, finishing it all up and holding the glass dish, letting it fall from her hands to shatter on the floor. Took her two days to inflate the gumption to sweep up the shards.

There was no way to get her stampeding feelings under control, and she feels the same now with this latest betrayal. All Sara can do is rest her head in a sticky spot next to a pile of fingernails.

No text back from Nat.

No way to lasso a sex tape and bring it down.

Tires screech outside. Hank's home. Hank's dog, Bernard, barks from the porch. She hears her brother say back to the bark, "Your master's still got it, boy! Let's drink a beer."

Hank enters the kitchen, the dog trotting behind. Her brother's not wearing a shirt and goes to the fridge for a cold one, drinks most of it in a sip, slams the empty on the stained counter. He has another beer in the same motivated way, then belches. The other finished bottle crashes down, too. Hank stares out the gauzy curtain into the backyard, the only item out there besides brush and bugs is an aboveground pool that hasn't had any water in it since the death of their parents.

All of this done without looking at or saying one word to Sara.

She watches him surveying the arid yard, wondering what her brother is thinking. Does he have moments of personal reflection? And would he ever open up to her? These are important questions for Sara, given the circumstances.

Because she's going to have to tell him. Sooner rather than later. She's going to have to come clean about the sex tape. She has no choice. If she lets him find out about it from anyone else, Hank will lose his shit. He's going to be so pissed, so disappointed. Hank has never turned his temper at Sara, not really. There's been yelling, but never any violence. He's gentle with her. Or he was. Until he finds out about this.

"Is Rodney all right?" Sara says, flexing her hands, in and out. Her heart rate stays too high and her armpits stink.

"He'll live," he says.

"Will you sit down?" she asks.

Hank grabs another beer from the fridge and moves a chair back from the table, fixing it into a few potholes. "Well, that was fun."

"What was?"

"Stomping those fools."

"What did you do to Rodney?"

"I gained some respect for him today," says Hank. "He didn't have to square up with me. I'd already whupped the other dumb asses. But he wanted to take a go. It was impressive."

"Does he need a doctor?"

"He's needed a doctor ever since the balloon."

"You know what I'm asking."

"He's fine, Baby Sis. He'll have a headache, but these things happen."

Sara swells with conflicting sensations, a different kind of conjoined twins. On one hand, she's happy that Felix got hooked, glad that the buffoon learned that there are consequences for being nasty. But she has guilt now, too. Some shame that it's her fault that Rodney got hurt. She'll apologize. It's easy to be honest with him because she once loved him, probably still does deep down, in some unhelpful ways. They'd still be dating if he'd never mounted that balloon, and because of that he deserves the truth.

And so does her brother, her protector. She loves the fact that he went down there for her. She loves that there's no thinking with Hank, no weighing the pros and cons, no looking at problems from all sides and selecting the prudent course.

No, Hank only leaps.

He loves her and he leaps.

He loves her and he leaps and she is protected.

It's going to be a hard conversation, but Sara has to be strong. He's been strong for her, and Sara has to meet his brawn with some of her own.

"There's something I need to tell you, Hank," says Sara. "I'm sorry this happened, but you should hear it from me."

Her brother's face, its mass of freckles and moles and some acne from the steroids, has a tenderness to it that Sara hadn't expected to see. Normally, he wears his rage like war paint, but now he looks gentle and concerned.

"Everyone already knows," he says, shrugging his shoulders.

"You know?"

"I'll beat Nat's ass for you," says Hank. "Wanna beer?"

"Sure."

He gets two more out of the fridge, and they sit at the sticky kitchen table. "You okay?" he asks.

"I ruined my life."

The dog rests his head on Hank's huge thigh. "Don't say that."

"What's left for me?"

Hank rubs Bernard's head. "Why are you asking that, Baby Sis?"

Sara loves it when he calls her that. Baby Sis. So familial. What you call someone you love, no matter what they do.

"I trusted Nat," Sara says, checking her phone again to see if he's responded to her texts, which he hasn't. She sets the phone on the table next to the pile of fingernails and turns it over so she can't see its teasing face. "I'm so stupid."

"You can't ruin your life, Sara, because our lives were already pretty ruined."

"Don't say our lives are ruined."

"Pretty ruined."

"That's not better," she says.

"Look around," Hank says, pointing toward the squalor drenching their house, and right on cue the fridge burps and snorts. "This ain't the Ritz. Hell, people probably thought you'd have six sex tapes by now."

For the first time all day, Sara laughs. For the first time since hearing about what Nat had done, she's unaware of her body. She's not thinking about her vibrating hands. She's unaware that her heart has slowed to its normal resting rate.

The laughter is pure. It is encompassing, taking over all of her conscious mind, freeing her. For that moment she is a human being without a digital twin. She has no mirror in cyberspace. Hers is an identity unmarred by technology. Sara is a laughing woman drinking a beer with her brother.

"Six sex tapes!" she says, leaning over and punching Hank in the arm.

"At least five."

Another punch.

"Hank!"

"So one's pretty good," he says. "Baby Sis, you're ahead of the game as far as I'm concerned."

Hank holds his beer toward his sister and they let them clink. No one says anything corny like cheers. They let the bottles do the talking.

"I've already been to jail four times," he says, "so you're doing better than me."

Maybe he's right. Maybe it's the best that can be expected of them. In the grand scheme, maybe they're not doing so badly.

That lone gust of bravado dissipates quickly, though. Perhaps her brother can be unaffected by all of this, yet Sara doesn't know if she's up to the challenge. She wants to be a badass. She wants to be unflappable, poised for whatever comes her way. Problem is it's coming back, these symptoms, the buzzing hands and heart and breathing. Quickly, she's back to being a wretched twin.

"I don't know how to face everyone in town," she says.

"Don't worry about those bozos."

"I mean it, Hank."

"So do I."

"They all think I'm a whore."

"You're a whore; I'm a caveman. Fuck 'em."

"It's that easy?"

"Fuck 'em, Baby Sis."

"I want to be a kid again."

"Me, too."

"I want to move."

"Everybody has sex, Sara. I know it feels like the end of the world today, but it will get easier living with it."

"What if I don't want to live with it?"

"People live with worse," he says. He finishes his beer and goes for more. "Hey, what do you want me to do to Nat when I kick his ass?"

"I don't want that."

"Any requests or shall I improvise?"

"Don't hurt him."

"Not even a little bit? A black eye?" says Hank, coming back with two more cold ones.

"That would make me feel bad for him and I don't want to pity that asshole."

"What about a liver punch? Hurts like hell and no visual evidence."

Bernard barks and Hank scratches his head.

"Even the dog thinks Nat needs an ass kicking," says Hank.

"Please leave him alone."

"Let me know if you change your mind."

Sara doesn't change her mind as they sit in the kitchen drinking beers, but she would like to hear how her brother would defend her. She'd like to listen while someone outlines exactly how he'd protect her. It doesn't matter that their house is made of cinderblocks. It doesn't matter all the broken down things scattered about, a linoleum floor lined with potholes.

"Will you tell me about it?" she says.

Hank smiles. "You want details?"

Yes, she wants to hear about every punch, every kick. She has to hear every single way he will defend her. She has to know.

A MOMENT PASSES and then Hank says, "Come with me," getting up and opening the back door.

"I don't want to move."

"You said you wanted to be a kid again. Come on."

Hank waves for her to follow, and he walks through the back door.

Sara sighs, knows that it's easier to do it by herself so he doesn't come back and carry her over his shoulder.

By the time she's in the backyard, Hank is already standing in the pool. She can only see him from the chest up. She peeks around the whole dusty rectangle of yard. It's all dirt and weeds and fire ants. Flat as a grave.

"You used to love swimming," he says and pretends to do the breaststroke, walking in a circle. "The water is perfect, Baby Sis."

Sara can't get in the pool fast enough, tearing toward it and leaping in. There are a couple inches or so of dust and sand at the bottom. The walls are cracked and puckered. But right now Sara doesn't see any of that. All she sees is water and her brother and her parents sitting in chairs on the side, watching them swim.

There are so many memories back here that Sara can't pick out one, can't zero in on one day where they were all here, all alive. It's not one recollection from their past, but a hive of them, a colony of reconstructions, Hank showing off how long he can hold his breath underwater, Sara doing handstands, legs together, toes pointed perfectly. Their mom works her way through yet another Sudoku book. Their dad flips burgers on the barbecue. There are enough memories now to fill this pool.

"I like the backstroke," she says and mimics the motion, moving in the same circular direction as her brother, both of them walking around and swinging their arms.

"You're good at it," he says.

Hank laughs and Sara laughs, and they are both laughing.

They are laughing like children and walking in circles and sort of swimming and they spend the next ten minutes like this. Hank forgets to tell her what he'll do to Nat, and Sara forgets she wants to know.

She switches to freestyle.

Hank says, "How the hell do you do the butterfly again?"

He awkwardly flaps his muscled arms like he's trying to fly and

Sara laughs so hard that she sits down on its sandy bottom, then lies down completely. She doesn't say anything, straightening out and moving her arms and her legs back and forth in the dust, a desert snow angel.

"Is this right?" he asks, shaking his arms in quick small circles.

8.

The day Balloon Boy was born, Rodney had been with Sara. They left their junior high and kissed in the park and then saw a man with a big balloon tied to a tree. It wasn't typical; it was flat like a big hunk of gray bread, about four feet across, hovering close to the ground. Rodney and Sara asked the guy what he was doing.

"It's a homemade weather balloon for some experiments," he said.

"What kind of experiments, sir?" Rodney asked.

"Do you two want to be my assistants?"

"Sure," they said.

"First thing I need you to do is watch the balloon for me. I have to run to the restroom. Can you do that?"

"We're not babies," said Sara.

"Don't touch anything until I'm back," the man said. "Then I'll show you how to measure barometric pressure." He ran off toward the bathroom.

Sara poked the balloon and said, "I wonder if this could make it to Spain."

"Why Spain?"

"We can go up, up, and away," she said.

Back then, Rodney's goal in life was to impress Sara. Making her laugh was his chief mission, and so he said, "Want to watch me fly?"

"Don't be crazy."

He strutted to the huge balloon and jumped into the middle of the flat gray thing. It took his weight no problem, kept hovering a few feet high.

Sara said, "Quit it."

He said, "Spain."

He reached for the rope and untied it.

"Get off there, Rodney."

He hovered a bit higher.

"This isn't funny," she said.

"Hey!" said the man, running toward them. "Son, be careful!"

And Sara said, "Please don't."

They kept screaming at Rodney in alternating sentences, but he wasn't listening. He smiled at her. He loved every second at first because this was all a joke. No big deal. Nothing to worry about. Rodney knew they'd all laugh once he was back on the ground learning about barometric pressure.

The balloon was fifteen feet in the air.

Rodney didn't feel any fear. He was a kid impressing his girl. Swept up in making her laugh. Sara wasn't saying anything anymore, only staring up at him, open-mouthed.

There weren't any clouds in the sky. He was up there by himself. He felt like a test pilot, brave and fearless. Someone reckless with liberty. The sun shone so violently that he couldn't even see its shape; it seemed to run and bleed like lava. It made everything a harsh blinding hue, and Rodney squinted into it, not bothered by the opaqueness but feeling welcomed by it, seduced.

There was also the unmistakable smell of burning hair, a scent that normally meant he was in the kitchen watching Uncle Felix fry fish, singeing the coils from his knuckles and hands. He despised the stink, but up on the balloon, he didn't mind it. It represented something else: The things that burned this high in the air were boundaries, limits, and a free Rodney flew, floated, soared. The sky was ready to take him wherever he wanted to go.

This must have been what it was like when they realized the earth was round, not flat—to understand that there were no edges to fall from, no end to the world. It would spin and spin forever, and they were all so lucky to be here. Rodney for the first time felt a great appetite to experience life outside of Traurig. He didn't care if it was Spain or not. All he craved was flight.

Lost in fantasy, there was no part of him that pondered the balloon tipping over. It wasn't even possible that he'd fall out of the sky, that his skull would jostle and crash. He'd never heard of aphasia or brain traumas or closed head injuries. Rodney had no idea that mouths could curdle and wobble and warp and never work right again.

How could any of those impossibilities be plausible when he was drifting on a balloon, feeling a warm breeze?

At first, it was a simple shimmy, a slight waver, a blip of turbulence that barely registered.

A few seconds later, though, the balloon buckled, shaking from side to side. Rodney tried to dig his hands into it for some grip. He looked down at Sara and she was the last thing he saw.

The falling was fast. It seemed to Rodney that he was on the balloon and then on the concrete.

He had two separated shoulders and a broken jaw and a broken nose and a broken wrist and a broken eye socket and three cracked ribs and a shattered ankle and a ruptured kidney and a traumatic brain injury. Everyone in town called him *lucky* once he was out of the hospital and limping around. All patched up on the outside, but they couldn't see the tornado unleashed in his head.

· · ·

LYING ON THE front yard's hot dirt, fresh from Hank punching him in the cheek and in the chin and in the solar plexus, Balloon Boy looks around for his dad and uncle. They both lie in close proximity, moaning and attempting to peel themselves off the dirt.

"I'll bring the damaged pole," Rodney's father says.

"Be gentle with it, Larry. Maybe it can be saved," says Uncle Felix.

Larry lays the broken fishing pole across his palms, carrying it like an injured animal.

Slowly, the three remaining members of the Curtis clan limp into the house. They lurch through the front door, onto the concrete floor, which Kathleen used to have covered with a knockoff Persian, the rug running the whole square room, concealing the cold cement underneath. Uncle Felix rolled up and torched the rug in the backyard once she'd left.

The only furniture in the room now is a small couch, a record player sitting on the floor in the corner, hooked up to a couple of cheap speakers. All of Felix's old vinyl is in a pile around it, Hank Williams, David Allan Coe, Johnny Cash. He's been known to crank up the volume and howl along to his records, Rodney always staying in his room until these recitals are over. He barricades himself away because he hates that old hillbilly shit, but more importantly, he doesn't like listening to his uncle sing—something he so badly wishes he could do—especially if a melody is being wasted on some redneck twang.

There's also a swamp cooler jutting from the living room wall, an ancient one that looks like a lawnmower has been turned on its side and jammed into the cinderblock. It makes so much noise when it's on that the whole room reverberates, the mewling ricocheting off the concrete walls and floor.

Not all three of them can sit on the couch at once. Rodney and Larry take a seat, while Uncle Felix lays the two halves of the broken fishing pole on the concrete floor and kneels down next to it, a doctor conducting an autopsy.

"He is an evil man," Felix says. "He wants to fight, fine. I am not opposed to physical violence. But ruining another man's fishing pole?"

"How's your head?" Larry asks his son, running his finger across the boy's cheek.

"I'm," Rodney says, then five seconds later, "fine."

"A fishing pole can't even defend itself!" Felix says.

"Do you need some water?" Larry asks his son.

Rodney shakes his head no.

"I'm sorry about this," Larry says to Rodney.

Uncle Felix takes both pieces of broken pole, waving them about like he's conducting a choir, and Balloon Boy dreads what's coming next. He's seen this look on his uncle's face many times, right before a bad idea: The look is like a whistle on a speeding train, telling you danger is on its way. The same face Uncle Felix had right before fighting Hank, or a couple weeks back when he rifled through the neighbor's trashcans looking for salmon skins, convinced they'd stolen a fish from the fridge, or a few weeks before that when Felix jacked a battery out of someone else's car in broad daylight, not even hurrying, calmly thieving, and then put it in his truck. Rodney knows this face and he fears it.

Uncle Felix brings one of the broken pieces of fishing pole up close to his face. "As much as it pains me to admit, this pole is a goner. Hank can't get away with it."

"He's already gotten away with it," says Larry.

"The battle has only begun," Uncle Felix says.

Larry stands up off the couch, clapping his hands, swelling with toxic camaraderie. If Balloon Boy has seen the crazy look in his uncle's eyes as he conceives and executes a bad idea, he knows this face from his father: a blank-eyed, abject agreement. He's going along with whatever plan his brother spins.

"I say we light her car on fire," Uncle Felix says. "Let's hold it responsible."

"Good plan," Larry says.

"Bad," Balloon Boy says, then four seconds later, "plan."

"Hush," they say in unison.

"But wait," Larry says, "won't Hank kick our asses again?"

Felix smiles and swings those broken poles about, keeping that deranged choir singing: "We need backup. Call our softball team. Call every Wombat. Get our whole batting order here and we'll light her bucket of bolts on fire and get some revenge on Hank." As he finishes his thought, he begins using the poles as swords, fencing thin air.

Balloon Boy isn't on the softball team, but he does go to the park to help with their practices, collecting equipment and whatnot. Sometimes a Wombat will look around the park and ask Rodney, "Isn't this the place where it happened?" and he'll say, "Yes," and sometimes a Wombat will say, "How high'd you get on that balloon anyway?" and he'll shrug with a smile, not wanting to talk about it.

Now Larry gets on the horn, calling Wombats, and Balloon Boy sits and watches, knowing there's nothing he can do to talk them out of this. But he can make sure that Sara stays safe, which is what concerns him the most. She might not love him anymore, yet that doesn't mean he's forgotten his own feelings for her. They're locked in him. That's what makes Balloon Boy feel so alone, all the swirling thoughts that can only clank around his brain like shoes in a dryer.

Alone, with no way to articulate himself.

The two halves of him, much like the busted fishing pole. Rodney and Balloon Boy. The same. Different. Permanent. Terrible.

"Excuse," Rodney says and gets off the couch, "me."

"Where you going?" Larry says, cupping the phone with his hand.

"Need. Fresh. Air." The whole sentence takes sixteen seconds to choke out.

"No such thing in Traurig," Uncle Felix says.

Rodney goes out the front door, walks over the small dune in the yard, and makes his way toward Sara's. He should have stopped in his room to get his pen and pad. This is going to take a lot of words.

But it was about time to Rodney, maximizing his time. So he decided to blow off the pen and pad in the name of getting to Sara as soon as possible.

The day is equal parts hot and achy, and Balloon Boy wonders if it's even possible for him to get a concussion, after the damage already done. Hank's fists connected hard against his body and Rodney feels a bit woozy.

He hears a ringing, which isn't a good sign. He might be concussed. Then he realizes it's Old Erma's wind chimes a couple houses up. Obviously, there is no midday wind, but she sits on her porch, clanging her cane along all the chimes, like a prisoner running a tin cup across her cell's bars. She smiles as Rodney passes and calls to him, "Hey there, sweetie. You good?"

"I'm," he says, and six seconds later, "good."

"I love music," she says, sending her cane over the wind chimes again.

He sees a lizard darting up a wall and a swarm of ants slowly mutilating a moth and carrying the bits off.

A toddler on a tricycle rides it in slow laps around an above-ground pool in a front yard. Rodney waves at her. The young girl doesn't break concentration, slowly circling while wearing a ratty red bathing suit.

He's at the end of the cul-de-sac, standing in front of Sara's house. There are so many other places he'd like to be—namely any place where Hank is not—and yet here is where he must be. Sara needs him.

Hank has a Rottweiler the size of a Mini Cooper, but even that won't stop Balloon Boy from warning her. The dog barks and froths on the porch, and despite being terrified Rodney walks right by it to ring the bell.

Hank comes to the door and stands, tapping his foot and smiling. He doesn't have a shirt on and Rodney hates how small he feels next to Hank.

"You wanna throw some more hands with me?" asks Hank.

"Sa. Ra," says Balloon Boy.

"Nope."

The Mini Cooper keeps barking.

"Sa," he says, "ra."

"She's busy not talking to you."

"Sa! Ra!"

"Don't poke a grizzly with a stick," says Hank. "We bite." He rubs Bernard's head. "We bite and it's no bueno for you."

"Sa! Ra!"

Sara finally comes to the screen door and says, "What do you need, Rodney?"

"They," he says, then five seconds later, "come."

"Who?"

"Dad . . . un . . . cle."

"They're coming here?" Sara says.

Balloon Boy nods.

"We no speaky the retard," says Hank with a brash Chinese accent, walking back inside with his hound in tow.

"Tell me what's wrong," Sara says.

These moments in Balloon Boy's life are the worst, the times when he needs words to make someone understand what's happening without the aid of his pad and pen. It would have only taken thirty seconds to run to his room and grab them. Now he has to humiliate himself in front of her, one syllable at a time.

And if she could ever see what's been written down in his pad, he thinks it might rekindle what they had. Balloon Boy has heard stories of people losing one of their senses and then the others gaining strength. For Rodney, this compensation happens in his pad. He cannot communicate orally and yet he is able to write down everything, not only jotting recaps of each day, but he even allows himself to write little one-act plays. He bought a copy of a Sam Shepard collection at a garage sale, the volume containing seven or eight plays, and Rodney has read them a hundred times. He's studied every line that Shepard put together. His favorite play is "Curse of the Starving Class." It's about a son who is doing his damnedest to avoid his parents' mistakes, the death sentence of turning into them, a story that Rodney can not only relate to, but holds as his biggest fear. He's already fallen off the balloon, but he so badly wishes that he doesn't have to go down the same pit that swallowed his parents. He doesn't want to be a coward that takes off, prioritizing herself above her family. And he doesn't want to be a coward that stays behind, drinking too much and wasting his life. He wants to shuck these curses, do better.

His one-acts are all set in Traurig, taking people and settings he knows and then spinning the stories from there.

So if Sara took the time to read a few pages, Balloon Boy has no doubt their friendship would wake from hibernation. Chances are he'll never kiss her again, and he's accepted that over the years, but there's no reason they can't be better friends, especially if she reads and understands that he is still the same person.

She exits the screen door and they're standing only a few feet apart.

"You know you can tell me," she says. "Oh, man. Your face."

"I'm," he says, and two seconds later, "fine."

"Hank did that to you. I never wanted that to happen. I'm sorry."

He says it again: "I'm. Fine."

"Oh, you're a tough guy now?" she says.

Rodney flexes his scrawny arms, nods, and smiles.

He guesses this conversation is something of a birthday present. Sara disappeared all those years ago after he got hurt. She was friendly to him, but no more camping in the backyard. So even if he felt dumb doling out his monosyllables, he was not only aiding someone he cared deeply about but he got a few minutes in her presence. Sara might have only been five feet tall, but she had a big personality. Rodney could be shy, obtuse, even before his accident, and Sara helped him with this. It was like their first kiss. It was Sara who finally came right out and said it.

If he could lean in and kiss her now on the porch, he would.

"What's going on?" says Sara.

"Burn. Car."

"Did you say burn my car?"

Balloon Boy nods.

"You mean Larry and Felix are going to burn my car?" Sara asks.

He nods again.

Sara calls in the house to Hank, "They're going to light my car on fire!"

"Those jag-offs never learn!" says Hank.

"Anything else, Rodney?"

"Hurt. Hank."

"And they're going to kick your ass!" she calls to her brother.

"I'm more worried about slipping in the shower," he says.

"They're coming here soon, Rodney?"

He nods again.

"They're coming soon, Hank! Let's get out of here. We don't want any trouble, neither does your PO."

"You go ahead," Hank says. "They wanna rumble, me and Bernard are willing to oblige them!"

Sara rolls her eyes at Rodney. "Some families we've got, huh?"

Balloon Boy shrugs.

Sara and Rodney stand there for a few seconds, smiling at each other.

If he had his pad and pen, he'd write a short note to her: *Do you remember me? Can't you see I'm still in here?*

"Birth. Day," Balloon Boy says.

"It's your birthday?" Sara asks.

More nodding.

"Well, if they want to stay here and kill each other, maybe me and you can go for a drive, just us," Sara says. "What do you think of that?"

Rodney doesn't nod this time, but tilts his head a little to the side, in awe, taking in every inch of her.

"You'll have to check my blind spots," she says. "Thanks to your uncle, I'm down a mirror."

IN THE CAR, Sara's speakers crank the same music Rodney had heard right before Uncle Felix kicked her car, a rapper once again going crazy over heavy metal riffs. Rodney likes hip-hop, mostly the old stuff. Tribe Called Quest. Wu-Tang Clan. Pharcyde. De La Soul. Anything with a beat that stays out of the way and lets the MC reign. Listening to tracks like that, Balloon Boy is able to hear the rhymes colliding off of one another, a pileup of fast and loose syllables sizzling from mouths. He's never been much into the whole chainsaw guitar sound of metal, but this he likes. It's aggressive and angry and crunchy, yet the singer is front and center, not drowned out by the fuzz. He's like a surfer riding the livid riff, staying on top of it, using the music's velocity to accentuate his cadences and all his rhymes are easy to make out. He's a beast. A barker. He's super-pissed and he wants you to know why.

That would be a great birthday gift: a day, an hour, hell, even five minutes in which Rodney can call out like that.

He points to the stereo.

"Sorry," says Sara, turning the volume down.

"No." Balloon Boy brings it back to its original level, which makes Sara smile.

"You like it?" she says.

He nods, listening to the singer rap something so deft, so on the beat that the syncopation makes Rodney bob his head.

"You've got good taste," Sara says.

Balloon Boy nods, not wanting to congest the car with any of his sounds.

"Where should we go?" asks Sara.

But she doesn't wait for him to say anything, not that Rodney was going to, only two or three seconds passing before Sara says, "Can I show you my favorite spot? You'll love the view."

The word *view* makes Rodney think about being on the balloon, think about the glory of all the open space he was able to see.

It's about three in the afternoon, Sara's AC working hard. They drive through what would be called downtown Traurig. It's only five square blocks, the population of the Nevada town around 2,000. There was a time in the 1970s when people thought that Reno was going to have a population boom, become something closer to Vegas, and so these towns in the outskirts, say within fifty miles, were thought to be up and coming. They pocked the desert and the dominant thought was that they'd all soon be connected, updated, the chain stores moving in and giving it that American cookie-cutter feel.

But it didn't happen. There was no great immigration to Reno or its "suburbs." The new people never showed and the chains never wormed their way in, and Traurig and towns like it became not ghosts, exactly—people lived here and worked hard—but there weren't any real opportunities. You could commute into Reno or Tahoe to find better employment, or you could burrow into a union gig like Rodney's dad and uncle. You could work those cracked and charred highways, repaving asphalt and cleaning up debris, scraping cooked carcasses like burgers from grills, feeling the meat jimmy from the road to your shovel, the slaughterhouse smell following you home. The nice and terrible thing about work on the highway was that it was never done, not with the sun's ruthlessness breaking what you'd fixed a few months back. Always fissures to fill. Always a rattler to peel off the road.

Sara takes the turn on the freeway, moving toward Reno.

"Where?" Rodney says.

"A great spot on the Truckee River," she says. "It will be a while. Enjoy the music." Sara turns the volume up and kicks the car up to seventy-five. If no semis clog up the way, they should get to the river in about an hour.

It's unfortunate about not having his pad and pen. He could've asked Sara to scrounge something up from her house before they bolted, but he didn't want to be there, with Hank, knowing that any minute his dad and uncle and the Wombats might attack and who knew what would happen from there. Rodney was wrong about heavy metal guitar—it's a good accompaniment for rapping. They challenge each other, and they bring out the best in one another. They are greater than the sum of their parts.

If he had a pen and pad now, this would be the perfect time to talk to Sara. They're stuck in the car, which is actually pretty clean, no trash or to-go cups or papers littered about. The only item is the broken side mirror, riding down by Rodney's feet.

This could be one of his plays. A one-act. A reconciliation. Something about long-lost friends on the run finding common ground.

But before his play gets the chance to start, Sara turns the volume down on the stereo and says, "I'm fucked, Rodney."

"Huh?"

Sara says, "Me. I'm. It's. Um. Uh. Shit."

She's talking like me, thinks Balloon Boy.

"Um, it's," she keeps going, "like, I'm, uh, I've been screwed and my life is ruined and I don't know what to do."

"What," he says and four seconds later, "happened?"

"I don't want to tell you what happened," she says. "I don't want you of all people to judge me."

"I. Can't."

Sara looks over at him. "You can't judge me?"

Balloon Boy shakes his head at her. "No. Way."

It comes out of her like she's the MC with his anger, and Sara meets his and tops it. But she's not rhyming or staying on the beat. She stomps on the car's accelerator and gets them up near ninety and the car works from one lane to the next, passing people, and her words mimic their motion, careening, zigzagging, snaking this way and that, telling Rodney about her boyfriend who posted a video of them having sex online and she probably lost her job this morning and everyone is texting her about the video and pretty soon there won't be anyone left on the planet who hasn't seen Sara in such a compromised position.

"It's like," Sara says, "it's like I'm frozen. The real me doesn't exist anymore. All that's left is the girl in the video. My whole life has been erased except for those minutes. That's all I am."

I know exactly what you mean, thinks Balloon Boy.

"Slow," says Rodney.

"What?"

He points at the speedometer. "Slow."

"Sorry." Sara brings the car back to seventy.

Rodney snatches the snapped-off side mirror from the floor and holds it so Sara can see her reflection. "Your. Face. Is. Great."

It takes him nineteen seconds to get it all out, and he expects Sara to get impatient, to roll her eyes. He expects her to deflect or joke away his sentiments, but all she says is this: "You're still the same?"

Rodney turns the mirror around so he can see his own reflection. "This. Guy. Likes. You."

Only eleven seconds. That might be a record for four syllables.

"I'm not going to cry," says Sara, reaching for the stereo, turning the volume back up.

They don't talk the remainder of the trip. They drive over a bridge with the river running underneath it, about forty feet below. Once over, Sara takes a turn off and wends down a dirt path and parks near the shore.

She gets out of the car and walks toward the water, kicking her shoes off as she gets close. The back of her shorts and shirt are covered in dirt and Rodney wonders why.

"Come on," she says. "I want to show you something."

9.

It's mid-afternoon when Kathleen Curtis flees the real world for the support of her AA sponsor, Deb, who has a tattoo shop in the Mission District. It's located only a few blocks from where Kathleen lives, so she stops by her apartment to drop off her art supplies—all the elements that tied her to this morning's unpleasant drawing of the pregnant girl with the black eye. Kathleen has never lashed out at someone like she did in the caricature, and she's rightfully scared by her actions.

I guess I'm a psycho now, she's thought to herself about a thousand times since the incident.

Deb is in the shop with one other woman, who is stretched out on a table, lying on her back, topless. The walls are painted turquoise, not that they're easy to see. Almost every inch is covered with pictures of Deb's artwork. Some are photographs of tattoos already on skin, while others are drawings, ideas for customers to peruse. She has some standards in the back—anchors and hearts and whatnot—but most of the wall space is allocated to her passion projects, the work she does with cancer survivors.

Deb, wearing a wifebeater and showing her full sleeves of work, two sugar skulls emblazoned on top of each shoulder, sits in a chair next to the woman. With her tattoo gun in hand, Deb dips the needles into an ink cap filled with yellow, then fires up the gun with her foot pedal—the shop filling with that buzzing sound—and colors in a sunflower on the woman's chest.

Kathleen looks at the tattoo, sees the whole tableaux, how the sunflower sits on her sternum, flanked by two lush vines that dangle over her puckered scars, a few tendrils of green running down her ribs. It's a huge piece, and Kat is utterly transfixed.

"I didn't know you could do that," Kathleen says.

"You can tattoo anything," Deb says, running the gun up against the sunflower's black outline, then wiping the excess ink and blood off with her rag. "Eyelids. Lips. Don't even ask where a man once got a barber's pole tattoo."

"Seriously?" the survivor says, then bites her bottom lip in anguish, folds a forearm over her eyes to block out the light.

"Unfortunately," says Deb.

Kathleen still hasn't stopped staring at the tattoo covering the scars.

"I started doing breast cancer survivors about five years ago," says Deb. "After my sister. I wanted to make her chest gorgeous again. Since then, I offer the same service to others."

"You look beautiful," Kathleen says to the woman.

"It hurts," she says.

"We're almost done," Deb says, arches an eyebrow. "Only a few more hours."

"Great," she says. "I'll try not to cry the whole time."

"It's worth it," Deb says. Then she turns her attention to Kat: "I thought I wasn't seeing you till later today. What time is the Craigslist guy coming to see the room?"

"Five o'clock."

"Her roommate left the country for a couple months," Deb says to the survivor, "and the sublettor bugged out at the last minute. Now my friend here has to find a replacement."

"That sucks," the woman says, her arm still covering her eyes. "But this sucks more."

"I need a buddy to make sure I don't get hacked up into little pieces by some creep," Kathleen says. "Deb will help me vet this guy."

"So why are you here so early?" Deb asks and takes her foot off the pedal, tattoo gun going silent, and stares at Kathleen.

"Well," says Kat, stalling, not sure she feels like getting into it with the survivor lying there, "it's sort of private."

Deb laughs so hard she snorts.

"Don't mind me," the woman says, finally looking up at Kat. "You've already seen my business. Might as well share yours."

Kathleen pulls the caricature from her pocket. It's folded and creased and has a small rip in it from when Tyler balled it up. Kat shows it to both of them—the exaggerated faces, the bruised fetus with the caption "Life beats babies!" coming from Tyler's mouth—then she tells the whole gruesome story.

"Let's take five," Deb says to the survivor.

"Let's take twenty," she says back, sitting up. "I'm seeing spots in my periphery. My body needs a break." She throws a shirt on and walks to the front door, props it open and goes outside for some fresh air.

"So what happened?" Deb asks.

"It's Rodney's birthday, and I guess I'm not handling it too well this year."

"You think?" Deb takes the caricature and inspects it closer.

"I wouldn't have been surprised if one of them hit me in the face," Kathleen says. "I deserved it."

"Stop," Deb says. "It's over. What I'm more concerned about is why you did it. What makes this birthday different than his others?"

Deb and Kathleen have talked about Rodney countless times, especially when working Kat's step nine. That's when alcoholics are supposed to make amends to people they've hurt over the years—the people they've betrayed and trampled. Loving a drunkard is like running with the bulls. But since Kat has already completed step nine, why hasn't she made amends with Rodney?

"I'm not ready," Kathleen always tells Deb.

Kathleen refuses to reach out to her son, saying that contacting him while he's still a minor would also open up things with Larry, and she's not strong enough to deal with that. She knows the first couple years of sobriety are brittle, and she needs to take care of herself. If she relapses, she'll never right this wrong.

"It's his eighteenth birthday," Kathleen says. "He's an adult. I'm out of excuses and scared about it."

"Scared?"

"I did the worst thing a mother can do."

"But that's done," Deb says and keeps scouring the caricature. "So what are you going to do now?"

"I don't have any idea," Kat says.

And that's the problem. She's lost. Kathleen can't get any grip on the *right* move. A part of her thinks that he's her only son and that entitles her to intrude back into his life, despite her unforgiveable behavior since his accident. Another part of her feels that's selfish—she's made her miserable bed and she needs to stew in these soiled sheets forever, forget about her son, she's ruined that relationship and must live with the consequences of her selfishness. Of course, she tries to dismiss the latter interpretation, but it rolls into her mind like fog. She never declares a winner in these warring debates. She hears both sides, then gets frustrated and tired and sad, settling for brackish inaction.

She had time, damn it. He wasn't eighteen. Not an adult. Under Larry's jurisdiction. Now that those excuses have burned off, leaving her free to make a decision, she's so bent up about it that all she can do is draw the meanest caricature in the world and hate herself.

"Good thing I have an idea," Deb says, "and you are going to sit right here in my shop while I finish tattooing that woman. You're going to watch her take that gnarled fucking scar and have it topped with something wonderful. That's what you're going to do. And maybe you'll feel inspired to get off your ass and contact him, Kat."

Deb hands the caricature back to Kathleen and begins to restock her station, filling up the ink caps with what she'll need to complete the work.

Kathleen actually relaxes after Deb calls her on all the bullshit. It's what she adores about her sponsor, her prying right into the matter's heart. Certainly, Kathleen could keep feeling sorry for herself, what she lost, what she gave away, the resentment she feels about how unfair it was, a child being injured like that. She can't ever imagine forgiving herself. She might be carting around the caricature that she'd done earlier that day, but she's been carrying her own since the day she left Traurig.

Kathleen can remember a time clean of any caricatures, any distortions. She and Larry maybe not fairy-tale-happy but far from mean to each other. When Rodney was first born. Their perfect boy making all the tiredness worth it, all the double shifts for her husband while Kathleen stayed up all night with the baby. She'd swear the first three months of Rodney's life were one long day—a repeating one, the opposite of a mythology-style punishment. Barely kept track of the time of day besides the dark or light. He would scream if he was set down, demanding to sleep straight on Kathleen's chest, so she carted him around everywhere. He slept while she listened to him breathe, worrying about SIDS, worrying about things much more practical than a weather balloon.

She was so sleepy and never changed out of her bathrobe. Covered in leaked breast milk. Smelling of Parmesan cheese that had been quickly aged in her son's stomach and spit back up, leaving pale stains on the robe that looked like clouds.

It actually became a joke, Larry saying, "You've sprouted another cloud," and Kat laughing like an overwhelmed but satisfied new mom, feeling a purpose she'd never known.

They were exhausted parents trying to figure out what they'd gotten themselves into. The loss of any semblance of free time. Loss of freedom and fun. Loss of identity. Loss of sex. Loss of any intimacy between spouses, juggling all these new responsibilities. The house was in shambles and rent was late and they hadn't grocery-shopped in who knows how long and hygiene was in dubious states, but despite all that they were happy—happy!—rallying together to figure all this out.

Back then they were portraits, not caricatures. No hyperbolic features. No funhouse remixes. No exaggerated facial details for comic effect.

Sure, she already had a drinking problem before her son fell off that weather balloon, but it was manageable, socially acceptable, *reasonable*, if that makes any sense. After his injury, she couldn't stop: It became an accomplishment—she thought it was an accomplishment—to not drink in the morning. Kathleen is talking about the true nature of craving and how she never knew what that word really meant until after Rodney changed. Craving. It wasn't simply something you wanted. No, craving in its pure, unpasteurized way was a religious experience. A compulsion that trumped anything else in the world. It became a biorhythm. A part of you. And maybe it started off as a small, controllable part, but that wasn't going to last. Its contingency will bully all others. Until everything was governed by that same thirst. Pretty soon what you were craving became a god. Jesus Christ, whiskey, whatever. The only reason to live was to worship that deity, and the only way to show your devotion was to consume another drink, and so Kathleen would get up in the morning and think about vodka and she'd scrub her teeth thinking about vodka and she wouldn't be able to shake these thoughts during her shower or getting dressed or pretending to eat toast, and pretty soon that craving buckled every reason she could think of to stay sober that day—all she saw was a knob to turn the volume down on her son's tragedy, her grief, never muting them entirely, but beating back the decibel level to a tolerable murmur, so yes, allow yourself one morning cocktail to take the edge off her hangover because she showed her devotion to this false god of craving the night before so why not treat yourself to one little innocuous cocktail and cauterize all the circular thinking, Kathleen, these mean thoughts about her decimated son might hop on a weather balloon all their own and fly off into the sunset and that first screwdriver did feel holy, her god stomping on her disaffections, all the blame her heart hoarded temporarily liquidated, and if the first drink worked, why wouldn't the second one make her feel even more human, holier, maybe even good, yes, actually good about the state of things, so she made that daily exception to have another morning cocktail but damn the law of diminishing returns and the second one didn't make her feel any *more better*, got her mind whirling about Rodney and her marriage and how things were so screwed up nothing was ever going to get fixed and then it was time to have another, chasing that first burst of biblical amnesia again but of course it was gone, and then another cocktail and another and she was an alcoholic piece of shit who couldn't stay sober one day in a train-wreck marriage with a son who should be in the eighth grade but talked like a toddler again and he will never be normal and will never have any kind of life and that wasn't fair and her marriage wasn't fair and Larry's fists weren't fair and Traurig wasn't fair and she couldn't think of one fair thing in the whole universe and she should leave town, why not, wasn't like she could actually do anything to help him, all they could do was sit around and watch each other die, Rodney was going to be that terrible toddler for all time with or without Kathleen's boozy presence, and so she bolted.

And here she is. Her whole world is a skyscraping caricature. Practically its own continent. Maybe that was her mythology-style punishment. Maybe being a caricaturist day in, day out is the worst fate a god addicted to poetic justice can cook up.

Kat has a rather convincing piece of evidence in her hand. She examines the girl with the black eye, her baby, and Tyler. She tries to get each crease out of the caricature, but it's no use. This is the way this family will look.

She feels so stupid and fragile for lashing out at them. She rubs her hand over it again and it dawns on her that it's only a drawing. It might represent how unstable she is right now, but the caricature is only a symptom. Deb wants her to deal with the disease—her guilt about abandoning Rodney—and her sponsor is right. She can do that; she has to do that.

"Let's get cracking!" Kat calls to the cancer survivor, who stands by the open front door.

"Do we have to?" she says back. "This doesn't feel good."

"It's worth it."

"Is it?"

"Carpe diem," says Deb.

Slowly and reluctantly, the woman shuffles back, takes off her shirt, and lies down on the table, putting her arm back over her eyes.

Deb gets the tattoo gun going again, dips her shader into the orange, and starts doing the work.

Kathleen spends the next three hours watching those scars disappear under a miracle of vibrant color.

THE GUY WHO found her online should arrive at any minute. All Kat knows about him is his email address, WesEinstein@gmail.com. That was how he'd responded to her online ad, and because he had been the first responder, Kathleen figured it was only fair to give him the initial crack at the room.

Since this is San Francisco in 2013, the new dot-com boom has pushed the rents sky-high; it's as bad as Manhattan. Because of that, Kathleen decided to jack the sublettor's share a few hundred to make some extra money. She rationalized that she deserved some severance for doing the work her roommate should have done before leaving the country.

Kat has only lived in the Mission for six years, but even in that small window of time the changes have become noticeable. At first, it was filled with artists and hipsters, college kids and Latino families, and she felt welcomed by all. Here it was okay to eke out a living drawing caricatures. Here it was okay to be poor.

But more dot-commers flocked in, offering landlords sums over the asking price. And some weren't interested in inflating rents and just bought the cheap apartment buildings, either converting them to one-house units for themselves, or they used the sale to convert to townhouses or condos and raise rents drastically. Kat knew damn well that if she ever got evicted, there was no way she could afford to stay in the city, maybe migrating over to Oakland, but even over there it was getting steep.

It wasn't only techie twentysomethings toting laptops taking over the Mission, though. There was also a steep rise in young, mostly white families, and this population brought Kathleen face to face with mothers of all kinds. Some days, they were all she could see. In all their various stages of development. Pregnant women outside a yoga studio, proud with their mats and hopeful, swelling bellies. Moms with babies bundled to their chests, cooing at them. Moms who took up the whole sidewalk with designer strollers that must have been mounted on Cadillac chassis. Moms who herded frantic kids, paroled from apartments to Dolores Park to tire themselves out.

In fact, Kat's apartment was right across the street from that park, and its big playground always sent the kids' happy shrieking shaking through her windows. All the howls and joys of childhood slapped Kathleen in the face. She couldn't keep their ecstatic noises out.

Everywhere were reminders that Kathleen was no longer a mom, and she dove out of the way while these mothers monopolized the sidewalk with their Cadillacs, casting her out, away from their club. No offspring, no membership. Something—someone—she willingly left behind.

Currently, Kat and Deb sit in the living room, waiting for Wes Something, who should have arrived exactly one minute ago, and Kathleen points at her phone and says, "This isn't a great first impression."

"What do you know about great first impressions, Caricature?"

"Ouch."

"Give him a few minutes," says Deb, "and if he doesn't show, I'll buy you some sushi."

"Don't you have a date tonight?"

"Yeah, but she's low-maintenance. No dinner. Just sex."

"Must be nice."

"You should consider having sex sometime," Deb says. "It's pretty fun."

God, Kathleen hopes he shows. This is the last thing she wants, the subletting turning into some time-consuming annoyance. She doesn't have the bandwidth to deal with that ordeal right now. Too preoccupied with what might be considered a breech in normal mental health, lashing out through the caricature, and how much Rodney's birthday torments her. She hasn't even thought about the brass band all afternoon, and not many people can say that: It dominates the Internet, the TV, talk radio, but Kat's too mired in herself to indulge much thought about anyone else.

Hopefully, Wes Something walks in the room and proclaims it a perfect spot. Hopefully, he likes it enough to move right in, so she doesn't have to hassle showing it to multiple people. Basically, if he's not wearing a grim reaper outfit, wielding a scythe and saying, "Death comes for us all!" she has decided the room will be his.

"Assuming he does show," says Kathleen, trying to get away from the topic of sex, "what should I ask him?"

"Feel him out. Go with your gut."

"Maybe I should've gotten a cheese plate," she says. "To distract him. It's pretty dusty in here."

She's not wrong. Kathleen's not a horrible housekeeper, but the rooms of the flat wouldn't hold up under close inspection. Nothing is filthy, but there's dust on the sills and floorboards, little tumbleweeds of her long brown hair pock the hardwood. There's one runner going up the hallway through the railroad apartment, and it hasn't been cleaned since the vacuum broke a year back.

What is nice, however, is that the apartment gets a lot of natural light. Both bedrooms, the kitchen, the bathroom, and the small living room—where Kat and Deb are—all have big windows and the apartment is always warm with natural light.

"What, you don't think he can see dust because of some cheese?" Deb asks, running an index finger on the sill and holding it up, a black inchworm of car exhaust and dead skin and cat dander dangling there.

Luckily for Kathleen the doorbell rings, and so she walks toward the door, truncating their conversation. The living room is right by the entrance, and she turns the deadbolt, welcoming the stranger into her home.

He looks to be in his early forties, a couple years older than Kathleen. His hair is short and black, and he has significant stubble, the jet whiskers near his chin mixed with some gray. Right around six feet and doughy, but he's not unattractive. Kat thinks that last word, *unattractive*, and scolds herself.

The detail that truly engrosses her is that Wes wears a lab coat, buttoned up. There are blue jeans sticking out from under it, along with navy Chuck Taylors. And a T-shirt is underneath the lab coat, which seems weird to Kathleen; she would have expected a tie and a pocket protector. Maybe this is called scientist-casual.

"You must be Wes," she says, smiling at him.

"I am here about the room for rent," he says.

Wes stares at her. It's clear that she's supposed to be in charge of steering the conversation, but what should she ask him first? For references? Should she demand a credit report? Show him some Rorschach inkblots?

Deb said that this decision is best left to the gut, but Kat doesn't trust her own judgment. That's why her sponsor is here in the first place. Yes, she's unofficial muscle, but Deb is really here to help Kathleen read him and see if this will work. If this will be safe.

Five seconds go by with the two of them staring at each other in the doorway.

"Are you a doctor?" she asks.

"A scientist."

"What field?"

"I work down at Fresno State and am up here doing a couple months of research at UCSF."

"That's such a relief," she says.

"May I see the room?"

"I'm sorry," she says, inviting him in with a wave. "I've never done this before."

"You've never invited someone inside your house before?" he asks.

This makes Kathleen laugh, which makes her relax some. Good, he's got a sense of humor.

"I've never invited a stranger into my house," she says, "to live for a couple months."

Deb is up off the couch and standing behind Kathleen, introducing herself as the "brash best friend," brandishing the title like permission to butt in and be in charge whenever she feels like it. Deb extends her hand past Kathleen, who regrets not shaking Wes's hand herself, and he grabs Deb's hand. Up and down their palms go.

"Solid grip," he says.

"I'm a badass," says Deb.

"Come in," Kathleen says, ushering him by Deb before the talk gets any more uncomfortable.

Once inside the door, Wes surveys the hallway. He looks up at the ceiling, down at the floor. Kathleen hopes that his scrutiny won't turn him off. She really should have purchased some cheese.

"What are the pounds per square inch of oxygen in here?" he says.

"Is that a serious question?" Deb says.

Kathleen says, "I have no idea how much oxygen is in here. How would I tell?"

"It's not a big deal," he says. "I like to know what I'm getting myself into."

"I haven't had any trouble breathing in here," Kat says.

"Good to know," he says.

"Let me give you a tour," she says.

They walk down the apartment's main hall, stopping first in the living room, then the kitchen and bathroom, which should have gotten a thorough cleaning earlier before the girl with the black eye, her baby, and Tyler distracted Kat from getting the house in order.

The two bedrooms are in the back and Kathleen decides not to show him hers, goes into the place where he'll be laying down his head, assuming the pounds per square inch of oxygen pass his inspection.

They arrive at the room. The door is closed. She should have opened it, made the room more inviting. Maybe some flowers. Daisies. Yeah, a vase of daisies to bring some cheer. No one wants to live in a hovel. It feels like the whole city has a pall over it because of the brass band. She could have thrown open the blinds and cranked up the window, even if she has to hear all the kids from the playground. Even if that makes her think of Rodney. Even if she's one of the worst people alive.

It's a small room. Ten by twelve. Walls painted maroon, except for the closet door, which is white. There's a futon in the far corner and an armoire next to it. A poster of Bob Marley smoking a joint.

The roommate's stuff is pretty nice, or so Kat thinks. She wonders how it must look to a scientist.

"How's the oxygen level?" Deb asks from the doorway.

Wes takes a deep breath, says, "Optimal."

Kathleen laughs again, harder this time.

"Do you have any questions for us?" Deb says.

"Not at this time. The room will do nicely. I have several garbage bags and small boxes filled with supplies out in the car," he says.

"Hold your horses, cowboy," says Deb.

"I can do this," Kathleen says to her.

Deb waves her away. "Did your other plans fall through?" Deb asks Wes.

"Other plans?"

"You must have had a place lined up before you got here."

"This opportunity came together at the last minute," he says, walking over and touching the mirror on the armoire's door.

"What are you doing at UCSF?" asks Deb.

"We're founding a new kind of mathematics. It mixes principles of thermodynamics and physics, even some psychology. It's a theoretical discipline called existential mathematics."

"Never heard of it," Deb says.

"It's new," he says.

"Sounds very interesting," Kathleen says, shooting her sponsor a look.

"It's a blossoming way of thinking about time travel," Wes says, stops and licks his lips, makes eye contact with both Kathleen and Deb. "Assuming we know what we're talking about."

"We?" Kathleen says.

"Me and my partner, Albert."

"Do you know what you're talking about?" Deb asks.

"We'll see," he says.

Kat is getting impressed at how he's handling Deb as she waterboards him with questions. Maybe she's doing it on purpose, being annoying, trying to get under his skin to see how he responds. If that's the case, it's a brilliant plan. If it isn't, Deb's simply being an asshole.

"You know," Kathleen says to her sponsor, "if you need to head back to the shop, Wes and I can take it from here."

"You can?"

"I'm prepared to pay both months' rent up front," Wes says, "and I'll be working excessive hours so you'll barely see me. Is cash okay?"

"There's one thing you need to know about this house," Deb says.

"What?" he says.

"This is a sober house," says Deb.

"I listed that in the ad," Kathleen says.

"I won't give any alcohol to the house," he says.

"This isn't a joke," Deb says.

"I understand," Wes says. "I'll be working the whole time. Your sober house is safe with me."

"Thank you," Kathleen says.

"Not a problem," he says.

"Would you like to go into the kitchen and have some coffee?" Kathleen says. "We can talk and make sure this is a good fit."

"We are talking now," he says.

"Right, but let's continue to talk in the kitchen. Would you like some coffee?"

"Sure," he says, "but can I use the bathroom first?"

"Of course."

He leaves, and Kathleen hits Deb on the arm. "What are you trying to do?"

"I gave him a test and he passed," Deb says. "My gut's telling me that he's the one."

"Assuming he's not shimmying out the window because you scared him."

"Please."

"I can take it from here," Kathleen says. "We'll be fine."

"Don't come home after curfew," says Deb, kissing her friend and walking out the front door.

Kathleen goes into the kitchen, puts a kettle on, and gets out her French press. She should have watered the two plants on the counter. They're not dead, but the leaves are droopy. She fills one of the coffee mugs up with water and soaks both plants, hoping for some immediate improvement.

Wes walks in and says, "The bathroom is optimal, as well."

"I'm glad to hear it. What do you take in your coffee?"

"Black."

"You're hardcore."

"All the long hours in the lab," he says. "Coffee is a man's best friend."

"I agree," she says. "I think we'll be a good fit. The room is yours if you want it."

"I want it," he says. "Do you mind if I hang something on the wall in the room?"

"What is it?"

"Just a poster of Einstein. His equation is the basis of my research."

"Sure, you can take down Bob Marley and hang yours right there. I think he'll understand."

The kettle lets go of its whistle, and Kathleen turns the burner's knob. The whistle slows, stops, and that's what she feels like herself. Meeting Wes had been fraught with so much danger for her, so much faith. It felt so intimate, so unnatural letting someone you don't know stay at your apartment for a couple months, but she likes how the facts have lined up. One, he's here for work and will be in the lab a lot, which means he won't be sitting in the living room, making her feel uncomfortable. Two, he's nice. That's huge. When their paths do cross, she can imagine having a casual conversation with him, maybe a meal or two. It's a temporary situation and Kathleen feels relaxed about the decision.

The plants haven't miraculously perked up. But it doesn't matter. Wes seems lost in his own world. He didn't even take off his lab coat before coming over here.

"You said you take it black, right?" she says, pouring the water in the French press.

"Black, yes. Do you like it here?"

"In this apartment?"

"In general."

"In San Francisco?" Kathleen says. "Yes, I do. It's changing a lot. It has a lot of history and each year it evolves."

"We are our history," says Wes. "That's what makes us."

Kathleen thinks about the crinkled caricature she drew this morning, thinks about Rodney. She pushes these things from her mind and thinks about the cancer survivor at Deb's shop. Life doesn't always have to end in disaster. Sometimes, there are disasters, sure, and afterward, those scars are turned into something else.

"History is important," she says, "but so is tomorrow."

Wes nods his head. "Tomorrow. Indeed. Yes, there is tomorrow to consider."

She pushes the plunger down on the French press and pours coffee into both their cups. It's a dark roast and she inhales the rich, pungent scent. Kathleen hands the mug to her new roommate, looking at his lab coat, feeling gratitude at her luck.

10.

Since the morning of the mass suicide, since Paul and his son saw the band members jump, since Jake posted the clip online, since he saw his boy tearing up his room with a baseball bat, Paul hasn't had a bowel movement. It's like everything is dammed up behind a wall of worry. Fear, concern for his son. For his whole generation, really. Their crass way of publicizing everything. Paul didn't even know how to play fantasy football, so he doesn't know the first thing about Twitter or Instagram and the like, these technologies that make it seem like a good idea to share shrapnel from your life, meaningless slivers of each day: *Here is the frittata I had for breakfast and check out this cloud pattern in the sky and here is a pic of me laughing with old friends having the greatest time ever and isn't this a clever way to decorate cappuccino foam?*

None of it made any sense. The whole thing has been easy for Paul to dismiss. They're kids. And kids are stupid. If these inane devices were around when Paul had a full head of hair, he'd probably have pecked his days away, too, mark his every thought with photos or emoticons. Which, if he's being honest, is his least favorite thing about texting with his son. He's accepted that he has to do it. A phone call is like a unicorn. So he texts like all parents clumsily do, but it would make it so much more digestible if his boy didn't include an infantry of emoticons with every communication.

And what's the deal with all the exclamation points? Why is that the preferred way to punctuate each prosaic phrase? From downstairs, he's texted his son if he'd like a bagel for breakfast, and from upstairs, the boy texts back, "Sesame!"

It all makes Paul feel so old. So irrelevant. He's sexually irrelevant and emotionally irrelevant and socially irrelevant, and if he keeps pretending that certain advancements in the workplace don't exist he'll soon be occupationally irrelevant, and in a few years Jake will go off to college and his wife's already gone, so Paul will be left familially irrelevant, and that will be the end result of his life.

It's not just kids, though. That really bugs him. Paul has to basically police his coworkers, or they'll fiddle around on Facebook all day. He might not have his own account, but he gets the gist of how it works. What's so satisfying about *liking* something? How could that ever fulfill you? Why scroll through posts and pictures and links? Why comment on other human beings' updates when you've walked by twenty people on the street and didn't take the time to talk to any of them?

If he tried to pinpoint his disdain, that would be the bull's-eye— the isolation. He wants to tell his son, *Don't rush to spend time by yourself.* Don't hurry to alienation. It's an inevitable destination. Time will eventually shroud you like velvet curtains, blacking out everything.

You'd think Paul would be a perfect candidate for social media, someone jettisoned from his family, his real-world community, somebody without any outlet, no way to express his feelings except one sour thought at a time, but this loneliness has the opposite effect. It's made him irate at smartphones and computers, and he's convinced that Jake wouldn't be in this current mess if it weren't for the Internet. If it weren't so easy to share things online. Paul protests its existence by staying as offline as much as he can without getting fired. He pickets each technological advancement by pretending it doesn't exist.

What does exist, and what is currently being digested by Paul, is a laxative. He and Jake stopped by the pharmacy on their way to Jake's therapy. The boy waited in the car, and Paul ran in and asked for "the strongest laxative alive."

The young lady working the register made a food-poisoning face, shook her head, then said, "Try aisle eight."

He bought the one with the best copy on the box, and he tore into it in the parking lot.

With the laxative in his system, Paul climbed into the driver's seat with renewed faith that things were about to get better—if not better, at least he'd drop this extra freight—and this assured feeling lasted until he realized that Jake was in the back seat now. He had been up front during the drive over. Paul had squawked about breaking that habit of sitting back there, get up front, act like an adult, etc., and Jake had caved and sat sullenly next to him, listening to music on his iPhone while they drove to the pharmacy.

"This is my reward," Paul said aloud as they made their way.

Jake didn't hear him, of course, kept bobbing his head to the beat of the song only he could hear, and Paul could only wish that laxative luck—things were bottled up and backing up further with each infuriating second.

So seeing him in the back seat, right behind the driver, he said to his son, "What does it accomplish, sitting back there?"

His ear buds weren't in, so Paul expected an answer.

"Accomplish?" asked Jake.

"Yeah, what do you get from being behind me?"

"Nothing."

"Am I that embarrassing?" said Paul.

That wasn't what he wanted to say. Not to his son, at least. Yes, it hurt his feelings having his boy prefer the separation. It created a swollen paradox for Paul: He wanted so badly to help his son, and yet Jake made it so hard to want to help him. Always distant. Always antagonistic. Paul knew that as the adult he had to rise above these petty feelings—he accepted that intellectually—but it was so hard on an emotional level. Not ever getting anything positive from your kid.

Jake hadn't said anything, so Paul said, "Am I embarrassing you?"

"I don't know," said Jake.

"You don't know if I'm embarrassing?"

Again, he didn't want to do this. He didn't want to feel wounded or go on the offensive. He wanted to be the calmest, most supportive parent ever. He wanted to help his son come back.

"Don't answer me," Paul said. "Sorry. Forget it. Listen to your music."

It was almost laughable, how immature, how childish Paul could be. He had to be the one to rise above any squawking. He had to be the one to take care of his son.

Jake stayed in the back seat, put the ear buds in; Paul drove them to the therapist's office. They waited till Jake was ushered in by the doc, leaving Paul alone looking at the closed office door, yet another separation from his son.

He stayed like that for ten minutes. He stayed like that until right now, only staring at the closed door, wondering what it means.

The most important thing is that they're trying to get Jake help. The goal is helping his son. Despite Paul's stillborn dreams or feelings of futility or all the ways he can tally his irrelevancy in life, the only thing that matters is that they are in this office. They are—father and son—here.

Even in such a dull waiting room. A Formica table in the middle of it, decorated with a fan of magazines. A few IKEA chairs, which at these prices seem ludicrous. They should all be lounging in authentic Barcelona chairs.

Paul tries to beat down the worry about money. To allow himself to see only what matters, that closed office door. On the other side are a doctor and Jake. They are making headway. They have to be. They are erasing the damage done by the brass band and the divorce and all other collateral damage that haunts his son. They are in there doing the work and everything else is moot.

Well, he wants it to be moot. But Paul can't help but blame himself for how little he knew about Jake's online life. It never occurred to Paul that things he filmed on his iPhone were ending up on the Internet, and it certainly never crossed his mind that he'd publicize something as awful as a mass suicide. It felt odd to Paul, that mechanism to share pathos. Paul's instinct was to hoard it. To keep it like a baby bird, feed it from a dropper. He figured that since his own sorrow was private, everyone felt the same way. And by everyone, he really means Jake.

Paul doesn't know one thing about the boy's virtual life, which begs the question: What else doesn't he know? He's operating under the assumption that posting the clip of the brass band is the worst thing his son has ever done, but maybe that's untrue. Maybe it's only another upload in a series of dubious, ignominious posts. Maybe his son has a whole cache of public pathos. Maybe his YouTube channel is a hive of sadness, and Paul makes himself a promise in his uncomfortable IKEA chair: He is going to get computer-savvy. He is going to unearth the side of his son that lives in the computer.

He has to know *that* Jake. The avatar. The username. TheGreatJake. He has to know if his son's username has any concept of morality, needs to see if there's remorse for sharing the suicides or if TheGreatJake doesn't see anything wrong with what he did. His son will barely engage him in conversation; hell, he won't even sit next to him in the car. So getting to know this other son is his chief priority.

Paul has to stop limiting his perceptions of his son based on his own biases. He has to swallow whatever odd clump of pride that keeps Paul from joining the rest of the free world on social media, if not to assuage his own loneliness, then in the name of finding out who his son really is.

It breaks his heart, thinking like that, but perhaps this is what love looks like in the twenty-first century. There's the heart pumping in our chests and the one that thrums online, beating a binary rhythm, zeroes and ones. Paul has to find that version of his son. He has to interrogate that son and find out if TheGreatJake comprehends how grotesque it is to use these suicides as something captured, something worth sharing, something like entertainment.

Paul feels a low rumble in his stomach; it might be the first showings of some movement. He has no idea how long a laxative takes to kick in, but he wants to see this feeling as progress, the beginning. He has to believe that this might lead to something better.

The therapist's door opens.

Paul rises, and the IKEA chair creaks.

Out comes Jake, slowly shuffling. He doesn't even look up at his dad.

Paul sees his son's whole body but now knows this is only a fraction of him.

The doctor walks out behind the boy, a fiftyish black man. He has a European accent that's on the cusp of reminding Paul of his ex's new boyfriend, Simon, but he won't let himself go there. He has to remain here, to absorb everything that comes from the doctor's mouth.

Words, though, aren't Paul's number-one concern at the moment. It's body language. Jake's eyes fixed on the carpet, hands jammed in his jeans, swaying a bit. The doctor has a furrowed brow and motions Paul into his office with a nod.

"Jake, will you give us a couple minutes?" the therapist asks.

Jake takes an IKEA chair far away from the one that Paul had sat in and fires up his iPhone, staring at the thing barely eight inches from his face.

"I'll be right back, buddy," Paul says to his son, whose gaze doesn't budge from the screen. "I'll be right back!" Paul says again, but it doesn't prompt anything from the boy.

The last thing Paul sees before the doctor shuts the door is his son, sitting alone, and yet he knows that TheGreatJake is somewhere else entirely.

THE 212, 212TH person to ogle Sara's porn clip is Jake, who still sits in the waiting room. It's already been fifteen minutes and no sign of his dad. He has been by himself for the bulk of the time, but a middle-aged woman comes in. She must be the doc's next download, receiving all the data from her servers so he can find the bug in her system.

The waiting room has a small palm tree in the corner, a coffee table with magazines for old people. There are only four chairs, and Jake is glad that the woman took one across from him. She can't see his screen. In fact, she fires up her own tablet. He can keep watching his porn in peace.

There's also a dispenser filled with hand sanitizer mounted on the wall that has a drip hanging off its spout, hardened into a pale meringue.

It is 9:44 in the morning, and the boy's appointment—only their first time meeting together—ended at 9:30.

He knows they're talking about him. Jake, the problem. Jake, the strange. He needs fixing. It's like he's hacked into their conversation and can hear each indicting thing through the closed door.

Jake watches the porn curled in the uncomfortable chair, and his eyes move to the tally telling him he's the 212, 212th person to take this clip in.

Lucky me, he thinks, *I am a palindrome.*

And he might be a palindrome, but there's one thing he's not: a virgin. He can't be considered a virgin anymore, not with all the hours he's spent watching strangers.

Or that's how it should work. Watching all the perversions he can, surely he's no virgin. He thinks of it like a currency exchange, trading in a stack of devalued bills and getting back one gleaming coin of visceral contact.

That doctor and his dad are in there gossiping about him. If he could post a comment on their conversation he'd say, "It's rude to make me wait out here."

Thinking about that inspires Jake to post something on Sara's clip: "Makes me hard!"

Which is a lie.

His penis has been trained to stay soft while watching porn in public. At first, it got hard whenever he indulged. But not lately. Lately, it minds its manners. Unlike Jake.

Pavlov's penis, thinks Jake, so he laughs.

The laughter startles the woman in the waiting room from her e-haze, forced to avert eyes from her screen, totally interrupted and inconvenienced by this boy's inconsiderate snickers, and she scowls, then turns her scorched eyeballs back to her media.

Jake doesn't want to comment on the porn, not really. He wants to comment on his own video, and so he hits YouTube and posts this comment:

```
TheGreatJake
This is my property and you should do what I
say, and I'm looking for Noah911. Where is he?
We need to talk about who is SAD and who isn't.
```

Refresh, refresh, refresh . . .

Nothing.

The problem with this therapist is his lip-pursing. It's the only emoji he has and he sends it to users after every sentence he speaks, every point he drives down on Jake. Every forming of his important and arrogant words ends with the same annoying expression.

"How are you today, Jake?" he had said at the beginning of the session.

Lip purse.

"I am optimistic about our time together, Jake, how about you?"

Lip purse.

"Will you tell me about what you saw on the bridge that day?"

Lip purse.

"Why did you decide to share what you saw, Jake?"

The boy tries to focus on this porn clip. It's the first time he has watched it. He likes this site because it deals only with amateurs, no actual porn stars with their fake tits and too-big cocks. Jake likes watching real people, what real people do.

The site also curates its content, helping users find the good stuff without having to scroll through pages and pages of boring material. The clip he's watching right now is featured at the top of the homepage because it's the winner of their "Skank of the Week" video contest. That's why it has so many hits.

Jake has more hits with the jumpers, but 212,212 views is respectable.

He isn't in the habit of rating videos, but if he did, this one would get a solid score. He likes the girl because she's young and small, like him. He enjoys the sounds she makes. A lot of them try too hard, overselling the sex, making it seem cheap and staged, but this girl remains simple and honest, which is a huge turn-on.

The rating categories on this site are as follows: Gold Medal, Hot-ToTrot!, Boring, Weirdest Boner Right Now, WTF, Flaccid Central.

This clip's called *Naughty in Nevada* and Jake copies the URL on his master sheet of personal favorites. He keeps this litany handy, ready to peruse his merchandise whenever he gets to steal a few minutes for himself. He doesn't only shepherd disasters; he has a separate stable for orgasms as well.

In the waiting room, the middle-aged lady yawns and brushes back her bangs but never takes her eyes off her tablet.

The clip ends and it's 9:49 and Jake starts it back at the beginning.

The simple fact that he knows enough about sex to classify all these clips, ranking them on a spectrum from good to bad, convinces the boy he will be a good lover—or that he already is a good lover but hasn't yet started using his skills. He thinks all his observances have taught him stamina, technique, positions, postponement, thrilling ways to pleasure someone.

His father had told him, on a rare day he felt like talking to his son on their commute into the city, about a theory that claims it takes 10,000 hours of practice to get good at anything, which was how the boy arrived at his own conversion.

Ten thousand hours of watching porn = 1 genuine sexual encounter.

Therefore, he's no virgin.

"You can get good at anything from practice?" the boy had asked.

"Literally anything."

And it isn't only the constant lip-pursing that makes the therapist terrible, it's his whole deal, his whole office, his whole face, his whole set of questions and phony way of instilling camaraderie that the boy had seen through immediately. He knew he couldn't tell the doc the truth, not with his incessant badgering about the clip.

"Why did you post it?"

Lip purse.

"What made you want to share it?"

Lip purse.

"How do you feel about putting it online?"

I can live-tweet this betrayal, thought Jake. *I can share our confidentiality with all my 281 followers.*

It will need its own hashtag.

#ShrinkStink.

#MeetMyMentalIllness.

He tried to pull his phone out during the session to tweet, but the doctor wouldn't allow that, threatened to take it away, and that's the one thing that can't happen.

But there's no one in the waiting room to tell him what to do. He's in charge. If he feels like live-tweeting, that's what he'll do.

The real travesty is that hanging meringue from the hand sanitizer dispenser. Looks like a tiny stalactite. Someone should wipe it off. Not the boy. Somebody has this job. They're supposed to dab and clean the contraption but they might have called in sick, might have seen TheGreatJake's clip, might have seen the brass band jump, too, and feel too confused to swab.

Virgins are clumsy lovers. Quick cummers. Make ridiculous faces. Keep their socks on. Only know two positions.

None of these describe Jake.

It is 9:51.

The therapist obviously doesn't care about this woman, who he makes wait while he's in the other room talking shit about Jake. Which makes him mad, and feelings are like Spotify, how each user gets to decide on a certain song that he needs to hear *right this second!* and he searches for it and finds it and clicks play and it's right there—this thing that you needed—it's immediately available, faster than sneezing.

That's what Jake's doing right now—he's streaming anger.

Good thing there isn't a baseball bat here, thinks Jake.

Then he immediately wants to share that thought, wants all his Twitter followers to grip his fury.

First live-tweet: *I'd smash this whole place.*

On the porn clip, they switch positions again, go reverse cowgirl. He is sure that this is the angle that feels the best, and it's how Jake would like to start his sexual career.

Here's the thing he didn't tell the doctor or his dad or anyone, didn't utter one syllable of this because he knows that no old person will understand: He didn't do anything wrong. This is what people do. This is how the world works. This is why we're smarter now: We share everything with everyone, have access to each sight and sound. We are informed and connected!

If they stop living in the past, they'd plug into this broadcasting consciousness, synapses firing all over the globe. The world is round like a brain, and we are all cells in it, firing all the time.

His dad doesn't get it and thinks that Jake is behaving badly, but he's totally missing the point, which is that good and bad don't matter.

All that matters is content. New content. More content.

Those are the nutrients that keep the great brain going.

Content is Jake's purpose.

It is everybody's purpose.

And each single frame uploaded is a public service.

He's doing what he's supposed to do, what his generation understands as their responsibility. The time is 9:54, and the woman's appointment is basically half over and Jake's day is basically ruined and behind that closed office door are two men talking about nothing, agreeing with each other, so sure that they know what's right and wrong and just and important, making decisions about Jake that he's not even being consulted about, and under these circumstances he can't stomach another second sitting here.

He puts his iPhone in his pocket and launches himself in the direction of the Purell dispenser and forms a fist and uses it as a tomahawk, bringing the edge of it down and breaking the whole dispenser from the wall and whoever thinks that hiring a cleaning lady who's too lazy to wipe one bead of hanging meringue gets what's coming to them.

An emoji of the boy's face would be someone plugging a power cord into his ear and the cheeks going a crazed red and bringing his battery to a full charge.

The woman looks up from her tablet but doesn't say a word. She's wearing a quaint yellow dress that reminds Jake of old movies, and for a moment he's bummed if he's scared her. That's not what this is about.

"Sorry for the disturbance," Jake says to her.

He sprints out of the waiting room, down the hall, the stairs, exits the door.

He's outside, still going full speed, composing his second livetweet in his head, which he'll post once he can safely stop running: *I am on my own.*

11.

Noah911 stands before an empty suitcase, staring into its maw, scared of it like the thing is a pagan god, demanding worship, sacrifice, and in a way that's exactly what it's doing, telling Noah911 to go against every instinct of self-preservation he has and fill the suitcase with his belongings, board a plane, attend Tracey's funeral back home. He's not sure he can bear witness as his sister is eulogized, remembered, and ultimately put to rest.

Because one thing he damn well knows won't be put down is every congregant's judgment, holding Noah911 responsible for her too-early demise. They know it's his fault, as he does, and the funeral would be a grueling torture chamber in which he's slowly eviscerated.

He is in his room, the black suitcase splayed on the bed, totally empty; the clock reads 9 PM and his red-eye departs in a few hours. Noah911 knows what's expected of him, after the belligerent phone call with his father.

It had been three days since Tracey's death and Noah911 finally got the gumption this morning to tell their parents, now only his parents. Pronouns, he is realizing, are going to be tricky from now on.

He called them even though that was the last thing he wanted to do. Seems like a series of unwanted tasks blossom before him: the call, the trip home, the funeral, the indictments, the life transpiring without Tracey.

It didn't take their father five seconds to turn his shock and sadness at the news into high-voltage rage, saying to Noah911, "What did you know about this band?"

Noah911 could hear his mom crying in the background.

"Not much, Dad."

"Why are you only telling us now?"

"The band didn't seem like anything."

"What's going on out there?"

"I'm sorry."

"Your sister is dead!"

Like the phone call with the cop, Noah911 hung up then. He couldn't cope with any more tar painted on his heart. And if he barely made it through that phone call, there was no way he could sit through the funeral. How could he pack for such an experience? How's he supposed to pick out socks? How can he be expected to coordinate colors? There's no way. To fill and zip this suitcase. To board a plane. To look his parents in the eyes. He's never felt this style of guilt before but it's like a hangover. Head aching. Clammy and sweaty. Nauseated. He can't sleep and can't go outside, even though he hates being in their apartment. It's now like a tomb. Tracey is everywhere. Her smell. Her stuff. The uneaten grapefruit still sits by the couch, flies buzzing around it. The toast and teeth marks and hummus. The note: *Make sure my sister eats this, okay?*

Noah911 has hunkered down under that same blanket and watched the YouTube clip over and over. Oddly, it's the only thing that temporarily conquers his symptoms. Noah911 can't stop watching it, watching her. In each viewing, he pauses it right before anyone breaks from the pack and jumps. Pauses it right before the moment becomes something else. Pauses it so he can gaze at Tracey, his happy sister, moving along the walkway and playing the clarinet with friends, and there's nothing wrong, just Tracey and her band doing the thing that makes them feel the most alive in the world.

Pressing pause: In that way he can stop time. He's not interested in trading futures; he's trying to prevent one.

Noah911 should be watching the video right now, god damn it, but the empty suitcase and the red-eye flight and their—his—parents won't get out of the way.

What he needs is an excuse.

The easiest way to get out of this is a text. It's so passive, so one-way, so devoid of confrontation. Empty of any opportunity to get talked into anything. Noah911 can type and send and the conversation is over. He talks, then no one talks. Delivering his news free from outside input. It's a perfect method to disseminate bad news. Flake on a dinner reservation. Blow off a massage. Skip your kid sister's funeral.

A few words and he's free.

Noah911 still has the programming of an athlete. He sees competition in every direction he looks. It certainly helps him professionally and it helps when he picks up women, not interested in a relationship but securing a one-night stand is its own short-term futures contract. He takes, or had taken before all this, impeccable care of his body, eating all the right stuff, lifting weights, tons of cardio, 7 percent body fat. But somewhere along the way he forgot to take care of Tracey as she needed him to, which reminds him of his senior season on the lacrosse team. A skinny freshman had made varsity. Kid was so quick and elusive, a little water bug out there that no one could keep up with, but the coach knew that other teams would target him, try to outmuscle the kid, render his skills meaningless if he was always being knocked around. Coach asked Noah911 to protect him out there, to take a penalty if he needed to put some people on their asses to alert them that any cheap shots on the kid would be avenged. But being a midfielder kept Noah911 busy in all sorts of ways, and during a particularly contentious game, he forgot about the kid. Or he remembered, but the responsibility to protect him plummeted down his list of priorities, and some muscle-head on the opposing side checked the kid so ferociously that he rocketed to the grass, separating a shoulder, his head hitting the ground so hard he lost consciousness for a few seconds. His parents never let the kid step foot on the field again, and Noah911 carried the taste of that around for a few years, couldn't shake it. He had been charged to act as the kid's protector and couldn't live up to the task. If it took him so long to get over something like that, Tracey's death will smother him forever. He'll replay it over and over, the things he could have done differently for her, the ways he could have been more involved, more accessible.

And if her death represented the end of the most important game of his life, then the funeral and seeing his parents were the post-game press conference, where Noah911 has to stand at a podium and answer for his terrible play. Reporters champing at the bit to skewer him, and the microphone isn't big enough for Noah911 to hide behind. He cosigned the death of his sister through his slack protection, and he needed to be held accountable for that.

"Don't you think Tracey deserved better?" someone will ask.

And Noah911 would break down crying. Right there at the podium. That would be his answer. That would have to do. Cameras going off, capturing him in this way, putting pictures of it in newspapers and online so everyone can see him for what he truly is: the brother who neglected his sister. Or worse: the brother who let her die.

Finding the right words to text his parents proves difficult. Or the reason he can't come home proves impossible to find. An illness will not suffice. This he knows from years of watching him and Tracey with stuffy noses and swollen tonsils, coughing and wheezing on the school bus. His parents won't accept any sickness as an excuse, their father always prescribing Tylenol as the cure for every ailment.

He sends this message to both his parents' phones: *I got beat up and can't travel. Sorry.*

Does his dad even know how to text? His mom certainly does, often lobbing phrases in the third person to make him feel like crap as he reads them: *Mothers would sure love hearing from their sons soon.* Or: *Experts say that sons should call their moms regularly to lead fulfilling lives.* A million others like these. She used to do it over email, a cyber-nag, but last year she switched to an exclusive text-only assault. No one can make you want to cut your heart out quicker than your mother.

But wait.

He's already made a mistake.

Seconds after sending his text to his parents he realizes his error. What he should have done is disable the tone that alerts him he's received a new text, should have minimized any temptations to analyze responses from them.

He's still standing in his bedroom, right in front of that splayed suitcase, its black material looking like a filleted seal. He's wondering what you do with this two-ton guilt and how you're supposed to live through this suffering and endure a life with constant grief, those sounds wheezing in his head like an old coffee maker, and then his BlackBerry beeps.

He knows that the text is from one of his parents, probably his mother, and he knows that reading a message from either of them is a bad idea, and he knows that if he reads it he won't be able to sever the conversation there, and yet he can't stop himself. He so badly wishes that he could resist this bait, but he's not strong enough.

Here's his mother's response: *What happened, sweetie?*

Got mugged. I was punched and kicked a few times. Broken nose. Cracked ribs. Etc.

Hold on . . .

There's about forty-five seconds of nothing, time for Noah911 to put his phone down. Go outside. Take a shower. Eat something. Do fifty pushups. Don't read any more of their texts. All these directives whirl around his head and yet he does nothing except sit there.

Another alert.

This is your sister's fucking funeral!

That's his father's foray into the conversation, and it sends a shudder through Noah911. A rictus jimmies onto Noah911's lips. Finding it funny, actually, reading and rereading the inaugural text from his father; he can't help but hear the message in his father's voice. Like he's in the room. Yelling it. That exclamation point is like a lightning bolt. Many a time in Noah911's formative years he's seen his father's exclamation points in person, punching holes in walls, chucking china. He never put his hands on his wife and kids, but he governed through fear and the possibility of violence.

Noah911 texts back: *What can I do? I'm injured.*

Be injured on the plane. Be hurt here.

I can't even walk.

Get your ass to the airport!

If he had it to do over again, he might have tried something surgical. An appendectomy. Or an exotic disease, like dengue fever. That's a thing, right? The kind so contagious that the authorities wouldn't allow him on a plane for fear of infecting others. He should have thought this through more.

From his father: *Call us.*

My jaw is sprained and broken nose kills when I try to talk.

Call us!

My jaw is SEVERELY sprained and nose throbs like crazy.

From his mom: *We're worried about you.*

And then this from his dad, barely a second later: *Prove it.*

Prove what?

I want to see your beaten-up face.

Camera on phone is broken.

Then let's Skype.

No response from Noah911 for over a minute.

From his father: *Hellooooo!!!*

Noah911 does what he should have done five minutes ago, before this fiasco started. He puts his phone down, actually placing it in the empty suitcase, if only he can send that as his proxy. He turns and leaves the room, the apartment, and heads out for a drink. A glass of vodka. At the very least it gets him away from the phone and the parents and the press conference and the suitcase and the flies.

They live—he lives—at 25th and Bryant, in the Mission District. There are a lot of bars on 24th Street, a major thoroughfare through the neighborhood. From what he understands, ten years ago this was a pretty tough stretch, but people like Noah911, rich and white, have been flooding this corridor, corroding its character. People tag sidewalks and walls with pejorative thoughts on gentrification—*This city used to celebrate diversity*—but it's too late. It's already happened. Such comments are as useless as bemoaning the weather from last Thursday. And as Noah911 now understands, once something has happened, there's nothing you can do about it.

He stops at the door of a bar, peeks inside. It seems too jovial. The room is filled with young and shiny kids. These people seem like they're drinking to have fun, and that's not what he needs. Noah911 seeks the kind of dive bar in which people drink to peel despicable memories from their minds like dirty socks. Is that REM on the jukebox? People still listen to them? The bar has perfect burgundy carpet, stools with shining leather, a bartender actually telling a joke to a gaggle of customers—*How many straight San Franciscans does it take to change a light bulb? Both of them!*—and Noah911 needs to get away from this cheery scene, sink into some squalor.

The next saloon he spies is a Latino bar, mariachi music blazing in a near-empty room. There are three guys bellied up, the faces obscured to him from the doorway, thirsty silhouettes resting elbows on the bar. Barren of any furniture. A concrete floor. No tables. This seems like a place to become a shadow, shrouded in blackness, but it's the music that keeps him from going inside. Mariachi features horns. Trumpets. Tubas. Which brings Noah911's mind to the brass band and there's no way he can sit in a room with horns hollering at him.

He continues his hunt for a just-right bar. Noah911 approaches and rejects five more, before finding the perfect place to slide inside.

It's the bar's color scheme, or lack thereof, that entices him. The place is painted entirely black—floor, walls, and ceiling. Noah911 is reminded of his suitcase, and knows this is what it would be like to climb inside the thing, zip it up, bathe himself in the darkness and quiet, keeping all the guilt away.

He walks to the center of the room and his eyes are brought up to the ceiling. He's wrong: It's not totally black. There are pieces of broken mirror glued up there, shining like stars in the sky, and it seems so beautiful that he chokes up.

Flies swarm back by the liquor bottles. There's a TV in the corner, playing the news. Ten guys, no women in the place. An old Jane's Addiction song hits everyone in the face.

Noah911 climbs onto a stool and the old man approaches, wearing a T-shirt that says SPANK ME, IT'S MY BIRTHDAY.

"Happy birthday," Noah911 says.

"Lay off, will ya?" he says. "Lost a bet with my niece and have to wear this stupid shirt all week."

"What was the bet?"

"Aren't you a curious asshole?"

If there was any debate as to whether or not Noah911 had picked the right spot, this seals the deal. He's home. This is the perfect pub for what he has to do. "I didn't mean any offense," he says.

"No, it's not your fault. My fuse is spent. People busting my balls about this shirt the whole time. What will you drink?"

"Ketel One on the rocks."

The bartender limps off to find the right bottle, and Noah911 peeks up and down the other stools. There are a couple men like him, drinking alone, cuddling dejection with every sip. At the far end, though, way over by the TV and its news program, is a group of four guys. They have the look he needs and are pretty brawny, too.

The Ketel One is placed in front of him and Noah911 says, "Hold on, please," and the bartender stands there for five seconds and watches Noah911 gulp down the whole drink and order another.

"I'm liking you more and more," says the bartender.

"Be careful or I'll spank you."

He shakes his head at Noah911 and goes to get another vodka, coming back with the bottle and filling up his glass, then pouring himself one as well. No ice in his glass, only warm vodka.

"That's hardcore," Noah911 says, motioning to the tepid vodka.

"I don't drink for the taste," he says. As a toast, the bartender holds up his warm vodka and says, "To being one day closer to death."

Noah911 doesn't say anything and they shoot the vodka.

The bartender gets summoned by the four men, who are wondering whose dick they gotta suck to get the baseball game turned on.

Noah911 can feel heat and testosterone pulse from them. It's written on their faces and wafts off of them, a violent pheromone, and Noah911 loves inhaling it.

"This ain't a sports bar," the bartender says.

"Just turn the channel, old-timer," one says.

"Just go fuck yourself," the bartender says.

Another starts clapping and howling. "Oh, snap, Willie. He sure got you!"

"Hey," Willie says, adjusting his backward baseball cap, "I like your bite, old man."

"You ain't seen my bite," the bartender says. "We're too busy barking."

This makes them lose it, cracking up, pounding fists on the bar, shaking their drinks, a few suds jumping out of pint glasses and slowly spilling down the outside.

Noah911 loses his capacity to follow the conversation, eyes glued to the TV. They're saying something about the brass band but he can't hear. They show a few stills from TheGreatJake's video; Noah911 has memorized every frame. Finally, the screen zooms in on one man's face, the last person to jump, the guy playing the bass drum. His mug is grainy, pixilated from being blown up this big on the screen, but Noah911 tries to soak up every detail. He's young, definitely in his thirties. Short brown hair. Sort of handsome. Not an imposing face, clean-shaven, not the crazy you can see in the eyes of, say, Ted Bundy or Jim Jones. Noah911 would sit next to this guy on the subway and not worry one bit.

He has to know what the newscasters are saying. Earlier, he'd been kept out of the mariachi bar, simply from the threat of being triggered to think of Tracey jumping by the horns. This, though, feels like something different—this feels like he might be able to learn. Why are they zeroing in on this man? Is he the leader? Is it his fault, too?

He asks the bartender to turn the music down, crank up the news. The men buck at this idea, saying, "God no, anything but that. Jesus, what's wrong with baseball? What do you have against the national pastime?"

This is the national pastime, thinks Noah911.

The cranky bartender agrees to Noah911's request, probably because his suggestion bothers the others so much. He shuts off the music, snatches the remote control, and turns up the news.

"This is an image of the man thought to be the mastermind behind . . ." the news anchor says, but Noah911 can't hear the rest of her thought because one of the men whines, "Boring! This is boring! Can we please turn the channel?"

"We are so bored!" another says.

"Bor-ing!" they start chanting, all four of them, bisecting the word into two harsh syllables. "Bor-ing! Bor-ing! Bor-ing!"

They pound their fists on the bar in rhythm with their chants.

"Will you clowns shut up?" Noah911 says.

They stop. Look at him. Stand from their stools. Flash greedy smiles. It's like an antelope has challenged a cackle of hyenas to a fight.

"I'm trying to listen to the news," Noah911 says.

"Mister, you should be listening to the common sense the good lord gave you," says the bartender.

"He's giving you sound advice," Willie says, readjusting his backward hat, pulling it down snug.

"I need to hear the news," Noah911 says, "so put your tampons in and deal with it."

"You assholes want to fight, you do it outside," the bartender says. "I'll call the cops, though."

"Believe me," Willie says, "he does not want to fight."

Noah911 hears another phrase from the anchor: " . . . it's not known if a reason has been explicitly stated . . . "

"What do you think, News Watcher?" says one of them. "Will there be anything left of you by the time the cops get here?"

Noah911 is off his stool. He backs up into the middle of the room. The news still tells people about the brass band, and Noah911 can't think of a more appropriate soundtrack.

"Not here," the bartender says.

"It has to be here," Noah911 says to him.

Then he turns his attention to the guys: "Are you made of chicken shit or what?"

"You must be off your meds, man," Willie says.

"I know exactly what I'm doing."

They saunter over and slowly circle him. The bartender has the phone in his hand, ready to dial 911, but no one will make it in time. Nobody can save him and they shouldn't. A piss-poor protector like Noah911 shouldn't get any shelter of his own.

Let his guilt have arms and fists.

Let him bleed.

The news still plays on the TV, not that Noah911 can hear much of what's being said. The brass band's enigma, their code, stupefies everyone, except Noah911 because he doesn't care why they did it. That's not a question that interests him. Futures contracts pay out or they bust. Those are the only two options, and Noah911 likes that simplicity. There's no time for why. Tracey was alive; now she's dead.

And that's when Noah911 hits him in the face.

It's a solid shot and drops Willie to the floor and Noah911 takes a deep breath, knowing what comes next. The first thing he feels comes from behind, a shot in the kidney, buckling him over, but he's not going to fall, no way is he going down yet, and now another fist finds his temple and he sees a bright light, loses any sense of where he is, might very well be zipped up in that suitcase, and here comes somebody grabbing him in a bear hug, tucking his arms so he can't defend himself, and Willie is up off the floor, saying, "Hold him still. Hold him still," and Noah911 feels two punches straight in the face, another in the stomach, and the hyena who's been holding his arms is now the only thing keeping him on his feet, a few more swings, a hook to the liver, an uppercut to the chin and he bites his tongue, tasting blood and freedom, and a wide hook lands on his eye socket and they let him fall to the bar's floor.

The bartender screams into the phone, "Send the cops, send the cops, send the cops!"

The other men who had been drinking at the bar all scurry from the premises.

Noah911 looks up, lying under the bar's starry sky.

He can't hear the news but knows they're still talking about the brass band, maybe a close-up of Tracey's face and the newscaster asking earnestly, "Who was looking out for this young lady?"

He sees the four hyenas huddled around him. They're looking down at him, inspecting their kill.

It doesn't make any sense to Noah911 why they've stopped. No need for mercy on somebody so useless, so unconscionable, so undeserving of sympathy.

He says, "You guys punch like pussies."

Which brings the boots, a couple of them kicking him while the others stomp on his chest and midsection, and he turns on his side so he can get enough air to take a breath, bringing his arms over his solar plexus to maybe defend his stomach but also maybe to leave his face free, exposed, open. Leave his face available for any gracious violence.

12.

Sara sees the river and knows she has to swim. It was one thing pretending with Hank in the empty pool, but here, in the late afternoon sun, she can't wait to be in the water.

She's without a bathing suit and that means stripping down to her bra and panties. The way she figures it, however, what's the big deal, with the sex tape broadcasting her bits all over the world? Hank says the sex tape will die down, and she's trying to believe that, trying to hurdle the initial shock and hoping the whole thing fades to a tolerable decibel. That it will become another clip in a wide sea of them online.

Sara kicks off her shorts, pulls her shirt over her head, and throws them on the shore. She walks into the water, up to her waist. The cool temperature feels amazing, as the day's still over 90°.

She floats on her back in about three feet of water, looking up at the white sky; without sunglasses it's almost impossible to stare straight up, but she tries, sees some rainbows around the edge of her eyes. She wonders if corneas smell like burning hair as they char. She decides to shut them, to enjoy the cool water and quiet.

To enjoy his company, assuming Rodney ever gets the nerve to exit the car. Maybe he's never seen a woman in a bra and panties before. It's a possibility that Sara hadn't thought about until right now. She's not trying to make him uncomfortable, not at all. She has no inhibitions around him, given their history. This isn't going to lead to a hookup or anything. Sara knows this isn't a big thing, but does he? Is he wigging out in the car, wondering if it's okay to approach the river since she's more than half naked? He's that kind of gentleman. Maybe the only one of those Sara has ever met. Rodney respects her, Sara knows that, and he's the last person in the galaxy that holds her in esteem.

It's also conceivable that Rodney watches a lot of porn, if he's not getting the real deal, and Sara doesn't think he is. Everyone needs to get off. She can't hold it against him. Not really. But it would bother her if she knew Rodney has seen her video, because taking it in would denigrate what he thinks of her. It would have to. In his eyes, Sara would be marred, spoiled, and she can't imagine losing his regard.

This is their first day together after so long and Sara enjoys his company, his honesty. Yes, it had freaked her out a bit in the car, him holding that busted side mirror up so she could see her reflection and talking his sweet words. He's so sincere that it takes her aback. It even did when they were inseparable, the way he could say something so real, so direct. One time during a backyard campout, they'd been kissing for over an hour, Sara letting him paw at her tits, and the tent was getting dimmer and dimmer. The battery in their flashlight dwindled, and they both knew the tent would be pitch-black in a matter of seconds, the light fading and flickering, Sara shaking it back and forth for extra juice, but there were no stashes left. "It's almost dark and I don't want it to be," she said, and Rodney said, "It's never dark with you."

Sure, it was schmaltzy, Sara recognized that back then, but what was wrong with schmaltz? Why not indulge in some when your life was surrounded by cinderblocks?

She actually says it aloud now, floating in the river, eyes still closed, feeling the sun warm her torso and feet and face: "It's never dark with you."

Sara has to help him get out of the car. She has to tell him directly that it's cool for him to come swimming. That's what she wants. That's why they're here.

"Hey," she calls, not opening her eyes or turning her head toward the car, voice stretching to a scream, "are you getting in here or what?"

"In," he says, speaking at a normal volume.

Sara's legs flail, eyes open, and she lets them find the bottom, standing up. "Jesus, what are you—a spy or something?" she asks. "I didn't hear you make a single sound slipping in the water."

"Nin. Ja," says Rodney.

There he is in his boxers, floating on his back only a few feet away from her. Sara relaxes and starts floating again, too.

"There's barely any water left," she says, "because of the drought, but I wanted to show you this place. My dad used to take me rafting here. Can you believe it? There used to be enough water for rapids, and we'd leave from this spot. Fight down the river through all the currents and twists. Now it's a puddle."

She pauses, seeing if he wants to say something, but Sara knows there's not much to add. She's bobbing in self-sympathy. Sara's not really talking to him anyway. Not talking to her parents. Not talking to anyone. Except herself. The river used to be something and now it's nothing and so is Sara and that's the truth.

"It. Will. Rain," Rodney says.

"What?"

"It. Will. Rain."

"It might."

"It. Will."

He's right, she guesses. That is a possibility. The puddle floods and swells and soon it's a river again. Soon daughters and dads will grab paddles and life jackets and fly down the rapids.

"You're right," she says.

"You. O. Kay?"

"No," says Sara, "but I like being here with you. I like thinking that it might rain again."

"What do you think our families are doing to each other?" Sara says. "Do you think Larry and Felix really attacked my brother?"

Rodney shrugs his shoulders.

They're both floating on their backs, slowly moving with the languid current. Sara wiggles her toes. Rodney does it, too.

This is what it would have felt like if she'd gotten on the balloon with him. Before he fell. When it was just a boy hovering. Sara stood on the ground, astonished, in awe. She stood there jealous, thinking that if he was going away she wanted to be with him. She was scared but not for his safety; she was scared she'd never see him again, watch him vanish on the horizon to a crumb in the sky.

"What if there's nothing left for us?" she asks. "What if they've torn it all down, burned everything up? What would we do?"

"Leave," he says.

"To where?"

"Cal. I. For. Ni. A."

"California?"

Rodney nods.

"Why?" she says.

"Mom."

"How do you know she's there?"

"Dad. Told. Me."

"I'd go to California with you," she says.

Rodney grabs her hand.

Well, *grab* isn't the right word. He slips his palm on top of Sara's and they slither their fingers together. He instigates it; she helps their hands find the right grip. They'll never be in the backyard tent again, but that doesn't mean they can't have a moment in this river.

Rodney is holding her hand, and she's holding his, and they're in underwear, and she looks over at him, though his eyes are closed. She sees his smile and Sara notices a couple dragonflies popping on top of the water and everything is silent so she closes her eyes too, straightens her neck to the center and the sun perfectly roasts her face.

Sara has found the only person besides her brother that will give her the benefit of the doubt. They'll float here, wet palm in wet palm, weightless and warmed, without any connection to the world.

SARA TURNS HER car onto their block, and everything appears normal. There are no police cars, fire trucks. The SWAT team isn't perched on rooftops with rifles. Animal control isn't wrestling with Bernard, fresh from chewing out Felix's and Larry's jugular. Sara can't see any amputated limbs littering the field of battle.

The block is quiet, and she slows the car in front of Rodney's house, but doesn't stop. The light is on in the front room, and they can see someone's silhouette through the window, either jogging around or dancing.

"That Felix or your dad?"

"Un. Cle."

"What's he doing?"

"Sing. Ing."

"He sings?"

"Dan. Ces. Too."

"Oh, shit, that's terrible," she says.

Rodney nods.

"Do you want to come over?" Sara says. "I don't really want this day to end."

She says it and means it, but it makes her pause. She should absolutely want this day to end. It's been the shittiest one since losing her parents. Finding out about the sex tape, getting suspended from work, but the last few hours have been great. She got a double dose of support: First, Hank handled all this so much better than she ever imagined he would, and then she got to reconnect with Rodney, holding hands in the river.

She checked her phone right before they drove home, and she still hasn't heard back from Nat. Sara's coming to grips with the fact she might never know why he did it. That piece of information might evade her, but what she did learn today is equally important. She knows Rodney is still in there.

"You. Sure?" he asks.

"Yeah, come over," she says.

He nods again.

Sara keeps rolling up the block.

Her house looks undisturbed from the outside. Either they had a quick dust-up and hillbilly order has been restored, or they decided to hold a finicky truce.

Sara parks in front of the house and says, "Don't forget your underwear."

His boxers, her bra and panties, are laid out on the back seat.

Rodney blushes and Sara wants to say something like *Getting shy now?* but it's so endearing she giggles at his red cheeks.

They park and walk up to the house, waving their still-wet undies around, being silly. They lope up the front steps and the door is wide open and she can hear Hank yelling into his phone.

That's when her hands go off, vibrating cell phones.

She can hear Hank stomping about, threatening whoever's on the other end of the call, saying, "So you're saying this is everywhere, and I can't do nothing to stop it?"

"Hank?" says Sara from the front doorway, still holding her bra and panties, Rodney a step behind her with balled-up boxers in one hand.

"Gotta go, Colby," Hank says into the phone. "She's here. I gotta deal with this shit."

Hank stomps into the front room with Bernard trotting behind him. "Why's he with you?" Hank asks, pointing at Rodney.

"Don't worry about it."

"Why you carrying your panties, Sara?"

Sara. He calls her Sara. Not Baby Sis. Not anything with affection. Agitation. Letters, two consonants, two vowels. Sara doesn't understand what could've changed. He was so supportive earlier, drinking beers in the kitchen and swimming in the empty pool and now he has hate in his eyes. He doesn't look drunk, though, only ornery.

"What's wrong, Hank?" she says.

"That was Colby."

"I heard."

"I guess congratulations are in order," Hank says.

Poor Rodney is glued in the doorway with his dripping boxers. Sara peeks at him for a second and wishes to flee this house, this block and town, but it's too late. They're here. She's here, and she doesn't know what's coming next, but she knows it's not good.

"I don't know what you're talking about," Sara says.

"Skank of the week!"

"What does that mean, Hank?"

"You are skank of the week on some porno site. Colby says it's already had over 100,000 hits. It's viral, Sara. And from the looks of it," Hank says, coming over and grabbing her panties out of her hands, "you were out making another dirty movie. Did you fuck the town retard, Sara?"

"Don't talk to me like that!" she says.

"No!" Rodney says, stepping into the room.

Hank takes the panties and throws them right in Rodney's face, tries to step up to him, but before her brother can get to him, before Hank can hurt him again, Sara stands between them, saying to Rodney, "I need you to leave."

"No," he says.

"Leave," she says. "Please."

"Ten seconds till I make you leave," Hank says.

"I'll be fine," Sara says and ushers him out, shutting and locking the door, feeling fear—actual fear—she's scared of her brother. He's never raised a hand to her, but it doesn't seem impossible tonight.

She turns to him.

"What's it feel like to be skank of the week?" he asks.

"Why are you talking to me like this? You knew about the video. Who cares what Colby thinks?"

"It ain't Colby. It's everyone, Sara. 100,000 hits in a day. A million in a week. Everyone will see it!"

"Why is this making you so mad?"

"And I no longer care what you think about Nat," Hank says. "I'm going to destroy him."

"Please stop, Hank," Sara says.

It's almost a whisper, which he can't hear. His eyes are far away, clomping around the room. His eyes are submerged in violence. They've tasted the chum and now need real meat.

Sara doesn't require his help, anybody's help hating herself right now. Some website can't brand her the skank of the week because she's been tagging that on her skull's walls all day, with almost every breath.

"What do you want me to do about it?" she asks. "How can I make this better?"

"And then you flit in here holding your panties?" he says. "Rubbing my face in all this? Making me have to see you slut around?"

"You're breaking my heart," she says and starts crying and runs to her room, throws the closet open, gets a ratty suitcase and unzips it and stuffs whatever clothes she can fit. Snatches her emergency money. Her hands aren't only vibrating cell phones on the inside anymore. They're flat-out shaking. She's shaking. And crying so hard that saliva runs from the corners of her mouth. To walk in the house and be shamed by her brother is the day's final disgrace.

Next she takes the suitcase into the bathroom and flings her toothbrush and hairbrush and there are probably ten other things she should grab, but she can't think of what they might be, zipping it up and turning to the door. She can't concentrate on any particulars because there are amplifiers blaring in her head, heaving Hank's shames over and over, playing them like power chords.

All that matters is fleeing this house.

All that matters is speeding outside the city limits.

All that matters is not being here.

"Where are you going?" Hank says in the doorway.

"What do you care if a skank of the week leaves?"

"You're not going anywhere, Sara."

"Stop calling me that!" she says, wishing she were strong enough to slam him in the temple and topple him to the ground, telling him, *My name is Baby Sis.*

"Calling you what?"

"I'm taking a trip," she says.

"You're not."

And she and her ratty suitcase run full speed into Hank. He doesn't budge. The dog starts barking from the hallway. Obviously, Hank can manhandle her, but he's not. He's letting her slam into him and he's letting her drag the suitcase away and letting her amble through the front door and letting her shut it. Sara can't tell what would feel worse—him making her stay, or him allowing her to leave—and her thoughts are the loudest they've ever been, cranking through those amplifiers and her hands keep buzzing and buzzing and she's crying harder than she ever has, even more than when her parents died because that at least had shock as a component and there's none of that numbing here. No, there's only Hank crunching up her heart like an aluminum can.

Sara's at her car, looking over her shoulder to see if Hank will come out and stop her, but the house is quiet. Even Bernard has stopped barking. The quiet at the river had felt so peaceful, yet this one feels fickle and cruel.

She throws open the trunk and stows the suitcase and opens the driver's side door and notices someone's inside. She jumps back.

"Me," says Rodney from the passenger seat.

"What are you doing here?"

"You. Oh. Kay?"

"You need to go," she says. "I'm getting out of here."

Rodney nods but doesn't budge.

"I'm leaving now," she says.

More nodding.

"Do you understand what I'm saying?" Sara asks.

More nodding.

"What are you doing, Rodney?"

"I'm. Com. Ing."

"You can't."

"Can."

Sara looks up at the house. Hank hasn't come outside to stop her. He's not bellowing Baby Sis from inside. She tries to stifle her sobs, but it's worse when she sees Rodney, and she surrenders into it, wailing. "He hates me," she says and crashes into the driver's seat.

"Shhh," says Rodney.

He holds his wet trunks toward Sara, presumably for her to use as a hanky, and Sara laughs.

"No thanks," she says.

"All. I. Need," he says.

"All you need for what?"

He points out the window, into the distance and darkness.

She'd misread his offering. He wasn't presenting the boxers as a way to wipe her tears, blow her nose. No, Rodney was suggesting something else entirely: an escape, a copilot, a friend.

"Those are all you need to leave with me?" she asks.

Rodney nods again, and Sara feels a bit better, taking his boxers and running them under her eyes.

"Let's go find your mom," she says.

They have no haven here, Albert, they are all password-protected, they all have signs on their hearts that say SLIDE TO UNLOCK. *But those four-digit codes have been forgotten and so they can't get inside themselves, locked out and lost, and in their confusion they will hunt through the ones and zeroes for connection, to find out who they are, they will show their naked bodies for all to see, they will look for the people who made them, they will flounder for some sense of decency or self. It's all the time on their hands, isn't that a weird expression? Forget hands. It is the time in their brains, racing through neurotransmitters like mice in mazes. Time cannot be stopped but it is not a predator. Time is our friend, and it's willing to play nicely if we learn how to ask, if we exchange pleasantries, if we shake hands and kiss cheeks, and you and I know the clandestine language to indulge time in dialogue. Only the two of us can articulate this yet-to-be discovered world. I wish we could wait for them, Albert, I wish there were a way to let them figure it out for themselves but thermometers don't lie, this planet will face the big burn. It's fate, it's science, it's existential mathematics. Unless we save them. My brain sends a signal to your brain and you send signals to my brain and we are connected, we are the only unlocked devices left. We are connected across time, and soon we'll be able to bridge space as easily, and once we've mastered that advancement, you will be able to beam back. The space-time continuum will be tamed. There will be no such thing as pasts. Even the past tense will be irrelevant, archaic, known only in legend. Everyone across time will be alive at the same moment, all of us collapsing into one shining transcendent community, which will know no heat, no pathos. People born before the common* *era, people in the Middle Ages, the Victorians, the Huns, the ones who clutch technology like oxygen masks, they will all breathe at the same time, they will all pump blood. There will only be now. And you will be here. The two of us will stand in the ugliest Garden of Eden. No one here believes in anything they can't find in the search engine but our action will remedy that, we will show them the new religion, we will illustrate the perfect convergence of piety and science. No demagogues or deities or dupes. Just a simple way to solve $E = mc^{despaired}$. Space and time manipulation means we can remain uncremated, means that so many wrongs might go extinct in the process because people will love their second chances. They'll love this new life, they'll rise to the occasion, it's a way to reenter that passcode, it's a way to navigate around with a blazing fast connection, to awaken and slough off that residue of cynicism, to reorient their senses of self. We'll be able to swim through our own nervous systems. Can you imagine? And as we figure out who we are, as we remember that there's good in our souls, everyone will be fused together into a single bright consciousness and in that moment, we will remember what it is to be happy.*

PART 2:

RESET

13.

"What was he wearing?" asks the cop.

"What?"

"His clothes."

"What was he wearing today?"

"At the time of his disappearance."

The two of them stand in the parking lot, in front of the therapist's office. Paul keeps his phone in his hand, compulsively checking it every few seconds to see if Jake has responded to any of his texts (he hasn't), while Paul turns in circles every thirty seconds or so to spot his son's return (no on that front, too).

The police officer is somewhere in his late twenties or early thirties. Barely looks like he needs to shave. It bothers Paul that he's so young. He wants someone chiseled, battle-tested. Somebody who has worked cases like this his whole career, and yet there's nothing Paul can do about it. He'll have to hope that this young man is good at his job.

Paul is, for all intents and purposes, calm. He's not raising his voice, no cantering heart, no tears, no hysterics. He's concerned, but he's having trouble accepting this as reality: The whole thing feels too blasé, too relaxed to be about a missing child. Jake is missing in terms of no one knowing where he's at this second; however, it's temporary—Paul knows this is short-term. His son overreacted, much like taking a baseball bat to his room, but his tantrum will wane and he'll be back, he has to come back.

There is a suspicion, though, huffing all the air from Paul's lungs. His breathing grows shorter, so he's not as composed as he thought. Perhaps Paul wants to collect himself via a flurry of *Keep your head and things will all work out* platitudes, yet he can't really nourish himself on those empty calories. Fact: His son is missing. Fact: It happened on Paul's watch, which plumps him up with blame. Paul has been painted with parental blame plenty of times in Jake's life. All parents have had this experience, he knows. It's part of the job. He remembers a time when Jake was two feet away from him—no more than that—and Jake fell down and chipped his front tooth. The boy was only three years old, and the rest of the tooth didn't fall out until he was seven and Paul had to see the chip, that denunciation, every day for four years, a jagged reminder of his negligence. *I was doing the right thing*, he always told the chip. *I was standing right there. I wasn't being careless.*

That's the devastating thing about being a parent—the world doesn't care about your plans. There's no tally for intentions. Kids fall, teeth chip, and you live with it.

In the parking lot, Paul checks his phone again for texts.

He turns in another circle, scrutinizing his surroundings.

And now Paul has to make eye contact with this young cop and his questions.

His lungs aren't pumping out full blasts of air. They're a garden hose with a kink. Paul pants out the next couple breaths.

"He had on sneakers," says Paul. "White and red Nikes."

"Okay, thanks."

"I bought them for him about a month ago."

"What clothes was he wearing, sir?"

"Can't you track his cell signal?"

"We need to finish this report."

"I've seen that done on TV, the authorities locating criminals from their cell signals."

"That technology exists," the cops says, "but our priority is to complete the report."

"We don't need a report if we track his cell."

"A physical description of what he's wearing will help spot him, sir."

"Well, it was . . . uh . . ."

"Let's come back to this."

Paul doesn't want to, though. He doesn't want to admit that he can't remember what his son wore today. Doesn't want to feel the repulsive burden of *not knowing* because, he guesses, other parents always know what clothes their kids have on. His ex would be able to answer this question with no problem and Paul should as well.

There are so many things that he doesn't want to acknowledge, things he can't bear remembering. Like the feeling of being in the office, he and the therapist barricaded away from Jake. The feeling of being interrogated by the doctor, his questions about the divorce, the separation, the living arrangements. The feeling of being indicted, of being on trial. The feeling of guilt—something Paul didn't necessarily know he felt about his son's well-being until that moment. The feeling of sweating on a witness stand. The feeling that a sentence will be handed down shortly.

The feeling of listening to a therapist express "deep concern"—his words—about Paul's son. "Deep concern for what?" Paul had asked, and the doctor only got to say, "Jake is at a precarious intersection."

Then they heard a loud noise from the waiting room, a door slammed, a woman's voice calling, "Doctor!"

Both Paul and the therapist emerged from the office and saw the smashed hand sanitizer dispenser on the floor, clear liquid oozing out, looking like a dead jellyfish.

"Where's Jake?" Paul asked the woman, her tablet resting on her lap, a napping child.

She pointed to the door. Paul ran through it. Paul screamed his son's name. Paul was down the stairs. He exited the building. He stood in the parking lot and couldn't spot his son anywhere.

"Jake!" he yelled, turning in circles. "Jake!"

Soon he dialed 911. Soon he was alerted by the operator to the fact that this wasn't an emergency situation. Please call your local authorities, sir. They'll be happy to assist, sir.

And ten minutes later, here he is with this police officer asking him a battery of questions, equally if not more defaming than those of the therapist, and Paul wants one thing: to remember what his son was wearing.

"His weight?" the cop says.

"Jeans, I think," Paul says. "Yeah, blue jeans. Baggy."

"His weight," the cop says.

"You know how they wear them too baggy?"

"Do you know his weight?"

"Maybe 130 pounds."

"Height?"

"Probably five-five or five-six or around there."

"We need to be as precise as possible."

"Five-six then."

"What's his date of birth?"

"April 24th, 1999," says Paul proudly. As precise as possible. He can be more precise. He can go down to the minute. 7:18 AM. He can tell the cop all about that morning, can re-create the whole scene, his son with the umbilical cord looped twice around his neck, the doctors getting more anxious and agitated. Every time Paul looked up these doctors multiplied, two of them at first, four, eight, and because they'd administered such a heavy epidural, his wife couldn't push, not really, and the doctors were now using a vacuum on the baby's head to suck him out, and the worst part was that they'd broadcast his heartbeat over speakers in the room, and as his wife tried to push the baby's heartbeat would crank up and between these too-light pushes Jake's heartbeat would slow to this dismal *thump thump thump*, and Paul was convinced the baby was going to die. Paul stood next to his wife's bed, holding her hand, their foreheads touching, saying to her, "We're all going to be fine; we're going to be fine," and the vacuum wasn't getting the baby out, either, *thump thump thump*, and the doctors were readying for a C-section if this one final push from his wife and one final yank from the vacuum didn't work. But it did. Jake finally slid out, his head misshapen from the pressure created by the vacuum, Paul actually thinking the head looked like a layer cake, and the baby was this terrible purple color and he wasn't crying and the doctors took him away, and Paul stayed right next to his wife, his wife that he loved so much, stayed right with her and whispered, "You did such a great job," and she said, "How is he?" and he said, "Are you okay?" That was when Jake cried for the first time, sitting on a table a few feet from them, having all the mucus sucked from his airways, and it was Paul who walked over to cut the cord, Jake's head already returning to a normal shape a few minutes later. Paul stared down at his son and felt relief that this was over, Jake was here now, Jake was safe, and Paul leaned down and kissed his child for the first time and said, "Welcome."

Paul could tell this young cop all of these details, and many more, so many more, so stop making it sound like Paul didn't know anything about his boy.

"You heard me about the jeans, right?" Paul says.

"Yes. Does he have braces? Wear glasses?"

"Neither."

"What color was his shirt?"

"I don't remember," Paul says.

"Jacket?"

Paul continues to peer all around the parking lot, hoping to see his son flouncing back. He simply needed to wander off, get mad, let his frustration out, something that would explain his departure, that he's not really running away. He's not trying to leave. He had been only temporarily carried away.

"Any other unique identifiers?" the cop asks.

"He usually has his ear buds in. Always playing music."

The cop doesn't write this detail down.

"He literally always has them in, so please put that in the report."

Sighing, the cop jots down a few words, then says, "I'm going up to the doctor's office. To get additional information about the boy's clothing."

"I'll wait here in case he comes back," Paul says.

"You should go home. Check and make sure he's not there. If you have keys, you should also look inside your ex-wife's residence. Be thorough. Closets. Under beds. The garage. Trunks of vehicles. Any place he can hide."

"Who will wait here?"

The cop looks puzzled. "Why would he come back?"

The officer meant why would Jake return here, to this parking lot, but his vague and stabbing syntax—*Why would he come back?*— travels through the skin, the meat, the bone, wedging in Paul's body, a wound already infected with blame. That parental blame. The way seeing a chipped tooth day in, day out can call into question if you're even fit to be a parent. The way there are so many reminders that Paul isn't doing a very good job of it.

"He's coming back," Paul says.

"I have all the information, and we'll be in touch," the cop says. "We'll also reach out to the FBI, talk about opening a missing person file with them."

"He might come back here to find me," says Paul.

The cop turns and walks to the building's front door. "You're right; we'll be in touch."

"That's it?"

"That's a lot," says the cop. The door is open, and he's marching through. "Normally, in these circumstances, the child hides in a familiar place. Go home and be thorough with your search. We'll be in touch."

The door slowly shuts and Paul is alone. He turns in another circle, screaming, "Jake! Jake!"

He texts his son again. This one says: *Let me know that you're okay, please.*

He even calls him, though he knows there's no chance that Jake will answer. "It's me. Where did you go? I'm worried. Please. I'm at the therapist's still. I'm waiting for you. I can pick you up wherever you are. I'm not mad. Only concerned. I want to help. Please let me help. I will meet you anywhere. Please call. Or text. I love you. We love you, your mom and me. We are here. Please call."

OF COURSE, JAKE isn't in a closet or hiding behind the water heater or buried in a pile of laundry, but Paul does his due diligence anyway, inspecting his condo from top to bottom, both floors, and once that turns up nothing, he knows his son hides in the computer.

Paul hasn't gone to his ex's—the place he used to live, where his alimony and child-support payments still fund the mortgage—but he'll get there. He's not dismissing the cop's advice. It's just that since Paul knows where his son spends the majority of his time, why not look there first?

Of course, that's part of why he's not champing at the bit to go to his ex's, but the main deterrent is the barrenness. It's one thing to be in his own empty apartment, because that's how a newly divorced bachelor is supposed to live. There's supposed to be a dearth of any intimacy. The walls should be stark white. The cheap carpet should have a constellation of pizza crumbs, so many of them that walking barefoot is like reading Braille with your feet. There aren't any throw pillows on the couch. There isn't a couch. The kitchen cupboards are packed with the slimmest essentials, olive oil and tinfoil. Paul hates all the vacant cupboards, but the idea of buying baking spices or casserole dishes seems devastating. The refrigerator is merely a brief cooling station for his pale ale, and there's a whole shelf dedicated to half-finished burritos. There isn't one vegetable on the premises.

Going over to his old house, to wander unaccompanied through all those memories, is too much. He'll do it. Of course, he'll do it. He'll make it over there soon, for Jake's sake.

Fact of the matter is that Paul doesn't want to search inside the computer for him, either, but that somehow seems easier, and if that's the wrong word here, it seems less bloated with the past, the prowling memories talking shit to him from inside the house's walls. The failure of the marriage haunting, rattling chains, slamming doors. At least looking for Jake online didn't have that ghastly baggage. Because he'd never done it before, and that now seems like another failure.

He had told his boy on his voicemail that Paul would meet him anywhere, and that claim will be challenged as Paul goes hunting for TheGreatJake. Paul has to let go of his disdain for social media. This is the only place he can find his son.

The site he hears Jake talk about the most is Twitter, and that's where the manhunt will commence. Paul opens the page and makes an account, choosing the humdrum username Paul_Gamache.

And he's in; he's a part of this; he's plugged in.

Of course, that doesn't mean he knows what the hell he's doing. Paul Googles various things on how to work the user interface, how to track down specific people, and it stuns him how easy it is to navigate, how effortless it is to find the single person you need to locate, and thirty seconds later he's found TheGreatJake.

He clicks follow.

He follows him.

He is following his son.

He thinks about all the historic reasons to follow your children. The time-tested ones, the traditional, the textbook: following kids for protection. For making sure predators are kept at bay. For ensuring a good life, all the advantages. For a balanced diet. High-fiber foods. Eight glasses of water a day. Shampoo and conditioning. To make sure they're never too hot or too cold. For sunscreen. For protective eyewear. For cleanliness. For cardiovascular exercise. To make sure they don't grow up too fast, see the world's forked tongue. Follow them so they shy away from greed, that god. Teach about the honor in a day's hard work. To build values. Grow optimism. Cultivate a social conscience. Stoke kindness in them. Shield them from the inevitable dullness and boredom that will grow on their bodies like fat once they're adults. Once they've settled into disappointing realities. Once they themselves are disappointments.

But before that, you protect them from themselves, which is the worst predator of all: the one they never see coming.

Follow children for the various kinds of support. Financial. Emotional. Psychological. Babying these kids way longer than is appropriate. Keeping them reliant on you for your own selfish means. Wanting them to seek out their own experiences but equally wanting them to need you forever. The ultimate Catch-22, because if you raise them right they strike out on their own, leaving you with curdling memories and their student loans.

For forced nurturing. Reminders about a proper night's rest. You follow and offer unsolicited advice about how to find the right friends and lovers. How to pick a partner. Paul loathes that part of being a parent—how it requires you to act as though you know so much, feigning wisdom, donning a pitiful costume of acumen that Paul knows is bullshit, but these sorts of hypocrisy are always and forever socially acceptable.

You follow them to bond. To communicate. To shuck their feelings from their hearts like oysters from shells.

Follow to offer crass and caustic editorials, spoiling any thoughts of a child's sovereignty with your intrusive monologues.

You follow your children because you love them and you know the world is contagious with depravity, and in one way or another, everyone gets infected.

Despite how adroitly we try to remain pure, it's impossible. It's only a chipped tooth but it's more. Everyone swims in the earth's dirty broth.

And yet parents do their best to shield children. They follow in every way they can, hoping for happiness and safety, even though those things don't really exist. They are artifices. Paul knows these things, and someday his son will possess this carnivorous knowledge, but let *someday* be decades from now. Let it only reveal the despair long after Paul is gone.

And what better way to accept the futility than to become Paul_ Gamache and enter the all-encompassing artifice—what better way to update these historic reasons to follow your kids, rooted in lessons learned in centuries barren of downloaded deities—what better way to follow them than to follow them.

Evolve into a binary detective.

Sleuth their profiles for clues that might tell you who they actually are, where they choose to reside.

No matter how much Paul hates this, it's the only way he can find his son.

His first tweet: *It's dad, @TheGreatJake. Where are you?*

Because Paul only follows one user, he can see no other people's tweets, has no other posts coursing down his timeline. It's empty, hollow, lifeless; it's a socket waiting for a bulb. He needs TheGreat-Jake to show himself.

And he'll also need to check his ex's house. He knows this and isn't being negligent. He was never negligent. Toward the end of the marriage, back when Paul had no idea they were nearing the end, he'd take walks by himself every night after work. This was 6 or 7 PM. The sun zipping down in the Marin sky. They lived in a circuitous web of residential streets, but if he kept following the forking roads to the left, he arrived at his destination: a yellow dead-end sign.

It never seemed poetic or metaphoric at the time. It was the marker he used on his walk to alert him to turn around, go back home, but with some space, if you spend your free time walking to the dead end, of course, your wife divorces you. Of course, your son leaves. Paul had been walking to the dead end for so many years that what if he actually reached it and didn't realize? What if he was living it?

Stop it. This isn't about me, he thinks, though he's not sure that's true.

That's exactly why Jake left; if his mom were here, were around more, with her presence the boy would be better.

Paul decides to scroll through TheGreatJake's old tweets while he waits, and Paul was right to look for him here. From the time stamps, he knows that there have been three tweets since therapy.

I'd smash this whole fucking place.

I am on my own.

Running away from home. Where 2 go?

There it is. Spelled out. Running away.

Paul winces, feels a stab in his abdomen, his lungs folded up like origami, every breath a labor.

All this could be from the laxative, he hopes. This could be the beginning of things getting back to normal inside of him.

But he knows it's not. He knows it's the news—the tweeted confirmation—that Jake is trying to leave. To flee. To be free. To be absent. To be missing. He is doing this on purpose. He is engineering a life away from Paul.

About eight minutes later, Paul gets an answer to his tweet, his plea to know where his son is, TheGreatJake saying to him: *I'm here.*

Where is here? Paul tweets back.

I'm here, @Paul_Gamache.

14.

About the time Jake answers Paul's tweet, Sara's adding more hot water to her bath. She does this with her big toe, moving the dial so the scalding reinforcements pour into the tub. First, her lower legs feel the temperature crank and the sensation slowly moves up her small body, the water working toward her head.

It's been four days since Sara's day zero. Her rebirth with a digital, conjoined twin. One without Hank, without a job, a home, a boyfriend. Those desired commodities ripped and replaced by a sex tape.

New Sara is four days old, and this newborn can't get out of the bath.

She and Rodney drove out of Traurig and made it into California, cruised down the mountain into the foothills, finally entering Sacramento. After five hours on the road, they needed a motel room. The room had two double beds. Pillows so scrawny that they were probably stuffed with creamed spinach. The carpet smelled like a campfire. Under a black light, the bedspread could make a porn star blush.

Right when they got into the room, Sara said, "I need a bath."

She locked the door, crawled in the tub, scrolled on her phone, reading more about the brass band, the jumper who lived. The article called the woman a survivor, but Sara didn't buy that. She was the exact opposite. An unsurvivor. If she leaped from the bridge because she thought a better world awaited her, what a tragedy to be fished from the water, wake up restrained in a hospital. She didn't want this life in the first place, and now the consequences of her actions would make it even worse.

Dead bodies could be survivors. Sara understood that. They were survivors if they escaped their pain. If they were liberated. If they occupied a consciousness swiped clean of appalling memory.

There were lots of things Sara hated about the media, but at the top of the list was their reliance on gaudy alliteration. It was insulting, dismissive. The local press had done it to Rodney right after his accident, naming him Balloon Boy. Such wounding insolence. It was vicious, the calloused practice of shredding someone's identity to a commodity, to a caricature. And the unsurvivor was the latest victim of this assault, the article referring to her as Jumper Julie.

If the media gave Sara a nickname it would be Slutty Sara, or Skank Sara, or Sex Tape Sara. They'd call her these things without any care of the malice tucked into these syllables, venom folded between consonants and vowels.

Sara lost track of time in the tub, or she knew that time passed and didn't care. She never expected to spend four days bathing, but honestly, the tub was the safest haven she'd found since her fiasco posted online. It was warm and nobody was talking and Hank wasn't yelling and decimating her heart and Felix couldn't kick her car and Moses couldn't suspend her from work and Nat didn't know where to find her to post another video, and on the other side of this locked door was sweet Rodney, her only friend left. She expected to spend half an hour in the tub, but being immersed in that womb proved impossible to slide out of—why leave such quiet and warm comfort?

She only exited for quick trips. To eat takeout that Rodney had ordered, Chinese, Thai, pizza. To sleep in spurts, toss and turn, think too much, retreat back to another bath, slipping into solace.

And four days later, they're still in this god-awful motel room. This is a capricious way to dole out her emergency money, but she can't find the verve to try. She feels bad for Rodney, trapped out there. She wouldn't be surprised if he took off on her—she certainly wouldn't blame him. But every time she briefly emerges from the bathroom, there he is, watching TV, using his own phone to scroll around the globe. He always greets her with a serving of food, something to drink.

"Eat," he says.

"Okay." But she barely does.

"Be. Nice. To. Sa. Ra," he says, hoisting a plate of pad thai at her.

It takes him almost twenty seconds to choke it out, but what Sara hadn't realized until right this second is that who cares how long it takes him to talk. It's the warmth behind his words that she craves.

"All right." She takes it, smiles at him, but sets it down somewhere in the room before crawling into another bath.

She can't believe they're calling her Jumper Julie. She hops from page to page, trying to learn more about her, details that will help Sara get a sense of who this woman actually is, but not much has been released about her. Details are sparse to guard her identity.

Sure, she gets her privacy protected, thinks Sara, *while my white ass shakes online.*

Sara should be feeling better. That's her mantra in the tub. *You've gotten away*, she tries to tell herself. Traurig and all its drama are in the rearview. Rally, Sara. Feel good.

What would really make her feel good is if Sara can pick up the phone and talk to Jumper Julie. Not for any guidance, just empathy. Empathy that spans all across the sky like storm clouds.

Cumulonimbus empathy.

Instead, she'll have to settle for another bath—the one that started as Jake tweeted back to Paul—and it's time to do it.

This is the time.

Sara points herself at a certain URL.

She opens the page and watches it load.

There is a still image, Sara on her hands and knees, Nat behind her, a banner above them that says SKANK OF THE WEEK.

And a link that says CLICK HERE FOR ALL THE ACTION!

It might sound like masochism, this impulse to watch what's ruined her, but Sara remembers some of her mom's advice. This was when Sara was seven or eight years old and she couldn't stop singing the song "Frère Jacques." It had been in her head for weeks and every time there was a lapse in conversation, that's when Sara started singing. It was in her head when she fell asleep and when she woke up, in her head while she ate and played.

"Here," her mom said, "let's listen to the whole song together. That might help get it out of your head."

She sat on her mom's lap, and they fired up a CD, hearing the entire track, and it worked. "Frère Jacques" was no more, though it was replaced by another song. Sara's life had music back then.

So perhaps that logic can be superimposed here. Perhaps watching her whole sex tape can stop its dismal loop in her head.

Her phone is like a hypnotist swinging a pocket watch, entrancing her. She lies in the bath and hopes this viewing purges all the sick congestion rocketing around her brain.

At first, it forms a trance for Sara, a molested daze: She stares at herself, on her knees sucking Nat's cock, licking down the bottom of his shaft to the balls, gripping him with one hand and playing with her nipple with the other, and she's barely fifteen seconds into the clip and that's all she can take. Her hands erupt like vibrating phones again and she puts the real one on the floor, flexes her fingers.

There's not enough room in the world for both these Saras. If they are conjoined twins, one is a survivor, the other an unsurvivor, and Sara has no idea which she is.

There are discussions that you can have with yourself in a bathtub in a crappy motel room when you feel like no matter what you do your life doesn't have any hope, any future.

She might not be able to escape in the literal sense, not yet, but escapism is a possibility. She can use her imagination to leave this room, leave the fifteen seconds of the sex tape behind. She can transform this place into something else. Transform *her* into something else.

Sara surveys the bathroom for props. Props are key. All that's around Sara are scratchy and cheap motel towels and a baby bar of soap and shampoo that smells like motor oil. All that's on the floor is a sad paper plate with two pieces of pepperoni pizza that Rodney asked her to eat—"Eat. Sa. Ra."—and his concern was so heartfelt that she brought the pizza to her bath, knowing she'd never devour them, slices sitting on the floor next to the tub.

Finally she spies something useful. She peeps a prop that can transform even the saddest motel bathroom into something better.

A bucket. A bucket for ice. A bucket so you can get ice from the machine at the end of the hallway and bring the cubes back to chill your bourbon. A bucket can transform into a helmet if you seize the day and quickly move from the tub to the countertop and place it on your head and scurry back to the water. It's a helmet with superior powers that makes her invisible, which is what Sara most covets right now.

No one can see Sara's sex tape when she's wearing that helmet.

She has been erased.

She looks down at the pizza.

She doesn't see grease. Doesn't see sustenance. Doesn't see ingredients.

Sara removes the pepperoni slices and plops them down, and the second they hit the bathwater they morph into lovely lily pads, bobbing on a serene pond, with crows cawing in the distance, and she swims through the pond, undetectable. No one knows where she is. Moving anywhere. Moving anywhere she likes. Moving anywhere she likes and nobody can zero in on her and make Sara self-conscious, feel like a loser, a slut. She slaloms between these lily pads and now she dives down, experiencing the depth of this serene pond. Swimming lazily through the kelp.

Is there kelp in serene ponds?

There's kelp in this serene pond.

This serene pond also has other sea amenities too. Such as jellyfish that don't sting but Sara can reach out and touch their illuminated shapes, tentacles waving in the current. Such as a gentle orca, a docile and mammoth presence that likes to have her belly scratched like she's the family's golden retriever. Such as a whole school of sardines, swimming tightly in a swarm, their silvery bodies moving in fast circles, looking like a shimmering tornado, and Sara swims through them into the center. Existing inside the wave of their rolling bodies. Existing and protected from the outside world.

Sara under the water.

Holding her breath.

Holding her breath for a long time.

A true explorer of this pond wants to experience everything, even if it means working to the very bottom. Where there's a coral reef, and it glimmers with iridescent life. Sara swims and inspects everything. She is invisible and she is happy and there is nothing that can take that away from her.

And languidly hovering by the reef is Jumper Julie. She's a mermaid, smiling at Sara. Jumper Julie says, "How are you feeling?" and Sara says, "Scared," and Jumper Julie says, "Your life will get better," and Sara says, "I didn't know people could speak underwater," and

Julie says, "We live in a mysterious and wonderful world," and Sara says, "Why did you jump off a bridge if the world is so mysterious and wonderful?" and Jumper Julie says, "I regretted jumping as soon as my feet left the bridge."

For a few seconds, she feels wonderful. Like she's been shot with a happiness bullet. She feels fixed. She is a good person.

"It's time to go back," says Jumper Julie.

"I'm okay down here."

"Please, go back," Jumper Julie says.

But why go back to the surface when Sara sees lobsters wobbling along the sandy bottom of the pond? There are seven of them. They march in a single-file line, drunken soldiers teetering in an awkward formation. It's an experience that no other human being has ever had, being so privy to the militarization of marching lobsters.

"Why aren't you wearing uniforms?" she wants to ask them.

But then there's knocking.

This knocking clamors and shakes and creates angry waves on the pond.

The knocking strips this serene pond to a muddy and barren patch of marshland.

Sara snaps back to her unwanted life. She floats up above the bathwater and knows that it's Rodney knocking on the bathroom door.

"Sa. Ra?" he says.

"I'm here."

"Oh. Kay?"

"Be out in a minute."

She takes the helmet off her head and crashes back into this world. Nothing mysterious and wonderful anywhere. Jumper Julie is a liar. Sara's in a tepid bath, surrounded by pepperoni slices, a film of grease from the processed meat, a sheen slithering on the surface.

The serene pond is polluted. The serene pond is gone.

Sara puts the bucket back on her head, takes a big breath, and slowly sinks under the oily water.

TECHNICALLY, RODNEY GUESSES, this qualifies as a quest. They did leave Traurig, drive off for an adventure. There was the promise of looking for his mom. But that's as questy as things have gotten. Besides that, he sits in this retched motel, waiting on Sara. He wants to help her, but he doesn't know how or when or what to do—wants to swoop up close to her ear and say, "Let's leave this all behind and be happy. We can do that, Sara."

Many times, he's hovered by the closed bathroom door, listening to her, working up the courage to interrupt. Sometimes she's crying, while other times she whispers to herself. For the most part, though, it's deathly silent in there, the only noise running water when the temperature needs to be brought up. Besides that, it's as still as a graveyard.

It's been four days on this crappy quest and Rodney is as confused as he's ever been, his cabin fever reaching all-time highs. He can't watch any more TV, nor can he walk around the motel's neighborhood, a Sacramento armpit, not as merciless as Traurig in terms of temperature but still in the nineties. It's a collection of stucco strip malls, concrete and asphalt and glass. Balloon Boy imagines his uncle standing in the middle of one of these capacious roads, launching his fly-fish lure, having the time of his life. And he should go home. Call it a day on this sputtering quest. He's tried leaving for greener pastures and ended up in scenic Sacramento.

It's like the moment on the balloon, before anything went wrong. It was everything, the whole gamut of human possibilities teasing on the horizon, and Rodney was so close, so very close until the thump-splat ouch.

In the motel room, Rodney tries to busy himself with his least-favorite task, talking. He hasn't called his dad since leaving Traurig, so no doubt Larry and Felix are up in arms. Maybe they've filed a missing person's report. Or they're so liquored-up it has barely registered that he's gone. Balloon Boy feels terrible about leaving them in the dark about his whereabouts, but he's scared to check in. He doesn't want to be manipulated into abandoning this quest. He and Sara have done the hardest part—they are outside the city limits, outside the state of Nevada, adventure at their fingertips— and now they have to dive in, seize this opportunity, bask in the open road. To find his mother.

But even if he doesn't call the remaining members of the Curtis clan, if he finds his mom, he will have to talk to her. Assuming the return address on the postcard is accurate, he might see her soon— later today or tomorrow even. If that's the case, he needs to practice talking.

He tries to familiarize himself with the following line: *Balloon Boy is here, Mom.*

He spent a lot of time constructing those words, deciding to call himself his nickname to prove a point, one he hates admitting—Rodney is Balloon Boy. They are the same. They live in one body. They have one mother, one who left, and he's happy to stand right in front of her, but he wants her to immediately remember the accident. *This is who I am now, Mom. You need to be okay with this reality.*

He detests speaking because it's the purest way for him to know he's not healing, that he'll never be whole again. Each time he tries, there's a sliver of him that hopes this next sentence will pour out of him, that things have miraculously repaired themselves. His old speech therapist, Mrs. Macmillan, had been optimistic when they first started their sessions, in the immediate aftermath of his accident. She called it a motor speech disorder, but Balloon Boy always felt that name didn't work, made no sense since his motor had seized up. No motor meant no ways to sync up his brain and his facial muscles, so even though he knew precisely what he wanted to work from his lips, all these thoughts hemorrhaged. No motor meant a lifetime of talking his terror sounds.

He attempts to block out all these impaling thoughts, as they won't help him. All he has to do is focus on the first word, the first syllable and attempt to articulate himself: "Ba . . ."

Damn.

That crushing and inevitable realization that there's been no progress, there never will be, he'll be broken forever. It took so much effort to bleat that *Ba*, one lousy *Ba*, all that energy to talk like a sheep. His mouth is busted and this quest is busted, and what if Sara is busted, too? What's going on in there?

The last time he knocked, she told him that she'd be out "in a minute." That was progress. Normally, she says, "I'm fine," and there's no mention of anything else.

But it's been much longer than a minute. It's been, if his calculations are correct, ten minutes, and that concerns him. It makes him wonder what's happening and if it's getting worse, she's getting worse. He tries not to worry, not to overreact. Saying to himself if she likes long baths—days in the tub—what's the matter with that? But it's different with Sara. It has to be. She's been so upset and Rodney can't help but think she said "Out in a minute" so he'd leave her alone. Alone for what, why? She might be dangerous. To herself. It's not normal to stay in the tub for so long. Rodney needs to know what she's doing in there.

He knocks and says through the door, "Sa. Ra?"

More knocking more knocking more knocking.

She finally answers and he's happy to hear her voice. "One more minute," she says, so Rodney walks back over to the bed, relieved. He gnaws a cold clump of pad thai, looks at the sentence he'd hoped to get out: *Balloon Boy is here, Mom.*

Should he try talking again?

No.

Rodney puts another tuft of Thai food in his mouth.

Five more minutes and she's still locked in there.

Something's wrong. He knows it. Sometimes you know these

things. Sometimes it's obvious, a tremble, a jolt. And sometimes it travels through your whole body, head to toe, toe to brain, blowing a shower of sparks.

More knocking more knocking more knocking.

She doesn't answer so he jiggles the knob something jugular. Tries to force the locked door open. Saying, "Let! Me! In!"

No words back.

More knocking.

"SA! RA!"

Balloon Boy will never forgive himself if she's hurt. He'll never be able to live with her injuries. He's learned to live with this own, dragging the mass of it through life, but there's no way to soldier on if something's happened to Sara. Not with him so close.

Sara can't be alone one minute longer. She might not know it, but she needs him, her Rodney, her Balloon Boy. She has to surround herself with people who care for her. People who aren't new, people who haven't just shown up in her life. No, she requires the retrofitted support of those who have loved her for a long time. And it's horrible that her parents died and horrible how Hank lost it and cussed her out, but there's still love, Sara. There's love and it's here.

Rodney tries to shoulder his way through the door like he's seen cops do on TV, but he's making no headway. Looks around for something to swing at it. A fire extinguisher, a suitcase rack, a microwave. But there's nothing.

Or there's one thing, but it's going to be painful. He can use his leg, his foot. Kick it down, though he's never done anything like this. A karate kick can force the door open, right? He moves two steps back for momentum, rushes forward with vengeance and vinegar, lifts his battering ram and connects with all this might, making contact next to the knob. Something cracks in his leg. A faraway pain that knows it can't be the center of attention, not yet, not until Sara's okay.

The door rockets open.

His leg heaves with electric shocks.

Balloon Boy looks over at the tub and sees Sara's naked body under the water. He limps in and falls to his knees and grabs her—falling and grabbing and hoping he hasn't waited too long to help her.

Luckily, she starts thrashing around in the water.

She comes up and coughs.

"What are you doing in here?" she says.

Rodney talks too fast for anybody to decode: "Don't. Huuuuu . . ."

"Get out!" she says, covering up her naked body with her hands. "D . . ."

But he's so worried, so concerned about what this is, or what it might be, that talking is impossible. He loves Sara. He needs her. He wants to show her every glowing cell that lives inside him. Wants to make her feel better. Wants to shine a microscope into his heart and then hers, and he wants to make Sara inspect both of them—wants her to remember.

"Get the fuck out of here!" she says.

Balloon Boy can't gather himself enough to articulate the simplest oral communications. There are no pens or pencils or pads around. If he hopes to speak with her, he'll have to use action.

Rodney stands and gets a towel and drapes it, concealing her small body.

"I'm so screwed right now, Rodney," she says, sobbing.

Rodney consoles her, watching the ice bucket float in the tub with a bunch of pepperonis. He leans over and hugs her, getting wet too.

"What if I never feel alive again?" Sara asks and grabs the ice bucket, wedging it on her head.

"I. Love. You."

It takes nine seconds for him to get this out, but really it's taken years.

Sara stares at him the whole time.

People don't pick when or where the good stuff happens. Some-times it occurs in shabby motel rooms, in Sacramento, with ice buckets for top hats and legs for battering rams. The good stuff happens at all sorts of asinine times, and none of that matters when Rodney hears her say, "I love you too."

He reaches into the tub and retrieves her, despite the frenzy going on in his hurt leg. Rodney carries a naked Sara from the bathtub to the bed. He strips out of his own clothes, cuddling with her until she's fast asleep and he's left awake, contemplating every detail that brought them here.

15.

Curiosity dismembers Kathleen: What's Wes doing in there?

He had seemed so earnest in his initial pledge to spend the bulk of his time at UCSF, in the lab, that Kat didn't question the validity of his assurance. But the first four days he's been here, he hasn't gone anywhere, barely left his room.

Which is why Kathleen finds herself gently placing an ear against the door. She can hear him. He's talking to someone. Skyping or some other video chat platform? She doubts it; Wes never asked her for the Wi-Fi code. It could be a phone call, but he's not really leaving time for anyone else to talk, running some kind of filibuster. Kathleen's been standing with her ear to the door for at least three minutes and he hasn't let up. He's not yelling. It's a steady drip of words, almost mutters. She can't make out exactly what he's saying; she can only hear the drone.

It's her house. Knock and ask. She doesn't have to be a hard-ass about it; there don't need to be any accusations, any talk of the bait-and-switch—*You said you'd be at the lab the whole time!* He's her tenant, and that gives Kat certain rights. Namely, the right to know if the rules have changed.

Of course, the reason that Kathleen knows he hasn't left the house in four days is that neither has she. The caricature. Rodney's birthday. It's left her in—not a depression, exactly. She's not depressed. It's a funk, a temporary dip in her morale. She'll rebound soon. Soon, she'll shake it off and go back to work, get scribbling on the Embarcadero. She rationalizes that she can take some "vacation" days because of the increased share of the rent that Wes is paying.

She had imagined herself to be left alone, but she can't slack off on the couch and feel sorry for herself with Wes mumbling away in there. It makes her feel uncomfortable, and that's not fair; this is her place, and she should always feel at ease. She should at least feel like she has the right to knock on his door and ask him some questions.

So why isn't she?

It's not that she's scared. He's a nice guy, some lab nerd. That's not it.

And she's no coward, either. She has had plenty of awkward conversations over the years and feels like she holds her own in them.

She guesses it's more of what she'll say. If something fell through with his job, is it really any of her business? He's paid to rent a room, and that entitles him to a certain amount of privacy. He's not being overtly loud, not being rude: There are no actual grounds for any interrogation.

There's a pause in his filibuster.

Kathleen takes her ear off the door and is about to walk away when Wes fires up another sermon.

Kathleen can't resist putting her ear on the door one last time, hoping to finally decrypt what he's saying, but it's no use. Just a gurgle of syllables, like her son.

It's hard not to wonder what his eighteenth birthday means. If the needle is going to move, she has to be the one to initiate it. Not a peace offering, or anything that's insulting to how insensitive she's been to him over the years, but a way to help him understand that a) she regrets her decision to leave every day and b) she couldn't imagine coming face to face with her ex-husband again, not after the violence she endured. Now it's time to find her version of their past and explain it to her son.

With a sponsor who earns her living tattooing, Kat should get some ink. She should get a portrait of her son. She has the perfect print. She left a copy of it on Rodney's bedside table, and now is the time to commemorate him on her body. A way to signal her contrition and at the same time indicate some hope for reconciliation. They can heal. As an eighteen-year-old, he's not under Larry's dominion anymore. Neither is Kathleen. They are free and if they so choose—if he forgives her—they can reunite.

That's it. A tattoo, a portrait, the perfect way to get back in contact with him.

There's another pause in Wes's mutterings. Instead of repositioning her ear, this time she chooses to knock.

"Yes?" Wes says through the door.

"Hi, it's Kat, can we talk?"

"We are talking."

He's so literal. This is what it must be like to live with a teenager. "Can you open the door, please?"

Kat wishes she didn't add the *please*. It's her house. If she wants to have a conversation, this guy should show her the respect of opening the door.

"I can and I will," says Wes. Soon, he's standing in front of her, still wearing that lab coat, and maybe still wearing the same clothes from when he first moved in. His stubble is pushing into a mangy beard. The room smells like a hamster's cage. There are papers strewn over the floor. A few empty plastic bottles of water, though she sees no evidence of food. It's a room of obsession, Kathleen muses, a scientist so consumed with his calling that the prosaic things suffer.

And, of course, his poster of Einstein's face on the wall.

"I wanted to check in," Kathleen says, "and hear how things are going for you."

"Things are in motion."

Kat points at Einstein. "What did you end up doing with Bob Marley?"

"I've never met Bob Marley."

"No, the poster."

"He is vacationing in the closet."

"I'm sure it's lovely this time of year," says Kathleen.

"Plenty of oxygen," Wes says.

"Do you need anything? Have any questions about the city?"

"No."

"Have you had any trouble commuting to UCSF?"

"I haven't had to go yet. My colleague has been delayed. But his arrival is imminent. Then we get to work."

Okay, now that makes sense. Much more sense than why Kathleen let this unnecessary tension build up. His schedule has been delayed some, which is out of his control, something innocuous. She immediately feels better. Between this revelation and the idea for her portrait tattoo, Kat hopes she might be snapping out of this funk.

"I was going to watch a movie soon," Kathleen says. "Would you like to join me? You can save me from eating all the ice cream myself."

"I'm under a deadline," he says.

"You are?"

"Our research is reaching its climax. We are about to change the world."

Kathleen knows she's supposed to ask *how*, tell me all about it, but she's getting tired of fishing. If he wants to hole away in his hamster's cage the whole time, so be it. She'll air it out before her roommate returns.

"Let me know if you need anything," she says.

Wes closes the door and not three seconds later the muttering starts again.

KATHLEEN GETS DRESSED, grabs the picture of Rodney for the portrait, and heads out. The neighborhood feels particularly congested. It's a weekday, and people hurry home. She heads down 18th Street to Valencia, turns toward the shop. Valencia has a bike lane flanking the traffic on both sides, which was supposed to ease the friction between the warring factions, but it's only made things worse: Bikers yell at cars, sometimes kicking bumpers, spitting on windows, while the autos trundle down the road, drivers too dumb or distracted to check blind spots before making turns, opening doors, almost breaking the bikers' necks with every action. Kathleen has seen fistfights about the rules of the road. All of it makes her happy to be a serial pedestrian. She's never had a car in San Francisco, and she's too clumsy to hop on a bicycle.

She walks down Valencia, sees phalanxes of diners starting to line up outside the posh places, sighing and checking the time on their phones every ten seconds; she sees a mother wearing a Baby Björn, her hands massaging the baby's head; she sees hipsters smoking outside the bars, which makes her miss being young—back then she could have a drink and it was fun, a cocktail or two, nothing that would ruin her life; she sees a cop tucking a ticket under a parked car's windshield wiper and sees a woman with tarot cards laid out on the sidewalk, sitting Indian-style, her iPhone playing a gypsy jig, a note on a typed piece of paper with an outstanding font saying KNOW YOUR FUTURE.

She sees all this and wonders what happened to the homeless in the Mission, the caravan of stolen shopping carts, the currency of empty bottles and cans, the bodies huddled in doorways after the close of business, the handwritten signs—not typed with pompous fonts—that asked for help, any help, any human grace? They used to be everywhere, and she assumes the police were ordered to kick them out. Obviously, San Francisco is trying to clean up the Mission; they're doing it to the whole city and she's heard the project being called "a reboot," which makes it so much worse, using the parlance of the industry that's taking over.

She sees the construction cranes downtown, looming across the skyline like huge prehistoric birds. The development is driving out all the character, and sometimes Kathleen imagines these cranes scooping up artists and plopping down tech employees in their place. She knows it's only a matter of time until she's ladled up, too, replaced by a twentysomething making six figures for speaking computer code, the only foreign language that matters. What happens, she wonders, to a city—especially one like San Francisco, a place that has always been composed of immigrants and outcasts and transients and artists, a whole surrogate family of people who weren't wanted other places—what happens when it becomes as homogenous as a suburb?

She doesn't want to leave this town, even though she doesn't like what's happening. But she likes even less the prospect of being forced out. This is her home, and she'll do all she can to stay.

She enters the tattoo shop, and Deb is there listening to an old Cramps record. She looks up at Kathleen, but doesn't turn off the tattoo gun, only holds it a couple inches off her client's skin.

"Permission to come aboard the bridge, captain," Kathleen calls.

"Permission granted," says Deb.

Her client is a young white man, one of the enemy. Kathleen's eyes dart to his laptop bag, his hilarious T-shirt that says CTRL+ALT+DELETE. He's even wearing those douchey shoes that have individual toes, making his feet look webbed. His oversized, probably cosmetic black eyeglasses are the perfect way to tie all his trying-too-hard together.

"We'll be done in fifteen minutes," Deb says to her.

"Pretty sweet, huh?" the man says to Kathleen, nodding at the tattoo on his bicep. "It's an Irish cross."

"Celtic," Deb says.

"Same thing," he says, wiggling his webbed toes.

"It's not," she says. "This is on your body. You're going to wear it forever; you should know what it means."

"It means that it looks cool," he says and alerts Deb that their conversation is over by picking up and fiddling with his phone.

Deb purses her lips and nods at Kathleen. "And how are you?"

"I have incredible news."

"What?"

"This."

Kathleen shows the picture of Rodney. "This is how I'm going to contact him."

"I could get the phone."

"I'll mail him a letter once you tattoo this picture on me."

Deb takes her foot of the tattoo gun's pedal, shop going silent, the guy still mesmerized by his phone. "The pony express went belly up. It's a post-mail world."

"I'll mail him a letter *and* a picture of my tattoo." Kathleen hands Deb the portrait. "Would you put this on my back?"

Deb takes and studies it. "This will make a good tattoo."

"Let's do it once you're done with him."

"Let's wait. I never tattoo someone who's emotional. That's one of my rules. Like I don't tattoo drunk guys."

"Why not?"

"Drunk guys bleed too much."

"I mean why not me?" Kathleen asks.

"Don't push me, or when I finally do it I'll add a Chinese character that means 'farter.'"

The man looks up from his phone. "Do you really think they have a character for that?"

"People fart all over," Deb says. "I'm sure there's a Celtic word for it too. I can add it on your arm if you want."

The guy smirks sarcastically, goes back to his phone. Deb hands the picture back to Kathleen and fires up the gun again.

"I need your help," says Kathleen, the photo in her hand uselessly. "I want him to know how much I've been thinking of him."

"What's wrong with email?" Deb says.

"Why can't you be more supportive?"

Deb starts laughing, looks at her client. "She says to her AA sponsor."

The guy flashes that techie smirk again.

"Right now you're just my friend," Kathleen says. "Not my sponsor."

"I'm always your sponsor, sugar. If I wasn't, I'd be a shitty one."

Kathleen has a plan to instigate contact with her son again, and it's a good one. She'd banked on Deb's eyes and ink and needles, banked on a portrait to show her son, his likeness forever on her flesh. *Look*, she'll be able to tell him through the tattoo, *I've always loved you and I'm sorry and let's start over.*

That's impossible, she knows. There's no such thing as starting over. It's a ruse. Memories are time machines, zooming us through our experiences, and because of this, people are never clean of their yesterdays. There is no transcendence. One minute, we're forty, then six, and ten, and twenty, and twelve. We remember our shames and humiliations. We remember trauma. Rodney might not recall one thing about Kathleen except that she left. All the good she did throughout the first twelve years of his life might be erased, and if not outright expunged, at least painted over. Covered up. It's the opposite of Deb tattooing cancer survivors, making the damaged skin into art. Kathleen is a breathing scar, her whole life hardened over by that one mistake.

All of this whizzes through her head as she stands there holding the portrait.

Deb dips the gun into a glass of water, flushing out her needles, then plunges it into an ink cap full of black, goes back to work. "If you mail him a picture of the tattoo, so what?"

"So what?" Kathleen asks.

"Why would that make him feel better?"

"Because it shows I'm thinking about him."

"The tattoo is for you," Deb says. "Calling and starting the healing process—that would be for him."

"I'm finally ready to try and you're not helping me."

"You're making this harder than it has to be," says Deb. "Call him."

"I can't."

"That brass band that jumped off the Golden Gate?" says Deb. "The one who survived is going to a mental hospital."

"She needs help."

"That's my point," Deb says. "The doctors can help her. The program has helped you; I've tried to help you. But you have to face this fear. You have to face him. I'll be right with you. We're all survivors, but even we need help, Kat." Deb takes her foot off the pedal and her gun goes silent. "How about a compromise? You call him now and I'll tattoo you after I'm done with this Irish cross."

"Celtic," the guy says.

"Now you're learning," she says to him.

"That's bribery," Kathleen says.

"Only if it works."

"Fine," she says to Deb, who gets the phone and asks, "What are you going to say?"

Kathleen dials her old number. If it's possible to get an adrenaline rush from a phone call, that's what's happening. Heart racing and sweating and all her saliva vanishes. And the crazy thing is how good this all feels. How freeing.

"Hello?" a man's voice says.

"Is Rodney there?"

One thing about mythological punishments: What if you simply stopped rolling that boulder up the hill? Refused to prop it up anymore? Moved out of the way and let it roll down to who knows where, not caring about the consequences?

"Who is this?" says the man's voice.

"Is this Larry?"

"Nah, this is Felix."

"Hi, Felix. This is Kathleen. I'd like to talk to my son, please."

There is a wonderful charge in her, an anticipation, a kinetic thump. Kathleen is about to hear her son's voice. She's about to communicate with him. They're about to talk. To begin, not from scratch but from a place that looks forward, not back. This is the first step toward healing, reconciliation.

"Cunt!" Felix screams.

The miserable syllable shoves through the phone and into her ear, worming around her body and kicking her in the heart.

Then the line goes dead.

That's all she gets.

And in a way, that's what she deserves.

She's earned someone calling "Cunt!"

It's stitched onto her.

Burned on the skin, its own scar.

Kathleen doesn't know what to do after hearing that fetid word. She's standing in the tattoo shop with the phone to her ear and Deb is looking at her and the guy with webbed feet is looking at her and she's been called that name, the noise of it still clanging, and she hands the phone back to Deb.

"What happened?"

Kathleen utters that wicked word and her sponsor sighs. Even the guy with webbed feet averts his eyes. The whole moment feels like a caricature Kat could draw. She could exaggerate the idiosyncrasies in such a perfect way: It would be easy to turn the guy's shoes into huge amphibian feet, the size of surfboards, and it would be easy to show Deb with tattoo guns for hands; it would be so easy to show Kathleen, stupid Kathleen, with a phone to her ear, her high hopes being speared by Felix's dismal syllable. The phone would have fangs. It would bite her ear, chew on her, chew her right up.

"Well, it's the start," says Deb. "Congrats on making that first call."

"I have to go."

"No. You have to stay."

Kathleen almost sprints to the front door: "I can't."

"Don't isolate," Deb says. "Be around people who care about you when—"

But she can't hear the end of the sentence. She can't hear anything except Felix's syllable, over and over, and she's off, not running, but not walking, somewhere between these two, as though she can't out-hustle the syllable, leave it at the shop. And there's still the various clogs of yuppies out front of three-star restaurants, still the mothers ambushing her with their babies and toddlers, and Kathleen sees the gypsy with her sign, its perfect font, KNOW YOUR FUTURE.

Kathleen already does.

Her future is in a bar.

Her immediate future starts right this second in a bar. Yes. Starts with pushing past the smoking hipsters out front and opening the door and bellying up and looking around at all the bottles and beer taps and hearing Jack White singing about a girl who had no faith in medicine. It starts with someone saying, "What would you like?" and this somebody happens to be the bartender, and she happens to be talking to Kathleen, who happens to answer with this: "Bourbon."

The bartender is young and Asian, and Kat pines for the simplic-ities of youth, yearns for an existence that hasn't marred so much that forgiving yourself is impossible.

"Any preference?" says the bartender.

"I don't care."

"We got Old Crow in the well."

"Fine."

Kathleen meant what she said before, about starting over being impossible. She cannot have this one drink without reliving all the ones she already had, without tasting every spirit that ever traveled down her throat, experiencing the aftershocks of every hangover, the shame she already feels and the bourbon hasn't hit her lips yet. She knows she shouldn't do this, knows that this won't solve anything, not really, but who said she was interested in a solution? Who said this was an exercise in making things better? No, this isn't about improvement. It's not about making things worse, either. It's just about this one moment and she wants a drink. She hasn't been rewarded for all her sober days; in fact, her life's been harder living clean, all that pure access to her mistakes. Her whole prison break fantasy is phony and faraway and pointless, and her palms are on that boulder again, the calluses ready for another shove. She feels that greedy eagle land on her stomach, ready to feast on her liver for the umpteenth time, appetite never tiring of the same square meal.

The bartender hasn't put the drink down in front of her yet. There's time. There's time to walk away, Kathleen. Go to a meeting. Tell them what happened and let their empathy wash over you. Be around other people who have disfigured their lives, amputated all kinds of happiness. They've died in a million ways and glowed electric with embarrassments and somehow lived to tell. Let them talk you out of this. Let them say *Don't give up*.

She hates that she's so easily rattled. That she's fragile. She thought her years in the program and working the steps would have given her the tools to deal with life when it reaches out and calls you a cunt, but here she is, one syllable from Felix, one phone call, and now she's watching the bartender put a shot of Old Crow down in front of her.

"Six bucks," the bartender says.

Kathleen throws down ten and tells her to keep the change.

She's alone. She has a picture of her son in her pocket, the boy she'll never see again. She has a caricature of the girl with the black eye and her hopeful baby. She has bourbon in front of her. She has a hand for grabbing the glass. She has a mouth and a tongue.

She should have stayed in the tattoo shop. With Deb. She should call her, text her; she should say, "I'm about to do something dumb," giving her sponsor the opportunity to crank some clarity. She should shove herself onto her feet and flee outside and ask the gypsy, "Will I ever see him again?"

She should do any of these options, but she can't.

She's trapped in the bourbon's gravitational pull. It's too close to her, or she's too close to it. There's no escape. She can feel her head being yanked toward the bar. She can feel her hand clutching the glass, can feel the bourbon reaching her face, the smell of it making her salivate. She can feel the shot pour over her teeth, puddle at the back of her throat, and she swallows, welcomes it into her system. She can feel her mouth moving and telling the bartender, "One more." She can feel the lid of a coffin close, blocking out the awful light of the world.

16.

Noah911 had imagined Tracey's funeral being the worst part of the trip—he'd pictured the whole parish casting eyes his way—whispers of the absentee brother, her bodyguard. He even conjured some confrontations after the service concluded: a couple people hopped up on the amphetamine of grief, unable to keep their heartache stowed away, telling Noah911, "We know this is your fault! We all know you did this!"

But truthfully, the whole visit has been a series of escalating invasions. It started at the airport. His mother picked him up and started crying as soon as she saw his beaten-up mug.

"Oh, sweetie, are you okay?" Her hands rushed up to his face, almost touching him, stopping a few inches away, like he was a dish fresh from the oven.

His body felt devoid of moisture. He was arid and achy and tired. He'd flown from San Francisco to Chicago, then after a three-hour layover, from 2 AM to 5, he'd taken the first flight of the morning from O'Hare to Little Rock.

"What are you connected to?" he heard the gate agent say in Chicago. But that couldn't be right. No doubt he had a concussion. His nose was broken. He knew at least one rib was fractured, knew that agony from a lacrosse check years back. He knew that breathing would be anguish, like it should be.

"What did you say?" he asked the gate agent.

"Where are you connecting to?" she said.

"Arkansas."

After an hour and forty-four minutes in the air, he arrived at Clinton Airport, stood in front of his mother as she took stock of his damaged face.

"Where's Dad?" he said.

"At home."

"Of course."

"Can I carry your bag?" she asked.

"Of course you can't," he said.

They didn't talk much as they walked to the car, or during the thirty-minute drive home. They didn't speak because there was nothing to say, and if there were, the words would only slide him back in the oven, baking Noah911 to ash.

His father didn't meet him outside, or at the front door for a greeting. His dad didn't seek him out as Noah911 entered his old room. It was the son who had to find his father, who was in Tracey's room. Or what used to be Tracey's room. Now, it looked staged, a fake room set up at IKEA to give consumers an idea what the furniture would look like in a home. The yellow paint on the walls was fresh, making the space smell sour. The carpet had been ripped up for hardwood. There was a desk, stained deep brown, with nothing on it. A big shelving unit was situated against the wall, its doors open, not one thing inside. The only other item was a potted plant with a braided stalk; it was young, only a few leaves, too small for the size of its pot, plenty of room to grow.

The father sat on the floor assembling a leather chair, the instructions splayed on his lap. "These directions are horrible."

"What's all this then?" Noah911 said.

"Your mother's new crafting studio."

Noah911 didn't enter the room, standing in the doorway. No one said hello. No one offered a hug. It was a father trying to understand instructions; it was a son trying to understand, too.

"Crafting?" Noah911 said.

"Arts and crafts."

"I've never seen Mom make an art or craft."

"She's wanted to for years."

"Has she?"

His father looked up from the directions. "She has."

"I'm going to take a shower," Noah911 said, turning to leave.

"You don't look as bad as I thought," said his father. "I'm glad about that."

"These things heal."

"The service starts at noon."

"I know."

"How am I supposed to even make sense of this?" his father said, eyes back on the instructions, fumbling to attach one of the chair's wheels.

Noah911 went back into his room, started to unpack his clothes. His mom entered with a steaming cup of coffee. "You're an angel," he said, then felt stupid for his choice of words. He had a sip; it was thin and weak.

"Will you need anything ironed?" she said.

"I can do it."

"I'd like to."

He knew better than to fight her on things like this. "Okay." He handed her a button-up shirt and slacks, both black.

His mother pursed her lips, inhaled to say something, but didn't.

"I saw your crafting studio," Noah911 said.

"There's a fresh towel in the bathroom." She left the room.

• • •

THE FUNERAL WAS a fist. It had tear ducts. The funeral was held in a lung, clammy and loud with mourners plucking clumsy ballads on heartstrings and razor wire. Grief felt tight to the body, like a wetsuit, squeezing Noah911's anatomy into a tangle of pall and regret. He could smell this funeral a mile away, pungent with feral, barnyard odors. People sat on platitudes with prayers that sounded like this: *Why why why, Noah911?* or a slow gurgling croon of *No no no . . .*

Everyone was numb and drunk.

Everyone was alive and dead.

And Noah911 was having trouble breathing from the broken rib. He was alone, might as well have been on a witness stand, everybody else jammed in a jury box, the minister banging a gavel on his Bible and belting out, "Guilty, Guilty, Guilty!"

THERE WAS A reception afterward. Platters of deli meat and bottled beer, homemade cookies and condolences. Noah911 was avoiding people, or they steered clear of him. It was his beaten-up face, his rumpled blazer. It was a two-day-old shave. It was nothing.

He watched people rally around his mother and father, watched all the pity and sympathy being expressed. He stood in a corner trying not to get wasted, hadn't eaten since a pastrami sandwich in O'Hare and this first vodka on the rocks went straight to his concussion.

His cousins were no better than his parents' friends. Both sets of grandparents were dead, so there was no one to shroud him in unconditional support. This whole room was full of rubberneckers looking at Noah911.

We live in a society of second chances, he thinks. *Should I confess? Should I tell all these leeches what they want to hear? Should I scream in all their faces, "I did it. It was me. I threw her off the fucking bridge"?*

Instead, he made small talk with the smattering of people who approached him. He drank too much vodka, though he didn't get loud or crass. They expressed feelings. Noah911 faked his. They stared at his injuries and excused themselves from his company at the first lull in the awkward conversations.

Even his favorite aunt—his mother's sister—said to him, "We need to know what really happened, sweetie."

"Me too."

"You know more of the story than we do. Or you should."

"I should. You're right about that."

Noah911 said he had to use the bathroom but went in a different room. Tracey's. The crafting studio. He stood in the sour smell of new paint, surrounded by these things bought to cover up his sister's absence. He pulled out his phone and switched his return flight so he'd leave later tonight. Catch the nine o'clock to Denver, and from there connect back to his new life.

ALL OF THESE events contributed to the pattern of escalating invasions. All of these were the worst part of the trip, a whole festival of betrayals.

But now Noah911 is in the kitchen by himself, eating an omelet. His mom is taking a nap; his father is finishing the assembly of that chair. It's 5 PM, the service and reception over, the friends and relations on their way back to their own miseries. The house is quiet again, and he hasn't told his parents that he's leaving tonight. He can call a cab, slip out, and be free of this place and its insinuations before anyone misses him—if anyone would miss him.

He cooked the omelet on too high a heat. The outside of it is patterned in scorched creases of egg, while the inside is runny and gelatinous, cheese barely melted in places. But this isn't about taste. He slops a piece of toast through the snot and hopes this helps soak up some vodka.

"Here," says his father.

He puts a Ziploc bag on the kitchen table.

To Noah911, it looks filled with instant oatmeal.

"What's this?" he says.

"We want you to have these."

His father picks the Ziploc bag up and thrusts them at him. A joust. A retaliation that means if you can't protect her alive, try this. Try carting this around. Never forget what you did, Noah911.

"I don't want that," he says to his dad.

"Why?" he asks, shaking the bag furiously at his son. "Why don't you want these?"

"Please stop."

"It's not all of her. We're keeping some. But this is your share."

"I can't."

"Take them, god damn it."

Noah911 imagines his dad divvying her up, like a drug dealer, weighing out bags of powder, and for the first time since she died, Noah911 cries. "I'm sorry," he says.

"It's your mess."

"Don't say that."

His father drops the Ziploc bag onto Noah911's plate, right onto the runny eggs, then walks out of the room. Noah911 sits there staring at the ashes, scared of them. Finally, after thirty seconds or so, he runs a sponge under the faucet and then dabs the baggy clean, like he's caring for wildlife after an oil spill.

He has one more bite of his eggs, retches. He knows he'll sneak back to his room, get his suitcase, and walk out. But he's going to leave this plate of leftovers on the table, so someone remembers he was here.

HE'S HOLDING THE Ziploc bag up for the TSA agent to inspect, cradling it across his arm like an injured animal. He says, "This is my sister. I'm bringing her back."

"We see a lot of cremains pass through here," she says, a sixty-something white woman with oxblood hair, "but they're usually in a . . . you know . . . proper . . . receptacle."

"I know; I will. This is my sister," he says again.

"I'm so sorry, dear," she says.

"Thanks."

"Let us x-ray her and then you can go."

Gently, Noah911 places them in one of those gray plastic bins, the conveyor belt carrying her through the machine.

"Take care of yourself," the TSA agent says to him.

He wants to reciprocate her compassion. The people in her profession have the rap of having no grace. Noah911 has had this thought many times, slowly snaking through these screening lines, but this woman, this one woman, has been kind to him.

"I like your hair," he says.

She smiles, averts her eyes, caught off-guard.

"Get your sister, dear," she says.

HE SITS ON the airplane, somewhere around 35,000 feet, and has the ashes sitting on his tray table. He's alone in his row, the plane filled with empty seats. Noah911 stares at the baggy. He's with her. A handful of Tracey.

He caresses the outside of the baggy and shuts his eyes, feeling a bit of peace, a sliver of it, being alone with Tracey.

It's not torture having these ashes. At least, not in this moment.

His face doesn't hurt and the broken rib isn't too bad, and he knows what he has to do with the ashes. It's obvious. Noah911 smiles and every jolt of anxiety and guilt subsides. He doesn't know if this feeling will last and he doesn't care.

Gently, he pets the outside of the baggy.

Tenderly, he brings the baggy up to his lips, kissing it.

Quietly, he says, "I know how we can find peace."

17.

Paul storms into the police station and says to the officer behind the front desk, "I need to see Detective Esperanto."

"Regarding?"

"My son."

"What's your name?"

"My kid is missing."

"Name."

"My son is actively communicating with me and the officer has to have this piece of information so we can pinpoint his location."

"Communicating how?"

"He just said to me 'I'm here.'"

"He called you?"

"Twitter."

"He posted that to Twitter?"

"We have to track his cell so we can find him."

"What's your name, sir?"

"Paul Gamache."

"Have a seat."

Paul does not have a seat. He walks toward the window, doesn't notice the weather or time of day. Those details from this world don't matter. Nothing matters except where Jake is.

It is also apparent that his ex, Naomi, would be so much better at all this. She'd never be kept waiting. She'd have earned the cops' trust and respect and would know everything about the case. Paul knows nothing, except that his boy vanished on his watch and the guilt that pumps like adrenaline. But specifics? Paul couldn't tell you shit and that embarrasses him so much. He needs to do a better job, needs to stop being so soft, so easily placed aside. He needs to demand, not ask, for the attention he deserves.

That was what made Paul stampede to the station in the first place: Jake answering him, reaching out. The boy might be missing in an analog sense but his voice comes through digitally. He is here, as he said he was, and now Paul has to unite his Jakes.

Paul is back on his side of the desk, watching the cop fill out an ancient-looking form by hand.

"What did he say?" Paul asks the officer.

"I'm sorry?"

"Esperanto."

"I'm finishing something up and then I'll call him."

"Call now," he says, wishing Naomi could see this.

"Excuse me?"

"Call him now."

"Don't raise your voice."

"My son is missing."

Paul opens up the laptop, logs on, refreshes his feed, sees there's a new tweet from Jake: *I am striking out on my own, @Paul_Gamache.*

"This came in while I was driving over," says Paul, turning his computer around and thrusting it at the cop, who only sits there.

The cop doesn't read from the laptop, doesn't make eye contact with Paul. She picks up the phone and says, "Paul Gamache is here. And he's pissed."

She hangs up and Paul says, "Thanks."

She doesn't answer.

"I'm not pissed. I'm scared," he says.

She's back to filling out that old form.

The door between the waiting area and the actual precinct opens, and Esperanto waddles out. If at first Paul lamented the young age of the initial officer on the scene, Paul wishes Esperanto were in better shape. He has the lumbering look of an old athlete with no cartilage left in his knees.

"What can I do for you?" he asks Paul.

"It's Jake. He's talking to me on Twitter."

"Is this how you normally communicate with him?"

Paul tells how he created the account and reached out to Jake. Paul hands Esperanto the laptop and he reads through Jake's tweets, then says, "At least we know he's not in some guy's trunk."

"Can we track his cell phone?"

The detective hands the laptop back. "It's not that simple."

"Why?"

"You're another parent who has gone to college on TV shows, watching police procedurals and think you know how this all works," Esperanto says.

"This is our best lead."

"Your son isn't inside the computer."

Paul waves his laptop at Esperanto: "He's right here, right fucking here, I can see him!"

"Your son has only been missing a few hours. FBI is on their way. They have all the good toys. Don't worry. You need to go home and wait. Keep him talking. Keep communicating with him. That way you know he's okay. And let us do our job."

Paul sits down in one of the plastic chairs in the waiting room. There's a bank of six of them. Besides that, the space is sparse. Linoleum and police propaganda posters on the wall. No music. Nothing.

"What are you doing?" Esperanto asks.

"I'm staying."

"No."

"Then arrest me."

"You can't have your laptop in a holding cell."

"I can't leave."

"Fine."

"I'll alert you if there are any advancements in here," says Paul, shaking the computer.

"Not *any* advancements. Only important ones."

Esperanto limps through the door, disappearing into the back, and Paul stares at the remaining officer, who has all her attention on the remaining boxes of her form.

PAUL IS LIKE everyone else now, plugged in. He tweets at his son and waits for answers but something changes: They are not alone.

Paul knew on some level that this was public, their back and forth, this online cat and mouse. But no one else had been butting in and interrupting their communiqués. It was a father and son talking—who cared about that; however, the luxury of isolation is over, with the introduction of a hashtag, #GoHomeJake.

At first, Paul has no idea what a hashtag is, but Google tells him with a quick search.

It's tweeted to Jake from a local TV affiliate, and their whole message reads *Missing teenager, @TheGreatJake, is live-tweeting. Join the conversation. #GoHomeJake.*

Paul follows the station. Maybe they'll have a clue to help his hunt. Right back, they follow Paul, probably for the same reason. It's instantaneous. He clicks to follow a few more and they return the favor. Four. Five. Nine. New alliances, greedy alliances, all for Jake.

Immediately, their tweet is retweeted and retweeted, and Paul watches their private conversation mutate. Paul is disgusted, all this attention, turning his missing boy into something else. It had never occurred to Paul until this moment in the waiting room how when a video goes viral, that's comparing it to an actual virus. Something that has the potential to spread out of control, infect all sorts of unsuspecting people, and this latest outbreak is his boy. Jake is the infective agent. Jake is the salacious contaminant. Jake is contagious.

These retweets lead to others intruding on their intimacy. Strangers feel the effects of the virus and, once tainted, they are pulled to patient zero:

It's not worth it, little man. #GoHomeJake.

B safe. B careful. #GoHomeJake.

Just worm home, you spoiled brat. #GoHomeJake.

Paul can't believe how quickly things evolve. How one father and one son, like grains of sand on a beach, can be singled out and picked from a million other nearly identical grains and their anonymity vanishes, as they're pinched between a thumb and a forefinger, held up for everyone to inspect.

@TheGreatJake tweets to his father, @Paul_Gamache, while he's MIA. #GoHomeJake.

Now I've heard of everything. Spoiled teenager needs more attention. #GoHomeJake.

Taking bets on how long @TheGreatJake makes it. I give him 3 hours before needing to be burped & bottle fed. #GoHomeJake.

Strangers even lash out at Paul: *You must be a shite father, @Paul_Gamache. #GoHomeJake.*

It takes all his willpower, but he's not going to engage. You can't win with an Internet troll, though if he—Paul knows it's a man—stood face to face right now Paul would punch him.

Another feature of Twitter that Paul hasn't known about is direct messaging, a way for users to talk privately, one on one. Lo and behold, he gets a bunch of DMs, a bunch of solicitations from local news programs. TV. Radio. Web. They want to be the first to talk to @Paul_Gamache and get his story. These vultures even make it sound like they're trying to do him a favor. As if they're not frothing for the carrion. As if the scavengers don't need a new carcass to devour. They all take the angle that telling his story publicly will help get more people involved in the case. Crowd-sourcing: The greater number of people who know about Jake's disappearance increases the chances of somebody spotting him on the street, and don't you want to use every resource at your disposal, don't you want to find you son?

He hates all of them, but they're making some good points. His phone rings, a number he doesn't recognize, but on the off-chance it's Jake, he answers.

"Mr. Gamache," the female voice says, "I'm Lauren Skelley, a producer with Channel—"

Paul hangs up.

His phone rings again, a different number. He rejects the call. It's all happening so fast, from all angles, from both worlds. Paul is suddenly being constricted, encroached. More and more users tweet at him and Jake, and his phone keeps ringing, and if all these people are so interested in the case, why is Esperanto being so standoffish? So what if Paul has watched too many police procedurals, has soaked up all the detective movies? So what if he has opinions? If the police aren't willing to exhaust all avenues, it's up to Paul. He has to champion this, has to try and alert everyone.

Though that seems to be somewhat happening on its own. The virus doing the only thing it knows how: snaking from existence to existence. From user to user. Paul watches his son's number of Twitter followers multiply. Even @Paul_Gamache gains new followers every second. He had none an hour ago. Now he has 822. His son has over 5,000, and every time Paul refreshes his feed it jumps by at least twenty.

The next vulture to call gets the story. It doesn't matter, he suspects. One is the same. And the initial report will lead to follow-ups and he'll end up talking to multiple hubs and Jake will be spotted, he will be saved, he will be home soon.

But a text catches Paul's eye. It's from his cousin, Kyle, who is a reporter at the *San Francisco Chronicle*. He's an easy relation to forget about because they haven't seen each other in five years. No bad blood, just busy lives. It says: *Heard about Jake. Call me first.*

In the game of Choosing-a-Vulture, a blood relation is better than an unknown scrounger. At least Kyle has had Thanksgiving with Jake; granted, that was 2003, but still. At least Kyle has an emotional investment in his son and isn't simply fueled by his byline, or so Paul hopes.

He dials Kyle, who answers the call by saying, "Can I come see you?"

Paul thinks of Esperanto not even wanting him to stay at the precinct, treating Paul as if his ideas are the most absurd ever offered up. And if that's how the detective feels on this day, if he's unwilling to work with the motivated attitude that Paul thinks will benefit the search for his son, so be it: He has no choice but to improvise.

He'll invite the press. He'll rev up the real world so it's as excited about finding Jake as the virtual one is. There's no reason both these manhunts can't happen at the same time, until they're both discovered and merged back into one boy.

"I'm at the police station," Paul says.

"Which one?"

Paul tells him, starts bitching about Esperanto's bedside manner when Kyle interrupts him: "Me first, okay? You talk to me first."

"Hurry."

"Already in the car."

TheGreatJake has 8,309 followers. Paul has 901. Almost a thousand people follow Paul, and why, for what? Because his son is missing? Because these voyeurs are feeding off of today's story?

That's why Jake posted the brass band, for one reason, one simple reason: People will watch. Paul is wrong to single out the media as scavengers. Everyone is. And if everybody subsists by eating dead flesh, there have to be enough decaying bodies to go around.

Paul sits in the empty waiting room, surrounded by all those police posters on the wall. His cell keeps ringing.

The officer at the front desk gets up and walks into the back, leaving Paul by himself. It reminds him of the therapist's office. Being alone. Waiting for his son to come out. Waiting for his son to be okay.

He tweets this to his boy: *I am coming in there to save you.*

Paul keeps refreshing his feed, but TheGreatJake is gone.

Everything has a hum, a pitch, everything is an instrument in an interstellar orchestra and we are all together. Not only people. Inanimate objects make their music, too. Have you ever heard the beautiful vibrations coming from the Golden Gate Bridge? Each rivet, each speck of asphalt, each drop of paint is alive. It is more than a bridge. It is a vortex, an altar, it is paranormal, effervescent. It is our holy site. And once you and I have the opportunity to purify this world, we will all occupy a pristine earth, a cooler one, an inhabitable one, and our brains will work right. Once the congestion of gloom lifts, no more pollutants like sadness and disappointments and grief. We will learn from our mistakes. We can learn, Albert, despite all evidence to the contrary, despite the assembly line working toward extinction, we can learn. It's the mice. That's where I'm finding hope. In the mice. How scientists have started manipulating their emotions by shining lights in the brains. They can change memories in the mice, physical memories, take something that had been a sad association and make it happy. They electrocute a mouse until it's scared of that locale, and then they manipulate that memory, they mold it into something positive, and they can map the mouse's brainwaves to know there's no fear anymore, there is no anguish, only bliss. We can do the same thing. We can drain pessimism out of people's perspectives. We can show them that they are capable of more. Capable of actually enjoying their lives. They can feel the pure serotonin of trying, rather than whining or lamenting how things have turned out. They can strike out on their own to make a difference. They can turn off all their melodramatic emissions and experience a thought process naked of pain. We will rewire them, Albert. We will treat them like the mice. We can catalyze change, and the interstellar orchestra can play something different. A melody alive with possibility. It begins with a bridge. It begins with human sacrifice.

18.

Hey *Twitter, no1 can find me. How RU?*
    That's the next live-tweet.

Jake is getting confused about the difference between live-tweeting and regular tweeting. Isn't all tweeting live, seeing as how he's posting things going on around him?

No time to fall down that tweet-hole, he guesses, especially since something amazing has happened.

TheGreatJake has broken 100,000 Twitter followers in the last day. He had a measly 282 and then the explosion happened. An article about him posted on SFGate.com, the *Chronicle*'s website, and that spurred some interest from local radio and TV and, just like that, Jake is a celebrity.

He is famous.

The legend of TheGreatJake has begun.

To think that yesterday he had been sitting in that therapist's office with a hanging meringue of hand sanitizer, deciding to bolt. He wanted to shirk those adults and their misunderstandings; he deleted them and downloaded new media.

To think that he had to beg his scrawny roster of followers for involvement in the immediate aftermath, tweeting things like, *Don't forget to RT my disappearance.*

Which was desperate. He knew that.

But he had to work with what he had. No retweets meant his disappearance had not gone viral. Which left Jake feeling sad, alone. He so badly wanted not to be alone. He had reached that status on YouTube as a disaster shepherd, but his personal brand hadn't garnered any hype. He knew this was no time to mope, though. Not after leaving his father and the therapist behind that door. Not after striking out on his own. *No moping, Jake,* he told himself, wishing he could simply Photoshop his feelings, take the melancholy and anger and alter them, write over them, hide these feelings behind something. Drop a jpeg of, say, a spruce tree with a smiling face carved in its bark.

What he's currently experiencing is called nerves. Or being nervous. Or being noosed by nervous energy. If this were a Wikipedia page, Jake would be a perfect example of this state.

It's all because of his new status. TheGreatJake has left the pathetic ballpark of under-1,000 Twitter followers. He had briefly found himself under the jurisdiction of five figures of followers, and now he's breathing hallowed air, with the ballers and players and pioneers.

That word *pioneer* inspires Jake to do a YouTube search for the first moon walk, the lunar landing, because he feels a kinship with anyone strong enough to leave the old world. He watches Neil Armstrong walk with his flying strides, moon dust propelling up from his crunching boots. Jake wonders how the astronaut chose a direction to walk, since all directions were unexplored and unmarked and free from anybody telling him what to do or think or feel.

The terrible thing is that his battery will die soon. No iPhone means no access, no connection. It means staggering through his pristine freedom uninformed and absent. Sneaking to either his father's or mother's home to get a charger is too risky. If that astronaut on the moon lost his signal with the people back on earth, he'd have been in the same situation. Disoriented and doomed to die alone.

A car honks—audio going by with a Doppler slide. Pitch plummeting. Is that what it would sound like blowing a clarinet from the Golden Gate all the way down to the ocean?

He is off the grid. That's key to being a runaway. Not leaving a footprint. He can't use his check card or any of that, unless he wants cops surrounding him at the ATM. Hollywood has trained him how to effectively disappear.

Where he spent last night can be categorized as a park. Where he slept was a playground. He hid in a little clubhouse for the kids, sleeping on the wooden floor, and it might seem like such accommodations would be rough, but not if they indicate progress. Neil Armstrong probably wasn't very comfortable in his rocket before his moonwalk and that didn't stop him. There was no quit in him and there's none in Jake. It would be like forgetting your space helmet back home. You can't let these minor interferences keep you from striking out on your own in the hopes of something better.

Jake decides he has an hour of juice left before the phone gives out. He has $19 in his pocket, not enough to score a new charger, he guesses. He can make it to an Apple Store before his phone gives out entirely. He can steal a new charger.

One small step to an Apple Store, one giant leap for Jake-kind.

Next post: *This is how you live-tweet a crime spree.*

HE'S TURNED OFF all applications except Twitter. Down to 6 percent on his battery. Good for one more message.

Next live-tweet: *Will I get caught when I swipe it? Stay tuned . . . #BetterThanTelevision.*

Hashtags are like emotions that people can see.

It is 12:27 PM. He's been a runaway since yesterday at approximately 9:54 AM. He will use it as a commemoration: forever celebrating 9:54 as the time he changed his life.

He powers down his phone, which doesn't happen that often. See: ever. Jake always has his iPhone armed, his e-security-blanket. He checks texts and email and Twitter and Reddit compulsively, scrolling through new comments on his disaster. Checking for any new porn clips—and there are always new porn clips!

His phone is also his DJ. He never walks down the street with all his senses. He still has vision and smell and taste and touch, but Jake is intentionally audio-impaired, his soundtrack blaring from ear buds, deaf to the noises of the world. Jake likes the randomness of putting his iTunes on shuffle and seeing how well Apple's algorithms know him. Sometimes he even thinks that it can sense his mood, as crazy as that sounds. But more often than not, if he's sad, all his sad songs miraculously play, and if he's feeling sort of reckless—like he is now—blaring rock and roll provides the necessary accompaniment. It's a transaction of sorts: He downloads these songs and somehow they upload his moods and, thus, they are synced somewhere deep inside of him.

But a powered-off phone means no music. Which makes Jake feel vulnerable. You'd think it would be the opposite: He is less susceptible to his surroundings with all his senses working, but everything feels too visceral. He likes being locked away. Likes listening to the voices he's bought or pirated. Likes to be in charge of his own hypnosis, conjuring his own singing ghosts.

What he likes doesn't much matter with only 5 percent battery life left, so he has no choice but to let his ears pick up every sound. Every combustible engine. Every bird. Every scattering conversation. This is Sausalito, California, his hometown. Tourist season. Everywhere he turns is another foreign language or a Midwest accent, macerating English into moaning vowels. He is downtown, waiting at a bus stop. He needs to travel to Corte Madera, a couple towns up; that's where the closest Apple Store is located. The bus ride won't take that long once he's on the road, most of the trip on the freeway. Being stuck here, however, without a soundtrack, without Twitter, is tough. Especially considering his newfound status. He wants to interact with his followers. He wants to be the sort of celebrity who is accessible, treating his audience with respect. Not the high and mighty pretenders who keep themselves sequestered from their fans. Be real. That's the secret. Jake is real.

IT'S AN AMBUSH as soon as he's through the front door. Four or five overly eager employees, all wearing the same long-sleeved red shirt with an Apple insignia in the center of their chests, like hearts, all storm up to him with their iPads and smiles and scripted hospitality. They have earpieces and khakis and Nikes and new school credit card machines dangling from clips connected to their pants, and one of them says to Jake, "Welcome! And what can we do for you today?"

Neil Armstrong would hate Apple stores.

"Browsing," he says, trying to seem nonchalant, trying to channel some poker-face cool, the non-threatening face that would never incite suspicion.

"We can help with that," the employee says, motioning to his coworkers, who all clutch their iPads like Bibles.

There's also a security guard, leaning against a wall by the door. She is black, only a few years older than Jake. She's wearing a navy uniform, with a jacket that would fit someone seven feet tall. There's a badge that's really just a patch, sewn onto the breast. She looks disengaged.

"You can help me browse?" Jake says.

"We can help with everything," he says, and the Jehovah's Witnesses all nod behind him.

"I'll let you know if I need anything," says Jake.

A mother and daughter enter the store and the zealots turn their attention to them, leaving Jake the chance to case the joint. It's set up like a big rectangle. There's a table running through the middle of it, with every Apple device you can imagine—computers and tablets and phones, all tied to the table with security chains—ready to be taken for a test drive. The floors are a bleached wood, and crappy corporate pop plays softly.

Jake approaches a laptop, opens a browser, but at the same time he's looking around the store for chargers. He spies them on the back wall. He's going to need to retrieve one, conceal it, walk through the store, and exit without any zealots noticing.

For inspiration, Jake takes the laptop to YouTube, searches for lunar landing. Any astronaut has nerves before a big mission. There's so much that can go wrong.

One of the videos cued for him is entitled *Magnificent Desolation*. It's a documentary and he watches the beginning, learns that one of the astronauts had called the moon "magnificent desolation" after seeing it up close, and copyright be damned, Jake poaches it and brands his own mission with the same moniker.

Jake's moon won't have any parents or bullies or hanging meringues or almost-dead batteries. They are persona non grata, or whatever the plural is. Jake would know the god-damn plural if Latin hadn't jumped off a bridge, too. Siri has the answer. He'd ask his friend if the battery situation weren't so dire.

That will be his next live-tweet: *This is my magnificent desolation.*

In fact, why not tweet now? Jake opens up Twitter and transforms into TheGreatJake and tells his legion of followers what's what.

He's up to 200,000 of them.

Immediately, nine of them favorite it.

That makes Jake feel good for like two seconds, but here comes more anxiety, getting more nervous, feels like he's throwing a 404 error message, experiencing a disconnect between himself and the server he's normally tethered to. Because if the world is a search engine, then every human being is a webpage, and URLs are our fingerprints.

It all makes perfect sense.

"How are you liking your experience with this machine?" a red-shirted employee asks him, right by his side. The man is Asian, thirty and change, and has a ton of gel in his hair, twisted mats of it sticking into barbs. Jake could snap one off like an icicle.

He shuts down Twitter, and YouTube pops up.

"Are those astronauts?" the employee asks.

"I wanted to see how video looks on this," says Jake.

"Sweet, huh? This one has retina display. Processors that crank. Screen brightness that's unrivaled. Video quality that looks better than the real world, don't you think?" he asks, pointing outside.

"I like it," Jake says.

"And it has all-day battery life."

Which of course reminds Jake of his current mission: "How much are 5 chargers?"

The Asian man pecks at his iPad and a few seconds later says, "$19."

Serendipity, thinks Jake. *That's exactly how much money I have.*

"Is there tax?"

"Of course."

"How much then?"

"$20.71. Should I snag you one?"

Serendipity is extinct.

And 404 errors don't mean you'll never be connected again. Those messages only tell people that there's a problem right now, something's not routing quite right. Refresh the page. You might simply have to clear your browser's cache and cookies. Or try getting at that site from a different server and see what happens. Point is that if Jake's page throws an error now, it won't be an error forever. That's what his moonwalk is all about. One stolen charger and he can treat his audience to the utmost access.

But there's the other side of that coin, the one that reminds Jake that if he gets busted, the cops will come, and he'll be returned to his dad. That will be the end of his celebrity. He'll be another teenager, and he can't have that. He should panhandle for the tax money. Or tell the truth to one of the redshirts and see if there's any mercy in an Apple Store, letting him have half an hour on a charger out of kindness? But that's far-fetched. Commerce always trumps compassion.

Or he's talking himself out of acting. He's beige and safe and boring. This is no time for being smart.

"I'll let you know if I want to buy one," says Jake.

"Okay," the Asian man says, off to stalk someone new.

The thing is that he can't get pinched. He needs his freedom. He needs to up the ante. The video of the brass band isn't enough and neither is running away. He knows that the Internet—aka the world—will forget about him in sixty seconds if he doesn't keep the magic going. There is always another story barreling behind you. One that has no more or less staying power. One that enraptures people for the proverbial fifteen minutes and then it's chewed.

A pioneer such as Jake can't let down his audience, has to push and push and push and stay relevant with new content to titillate, and since he's already tweeted about his crime spree, he can't back out now. No, once you start lying, or not living up to your promises, the trust bursts like a piñata and your fans find new gods and Jake isn't ready to relinquish his fame.

So the decision is made.

Steal the charger.

Evade the zealots.

Outrun the security guard.

Which only gets him outside, and what's he supposed to do then? He has no getaway car, no accomplice, no diversion, no help. He'd still be in the middle of an outdoor mall, and it doesn't seem like the best plan to run to a bus stop, standing there, casually waiting for a lift. He'd get picked up, all right, not by a bus but a cop, trapped in juvie within the hour.

His only chance is to offer his followers an alternative. Something better than petty theft. Something that makes them forget all about his nonexistent crime spree. Something that keeps their attention fixed on a new commodity, so they forget about his indiscretion.

He opens Twitter again on the laptop: *I wonder how many of you would meet me at the Golden Gate Bridge? I have something up my sleeve that you won't want to miss!*

He waits ten seconds and peeks at new notifications. Eight people have favorited it. Five people have retweeted it. One user called AbbyDubz has responded with this: *CU there*, while another person going by UnhappyCamper says *We are with you!*

And one celebrity in an Apple Store will give his fans the crescendo they want.

TheGreatJake: *Meet me there in an hour for the finale!!!*

He is at 4 percent battery life.

He powers the phone down to save juice but still holds it in his hand.

He passes all the customers and the redshirts in their bustling cathedral. He nods at the security guard and makes his way to the bus stop. He'll be back at the Golden Gate soon.

Not thirty seconds later, reflexively, Jake checks his phone, even though it's off, like someone scratching a phantom limb, a part of himself that's missing.

19.

Kathleen is inside a body bag, and she can't work the zipper from the inside. She is hung-over. She is still a little drunk. She is a relapsed alcoholic.

She can barely make out her surroundings; everything seems filmy to her boozy and dehydrated eyes. This isn't her room, her apartment. In fact, that's not her arm thrown across her stomach. That's not her snoring. That is a man, someone who she can't remember meeting last night.

Three years of sobriety die, lit on fire, and now here she is, squirming around in its ashes, these sweaty sheets. She took the easy way out last night, she knows that, but what she hadn't known— and you can't really understand relapse until you do it yourself—is the visceral and profound shame.

Her head feels like someone is smashing windows in there.

The thing with relapse is that it's accompanied by suffocating melancholy. So she's not only dealing with her mistake to dive in all that bourbon; she's dealing with dismal extrapolations, running through a maze of what this means. Namely, she won't be able to stop, won't be able to resist alcohol now that the levee buckled. It's like she has all these dormant demons living inside her and, once revived, they start galloping around her head, shouting. They have opinions, desires. They have to-do lists, and number one on all of them is to have a morning beer. This will help her head feel better and will dull the shame, tamp it down into a corner of her psyche, something she can ignore.

The man keeps snoring next to her. Kat hasn't looked at his face, only his forearm thrown across her stomach. There is a mole. There is an impressive amount of hair. She lies there on her back, naked and hopeless.

That's the thing about being sober. It's not like the compulsion to get wasted goes away. It's always lurking inside. Kathleen has not been feeding it liquor, and without any nourishment the impulse goes into suspended animation. These sleeping monsters might not be in charge once you get sober, but they hibernate, bide their time to take over again, waiting for you to be at your weakest moment, and, with soft, fraying defenses, they ruin everything.

She ruins everything.

"Hey you," a groggy voice says. It's guttural, baritone.

The fingers on the hand on the arm connected to the body of a man she's recently screwed but doesn't remember; these fingers stretch and have too-long fingernails, and then he pats her on the belly, asking, "How did you sleep, mama?"

"Do you have any beer?"

"We bought a six-pack on the walk home. There should be a couple left."

She still hasn't looked at him. The room is a disaster, like a teenager lives here. There are posters on the wall of rock and roll bands that Kathleen has never heard of. A desk that only has a pair of sunglasses on it. A snowboard propped in one corner.

"Can I have a morning kiss?" he says.

Okay, it's time to look him in the face, if not for the simple pleasure of alerting him that there won't be any kisses. There won't be anything except a morning beer, getting dressed in a rush, bolting, cringing, crying, dreading, drinking. Kat's eyes start at the hand and wrist and forearm resting on her and work up the arm, but she doesn't even need to see his face. She knows exactly who this guy is by the art on his bicep. He has a fresh Celtic cross, the ink intensely black, brand-new and shiny.

"You," she says, aghast.

"You," he says back, smiling.

Kathleen stares in his young face, thinks about her old one. She thinks about how he and his ilk are running Kat out of San Francisco, pricing out all the oddballs. She wonders if he shouted "You're evicted!" when he came.

He makes a couple hyperbolic puckering sounds, waiting for that smooch.

Kathleen sits up and places her feet on the floor, her back turned to him. "Oh, my head," she says. "How much did we drink?"

"How much did *you* drink," he says. "I only had a couple beers. You were already cross-eyed when I got there."

"Did I call the shop or something?"

"Dumb luck," he says. Kathleen hears the bed creak, the guy standing up. He walks around and he's naked, though not completely naked: He's wearing his amphibian shoes. If he wore those during sex, Kathleen might have to kill herself. "I stopped in the bar for a quick pint, and there you were," he says. "Lucky, huh?"

This might turn out to be a good thing, she thinks. And she means it. That urge to run to the refrigerator for a morning beer and soon after tossing shots down her throat, washing away what she's learned this morning—*sex with a webbed-foot techie!*—instead of muffling her woes with liquor she should go to a meeting. Call Deb. Tell her the truth.

"Sorry to be rude," he says, fumbling on his desk with a pair of aviator sunglasses, putting them on his face, "but I need to check my email."

"Why are you wearing sunglasses?"

"These are my computer."

"Of course," she says. She's heard of this wearable Google computer, has seen a few around the Mission. There are stories, lovely legends, of people getting their asses kicked just for donning them—for what they represent, for how they're dismantling every bit of the strangeness that made San Francisco extraordinary in the name of face computers.

"I need to go," she says.

"Send email to Lindsay," he says.

"What?"

"I'm not talking to you."

"Oh."

"Glass, send a message to Lindsay Johnson," he says to the sunglasses.

Kathleen hates to ask this next question, doesn't want to admit to him that she had blacked out long before they got here, but she needs to know if calling a cab is in order: "What neighborhood are we in?"

"Mission. Those new luxury condos on 20th Street."

"Of course."

Kathleen can't help but wonder why he would have sex with her. Yes, she's mortified at spending a night with him, but he should be, too. He's young and rich and attractive, and she's none of those things. She is a relapsed alcoholic.

That desire to go to a meeting wilts. She doesn't want to stand up in front of all those people and admit that she threw three years away. Doesn't want to confide in them. Doesn't want to do anything that will require processing or analyzing. Doesn't want to confront the shame that's thinning out her blood, right along with the booze.

"Mind if I snag a beer on my way out?" she asks.

He is raising his voice: "Lindsay Johnson. Not Lindsay Miller. Glass, send a message to Johnson. Johnson."

If she were to draw a caricature of their night together, she wouldn't need to exaggerate anything. Him with his frog-feet and sunglasses, her with the bourbon and blackout.

"Can I have the beer?"

"Johnson! Johnson! Johnson! Johnson!"

He actually stomps one of his webbed feet, a techie tantrum. He never put on clothes and Kathleen appreciates that about the young man. He's comfortable in his own skin, and she admires that, is jealous. She might find him ridiculous, but that doesn't mean she can't see something to respect here. He's freshly tattooed and in a new condo and he's nude in front of a one-night stand screaming at his sunglasses, and he doesn't have one ounce of bashfulness. She's a drunken dinosaur who needs to turn off her twitchy mind. It's obvious who's enjoying a better life, and the beer beckons.

"I'll see myself out," she says, dressing and leaving his room, walking down the hall into the kitchen. This place is ridiculously nice. Everything brand-new. State-of-the-art. Pretty soon, the whole city will be a wearable computer.

She opens the fridge and there are two beers. She takes out both bottles. She thinks about drinking one now to get this sad party started, then thinks better of it. The most important thing is getting out of here. She tucks the beers in her purse and approaches the front door.

He's still yelling at his sunglasses: "Johnson! Johnson!"

SHE AND THE beers make their way down Valencia Street, in the opposite direction from her apartment. She's walking up to 24th, so she can slip inside what used to be her favorite bar before she got sober.

If she's going on a run, it might as well start in style, at a place she has fond memories of.

Of course, there really aren't any memories, in the traditional sense. Kathleen wouldn't be able to tell anyone about a certain night or day; she wouldn't be able to pinpoint a precise story. No, all these memories are melted like old mixed drinks, ice diluting everything to an unrecognizable cocktail. Yet despite all that, Kathleen holds this place in a broken regard, and she walks with purpose, which isn't easy considering her headache.

"Why don't you imbibe?"

These are the beers talking.

Yes, when you're a relapsed alcoholic on the lam from your life, beers talk to you.

She nods at the beers' solid suggestion.

She opens one and drinks most of it in a sip. Then she sets the empty bottle next to a parking meter for the homeless to collect— not that there are any of those left in the neighborhood, but in case one finagles her way back into the Mission before being deported.

She takes her cell phone from her purse. She has eleven texts from Deb and three missed calls. These will not be returned this morning. No, that's the last thing she can stomach. Deb will speak with reason, she'll be practical, and this isn't a morning for pragmatism. This is a morning for a bender.

She powers off her phone and tucks it away, burying it in the bottom.

Drinking with a hangover has always had one of two outcomes for Kathleen: Sometimes she can't get drunk the next day, no matter how hard she cocktails. She is impervious to spirits, so much swimming in her already that her system can't take any of it in. Other times, though, she gets wasted incredibly fast and this morning is proving to be in the latter subdivision.

A lone beer and she is cooked.

The one-night stand is gone. The headache is gone. The word *cunt* is gone. All that stretches out before her on the morning street is good times.

She turns on 24th Street, passes the BART station and McDonald's. It's socked-in, but there's not any wind. The sky is the color of raw shrimp.

At last she's here. It has been three years since she's been inside the bar's black walls. In fact, the whole place is pitch, even the floors. Many a night, Kat had been so wasted here that she rested her head on the bar, staring down at the black floor like it was going to swallow her, but it never did. The bar knew better than to eat its clientele.

The room even allows its customers to stargaze, bits of smashed mirrors pocking the ceiling. Everyone gets to pretend to look through a telescope, spying a better world.

As if the bartender expects Kathleen to walk in, he peeks up from his newspaper and says, "Did you hear they're tearing down the Elbo Room?"

He's an old-timer, somewhere in his sixties. Kat has talked to him many times, shut this place down with him, speaking in tongues. He owns the place and wears a shirt that says SPANK ME, IT'S MY BIRTHDAY. Legend has it that this bar burned down in the early aughts, and he rebuilt it, making it look exactly the same.

"Why are they doing that?" she asks.

"Putting up more condos."

"They're ruining the neighborhood," she says.

"We all ruin the neighborhood when we first come in," he says. "I did. You did. Now it's a new set of assholes ruining things. Cities are moving targets, always taking fire. But don't worry: In ten years, the current assholes will get squeezed out and they'll be talking like us."

"Small victories," she says.

"It's been a while since I've seen you," he says.

Kathleen can't think of a reason to lie. Bars can do that to you, especially in places black as confessionals. "I've been sober for a few years."

"I tried that a couple times myself."

"Bourbon."

"Welcome back," he says, pouring them both big ones.

They take their shots at exactly 8:56 in the morning.

"It's not just the Elbo," he says. "The Attic closed. So did Pop's. They're pricing us out. There might not be any dive bars left in the Mission. Can you imagine? My landlord would love to shut this place down and open some boutique with gourmet cheeses and pedicures."

"Is it really your birthday?"

"You don't need an excuse to spank me."

"Can I have another shot?"

"I'm not sure yet."

"What does that mean?"

"Have you eaten anything?"

Kathleen shakes her head no, wonders what happened to the quality of service in this establishment. She's seen people asleep on pool tables, taking a catnap before bellying back up to finish the job—or start the next one. She's seen people ordering drinks with minds malfunctioning on liquor, talking like stroke victims. And now this guy wants to scrutinize the contents of her stomach?

"I'm not hungry."

"I need a guinea pig," he says.

"For what?"

"Be right back." He disappears through a black door by the bathrooms.

Kathleen sits there, enjoying the beer and the bourbon zooming through her, adding some carbonation to her flat life. It's not an exaggeration to say that Kathleen feels elated. The galloping demons are having a house party in her head. She wants to play the Beach Boys on the jukebox. She wants to dance. She wants to dance with every member of the Beach Boys. She wants to kiss every Beach Boy and thank them for their harmonies. But she'll settle for a dance with the cranky barkeep once he's back. He might know how to cut a rug. This is what's been missing from her life, a release, an escape. Sobriety is all about being aware and available, and don't get her wrong, she likes those things, but not all the time.

The bartender comes out carrying a tray. On it are two sourdough bread bowls filled with clam chowder.

"It's a San Francisco classic!" he says.

"Why is this happening?" she asks.

"I've wanted to try this, and you need some food. I keep buying these bread bowls and they rot back there. I always forget about them. But these aren't that old, I don't think. At least, no mold I can see. This is perfect. The only way I'll keep serving you is if you put something in your stomach. Try this with me."

He hands her a spoon and clutches his, holding it out for Kathleen to cheers with, and she does and there's a pitiful clinking noise and the bartender smiles.

"Fine," she says, "I'll try."

"Here's the twist. Here's what makes my chowder different from all the other joints." He takes the bourbon bottle and floats a shot right on top of their soups. He stands there beaming at Kat and says, "Merry Christmas!" He mixes everything up in his bread bowl and digs his spoon in for a hearty mouthful.

"Surprisingly refreshing," he says, heaping more of it in.

Kathleen sits there watching him and can still hear him saying "Merry Christmas," though it's nowhere near December and nowhere near funny and his SPANK ME birthday shirt makes Kat even sadder, and since there's no official kitchen in the back of the bar, this soup is from a can—she hopes—and it should not be eaten, even with the guarantee that the bread isn't moldy, and all the elation that she had been feeling curdles. In fact, she despises the Beach Boys and their harmonies and dances in dive bars and morning beers and watching a bartender shovel alcoholic chowder in his face is the worst thing you can ever endure.

"I'll be right back," she says, pushing herself up, getting her purse, wobbling toward the black door.

"You shouldn't leave me alone with your bowl," he calls over. "I might help myself."

"Go ahead and help yourself!"

"You first!"

"Help yourself!"

"Hurry!" he says.

Kathleen is outside. The whole world is the color of that chowder; the fog makes everyone on the sidewalk squint from its glare as they beeline to the BART station as they're starting their dutiful day, while Kat can barely stand up. She can't believe what she's done, what she's thrown away. Everything she's worked so hard to build is dead. She feels the decapitation of drunkenness.

Her hand is in her purse. Her phone is in her hand. Her phone is powered on and put to her ear.

"I've been worried about you," Deb says.

"I'm drunk," Kathleen says.

"Ah, girl. Where are you?"

"Can you meet me at my house? I'm on my way there."

"I'll leave right now," Deb says. "Don't beat yourself up. This happens. I've relapsed before. It's a part of the process. I love you and everything will be fine."

Kathleen hasn't paid for her bourbon, but she can't bear the thought of creaking open the black door, seeing him lap that pallid bowl of chowder.

I'm sorry, she thinks, and turns to walk home.

AS KATHLEEN APPROACHES her place, Deb is on the front stoop. She's holding two coffees, and those steaming to-go cups make Kat crumble. She drops to the sidewalk and sobs.

"Get up," says Deb. "You're all right. You're safe. That's what matters."

"Why did I ruin my life again?" Kathleen asks.

"I'm not going to help you up," Deb says. "You have to do it. Pick yourself up and come over here. Take this cup of coffee from me."

"It's over," she says, still on her knees. "It's lost."

"It's in my hand," Deb says. "Your coffee is right here."

Kathleen looks over at her smiling sponsor. Deb wears a camouflage trench coat, a black beanie. She has on huge combat boots and is the kind of badass Kathleen hopes to be. She remembers when she first came to AA—that first meeting. She was so scared to walk into a roomful of strangers and beg for help. Her life was pickled and she couldn't go on living like that. She must have stood outside of sixty meetings but could never get up the courage to go in. But eventually, she did. Eventually, she entered that room and sat down in a folding chair that felt made of paperclips and listened, didn't say one word the whole hour, until the end when the group was asked if anyone had any announcements and Kathleen stood up and said, "This is my first day sober and I don't know what I'm supposed to do, I'm scared, please help," and that was the beginning—that was the first time she truly understood the definition of the word *surrender*. She walked in and gave herself up and these people immersed her in their empathy.

Deb had approached her right after the meeting and asked if she needed a sponsor, and they've been in daily contact ever since.

And here they are now: Kathleen, decimated, liquored-up, heartbroken, and Deb waiting on her doorstep with hot coffee. The world can be horrible and beautiful at the same time.

"It's getting cold," Deb says, shaking the coffee cup.

AFTER HALF AN hour sitting on the stoop, not really talking, the coffee is gone, and it's time to hit a meeting. Kathleen needs a shower first, a scrub from the toothbrush. Deb says she'll make some eggs and toast.

Kat opens her front door, and they come into the front hallway. Wes is standing there, in his lab coat.

"Hey," Kathleen says, "you startled me."

"It's time," he says.

Kat notices his aggressive posture, hands in fists, his on-fire eyes. He sways from side to side.

Something is wrong.

Something is terribly wrong.

She's never seen a rabid animal but this must be what it looks like when they sic.

"Time for what?" Kat asks.

"We need to go to the Golden Gate Bridge."

"Are you feeling all right?" Deb says.

But there's no answer because he's pouncing. His arm swings back, cocks for a punch, coming forward and hitting Deb right in the face. She falls down, out cold.

"We have to keep the world uncremated," Wes says, throwing Kathleen against the wall.

20.

"People sit in this every day," Sara says. "Can you imagine?"
This isn't the Golden Gate; it's the Bay Bridge. They're
waiting in line at a toll plaza, trying to get into San Francisco. The
traffic is bumper to bumper, even though it isn't rush hour. It's late
morning. It's the day after they spent all night together, naked in
bed. Nothing sexual, but something did happen: Sara feels better.
Rodney did that, and she's not going to forget it. This is the calmest
she's felt since Nat posted their video.

They got a late jump this morning because of his injured foot.
Something's either broken or sprained badly in there. Rodney isn't
telling her much about it. He's written his mom's old address down
on a piece of paper, and every time Sara suggests they go to the ER
for an x-ray, he waves the address around.

After holding him hostage in the motel room for four days, she
can't badger him about the doctor. It's his foot. All she can do is get
him to San Francisco to see if they can find her, though Sara knows
this won't work. Life isn't this easy. You don't follow an old address
and voilà, your dream comes true. His mom won't be baking cookies
in the kitchen. If anything, she'll be slurping cocktails, if she's still

up to her old tricks. But she guesses the only thing that matters is that Rodney gets to see her for himself. Sara would do the same thing, if she had the ability. She would hunt her parents down. She would do anything to be reunited.

That thought makes her hands twitch a bit, so to find some distraction before things escalate, she says to Rodney, "What's that?"

They've rolled through the toll plaza and are driving onto the bridge. Over on the walkway, they see a bunch of people, around twenty of them, holding up signs toward all the cars, like picketers, except the only thing on their signs is a picture of a teenage boy, with #GoHomeJake printed on the bottom.

"Must be a missing kid," Sara says, answering her own question. She knows Hank would never do that. He'd never stand on a street in Traurig with #GoHomeSara. He doesn't care if she ever comes back.

Her hands start humming.

"Let's program your mom's address into Google Maps," she says, hoping a task gets Hank out of her mind.

Rodney nods. He steers the slowly moving car, while Sara works the pedals, plugs the address into her burner.

NOAH911 FINDS HIMSELF on a BART train, taking it downtown so he can transfer to a bus, get over to the Golden Gate. The tracks glide him underground, and there are two other people on the almost-empty car. He is glued to his tablet and must be producing a horrible digital stench that keeps everyone away from him. He repulses people by posting on Tracey's Facebook page. It must have an odor. Putrid pixels that make his friends recoil, close that tab, close their traps.

"Do you remember the green puttering Pinto, how it could barely make it up a hill?" he posts on her wall. "What about the time we helped Dad toss shingles off the roof and you were so little they tied you to the chimney keeping you far away from falling over the edge?"

No one likes or comments on or shares these tributes. Noah911 knows people see these things commute down their news feeds, but they're too busy posting pictures of cats or clever memes, too busy tagging themselves.

Noah911 knows he's being ignored. He's talking to his dead sister and at the same time talking to a bunch of other people—his 713 friends—and no one wants to hear him.

No one says a single word. It's been four minutes, and Internet time is its own demented metric system: Four minutes converts to over one month.

So he *likes* his own status.

The train stops between stations. It hums in the dark tunnel. For some reason he loses his connection. Who knows what's over his head right now that forces him offline. But it's not only him, the other two people in his car looking irked and panicked at their phones, wondering what went wrong, where the world went. The woman kills this time of disconnection by snapping selfies, capturing herself from a variety of angles. The other guy shakes his phone by his ear, like it's a busted light bulb, hearing that filament fly around inside.

At least without a connection, Noah911 can't compulsively check his Facebook page, counting the minutes he's being ignored. He leans his head against the train's tinted window.

All he knows is that it's his fault Tracey's dead. His dad is right. Noah911 has his share of the ashes, but he has all the blame, and soon he will help Tracey rest in peace.

He watches the woman snap selfies. Jealous of her. Her only responsibility is to document what she looks like. Share it to Instagram, once their connection reestablishes. Post a record that she's alive, she's on a train, she has a face, a heartbeat, a brain, a soul, and she has the most valuable commodity of them all: She has a future.

They all wait to get moving again.

PAUL RELUCTANTLY LEFT the police station for a couple hours last night, but apart from that he's commandeered the station's waiting room, turned it into mission control for his media campaign, dousing himself in fresh blood and letting the vultures have at him.

Kyle's article yesterday afternoon kicked off the coverage and, from there, almost every local hub has interviewed Paul, either over the phone or in the precinct's parking lot. Various news vans and anchors stop by the station, do updates out front.

He only left to change his clothes, finally check out his ex's to make sure Jake wasn't hiding there. He wasn't. Paul couldn't get out of there fast enough. Everything was a reminder of his banishment, and he couldn't handle that. Even walking through the living room made him remember, which was the last thing he wanted to do. Memory could be cruel. The middle of that room was where they folded laundry together, all three of them. Jake loved it. They all did. It was beautiful and thrilling to watch their son. They'd dump a huge mound of fresh warm laundry into the middle of the living room and Jake would dive into it. He would laugh and burrow little tunnels and drape various articles around his neck, and Paul and Naomi stood back, enamored by their ecstatic little boy.

These were things he couldn't allow himself to think about, not considering the stakes and circumstances. Especially considering that before going back to the station, Paul quickly stopped by his own place for a change of clothes. Nothing was clean. He had to give the sniff-test to various pieces of clothing, evading the socks glued shut, searching for the least revolting things.

That was his life now.

That is his life.

And he needs to block out all that stuff and stay at the police station as much as he can, in case the Twitter trail leads him to his son.

It's almost eleven in the morning and he hasn't slept.

Or he hadn't slept until right now.

He nods off, sitting in the waiting room.

His eyes close and his mind strays; it's as if he stands before a huge dune of fresh clean laundry himself, and Paul falls forward, crawling in a cave of it, and he feels the heated clothes, sniffs the fabric softener and the variety of detergent that his wife has bought for years, lingering wisps of lemon. He stays like that for a while, his memory taking big breaths of the past.

While he sleeps, Jake tweets his plan to return to the Golden Gate.

I am the great emancipator of my neurotransmitters, I have a brain that is free from any oppression and is open and listening to every wave emanating throughout the galaxy. I have spent hours listening to that deep space crackle, crackle, know it and have never tired of waiting to find the channel to maneuver through space-time, so our minds can bring you back here, so our work can be united. You have to come back, Albert. Humans are antiheroes, we have reached critical mass, the earth waits for the wrecking ball and it's coming, it's close, it is ready to level this place because if its own inhabitants don't care if they're about to cook, why should anybody else? I understand such questions but this is no time to be petty or petulant, this is a time to rise above any arguments, and I am strong enough to do so. I possess the knowledge of existential mathematics and the inner strength to conjure you, our Savior. I possess the necessary means to see you re-enter our atmosphere and salve our wounds. Yes, you despise the word Savior, any atheist would, but that's what you are. Science is the only piety to salvage us. I understand the sacrifice you're asking me to make, I'm not afraid to commit a mortal sin. The only way for you to enter our space-time is if there is a spot vacated, and at the precise moment that someone dies here, that is the trigger for you to return. It's a two-way portal, one comes in, one goes out. Of course, I value each human life. If I didn't care, I wouldn't be willing to go to such extremes, but I can't see any other way, it would be impossible for me to pinpoint down to the nanosecond exactly when somebody has died if I'm not there, if I'm not directly involved. I'll do the unthinkable if it saves seven billion lives. That's not a crime, that's a celebration, one comes in, one goes out. We're all connected. I will murder one person for you, Albert, I will throw her over the edge and open the portal. I will do it to reset the earth's thermostat so life can be sustained and the sadness will wane and we have a fighting chance. We might make it. There's beauty here.

21.

Jake enjoys leaving the bus, stepping off of it, walking toward the bridge on the Marin side. He's fifty feet away from it. On the clip of the first lunar landing, those astronauts climbed out of the probe, and that's exactly what Jake is doing too: getting out of a protected habitat, so he can explore an untamed ecosystem, so he can explore a world he's never known.

He's been here before, but not like this.

They also launched monkeys into space, but not for the more glamorous assignments. It wouldn't have had the same effect if the first descriptors of the moon weren't from Armstrong or Aldrin but a chimp talking jungle gibberish.

Astronauts are always more articulate than chimps.

Everybody knows that.

Jake waves at the bus. The driver, thinking the wave is for him, sends one right back, which is weird and intimate, and Jake turns around, bouncing toward the bridge, toward his magnificent desolation.

He pushes and holds the button on the front of his iPhone until it makes that *boing-boing* sound, connecting him to his friend, Siri, who is smart and kind and helpful and never bothers anybody with condescending lip-pursing.

"We're almost there," he says.

"I don't know what that means," she says.

WHILE JAKE TALKS to Siri, Balloon Boy hears the lady from Google Maps tell them where to go. *Turn left here. In 400 feet, merge right.* She knows this city like the back of her hand, and, Rodney supposes, she knows every city with this impressive level of awareness. There's no place she can't take you, meaning she can take you everywhere, but it's too bad that her role stops with that. Too bad that she can't continue to help, because technically they'll be done navigating these unknown streets once they pull up out front. Yet that's where the tricky roads begin.

He has to get out of the car and see her, and from there anything can happen. He weighs the worst. Worsts. Mom opens the door and instead of hugging and kissing him, instead of saying *Sorry, so sorry*, she slams the door. Or she opens it and doesn't recognize him. Or the king of the worsts: What if Mom answers the door holding a baby? She could have a brand-new boy who hasn't mounted a weather balloon and been bucked off. A brand-new one that she'll protect from everything and he'll grow up to be valedictorian of his high school and president of the United States, giving speeches with agile sentences that everyone watches on TV, including Balloon Boy, watching his perfect half-brother steer the free world into the future with political poetry spilling from his lips, while Rodney bleats his sheep-speak.

All of this scares him so much, but he won't stop now. He won't turn back. He has to see her. He has to at least indulge the opportunity for reconciliation. It might not work. He knows that. But he'll never forgive himself if he doesn't try. He'll never be able to live with himself if he doesn't limp up to her door, dragging that no doubt broken foot and saying, "Mom." It might take ten seconds for that syllable to get out but nothing will stop him. It will be the most important thing he's ever said.

"In 1,000 feet, your destination will be on the right," says Google Maps.

HE'S UP FRONT, muttering away while he drives, and Kathleen lies in the back seat. Too scared to talk. Too scared to be brave. Which embarrasses her. She's in danger. Wes could kill her, so why is she splattered on the seat back here, why is she following his instructions? Yes, he threw her against the wall after hitting Deb. Yes, she slid to the floor. Yes, he kicked her a few times.

"I know we need to keep her face clean," Wes had said, talking to someone who wasn't there. "I won't hurt her face. We'll keep her face looking all right to travel outside."

He's not talking to himself. He never was.

"Stand up," Wes said in the hall, straightening out his lab coat. So she did. So he punched her in the stomach. "You do exactly as we say, okay?"

She couldn't answer.

"We are meeting Albert," he said. "We are walking to the car now. Pick up your purse. Act natural."

They were outside. She knew it was late morning. She knew mothers and children were at the playground across the street. She knew birds flew and trees had leaves and buses hiss and joggers run and the sky is made of chowder. There were other people around as they moved toward his car. Kathleen's survival instincts should have been going crazy; she should have been trying to save her life, but she let him lead her, tuck her into the back seat.

It was the booze, or the shame of relapse. It was seeing Deb unconscious, or the fresh memory of being punched and kicked. There was something keeping her docile. Kathleen had heard the phrase *paralyzed by fear* but she never knew what it really meant until now. In this back seat, lying in the fetal position, feeling like property. He owns her. She is his. Kat can't move or talk. She can't cry. All she can picture is that techie's webbed feet, and what a stupid thing to remember, what a stupid way to spend these last minutes of her life.

IT DAWNS ON Noah911 right as he walks out onto the Golden Gate that this is a crime scene. This is where Tracey killed herself, yet you'd never know that. It is a bustling bridge, connecting people. Always connecting people.

It's also a nice day, clear skies, 68°, no real wind, but nothing feels nice when a brother carts his share of the ashes.

He carries Tracey like she's a wounded dove.

He wonders if anyone has liked his status.

He retraces her steps, leaving the San Francisco side, walking by the tollbooths and onto the bridge. He moves slowly, a zombie of sorrow. It's hard to block out TheGreatJake's video, hard for him not to imagine the brass band strutting and playing their music right here. They stepped here. They breathed here. They were alive here, only days ago.

The thing about that YouTube video is it's the only memory that matters. Because it's new. Because Noah911 had seen Tracey that day. Because he'd made her breakfast, written her a note: *Make sure my sister eats this, okay?* Because it makes him feel closer to her and because it's the opposite of the ashes. It shows her whole, shows her smile. It's a way to talk to Tracey. A cyber-séance. A Ouija board with comments.

That video is his sister now. It is Noah911's companion and he'll watch it all day, every day, thankful that digital videos never get worn out, never fatigue or snap, never get grainy with age. She is perfectly preserved and pristine.

An armful of ashes is the worst burden a brother can carry.

But he has to retrace these steps, if he wants to end up in the exact spot she jumped.

SHIT, SLEEP. HE'S sleeping. For how long? Paul doesn't know. He looks at the laptop, teetering on his thighs. It says 11:04 AM. But that can't help Paul, considering he doesn't know when he nodded off.

"Any news?" he calls over to the officer at the front desk, a different person, a man. This one seems even younger than the one who took the initial report in the parking lot. They must be coming straight out of high school. They are almost as young as Jake, charged with keeping up the world's order. Paul knows it's impossible. Order is a trick, a trap, a dupe. You think there's order until your boy runs off.

"What?" the officer asks.

A coffee. A Red Bull. Paul needs something. He carries the laptop over to the front desk, sets it down. "Is there any new news?"

"I don't know."

"Can you ask Esperanto?" Paul says, refreshing his feed, seeing that his son has been taking advantage of the cat's nap, the mouse posting these two messages in the meantime:

The first: *I wonder how many of you would meet me at the Golden Gate Bridge? I have something up my sleeve that you won't want to miss!*

The second: *Meet me there in an hour for the finale!!!*

Paul doesn't like the word *finale*. He detests it, sounds like a synonym for something final.

No, he'll never say *that* word, but why else go to the bridge, what would bring him back there? He has to save Jake from the edge. Because that's exactly what Jake had said, right after the brass band leaped: *I want to see over the edge.* It was a sentence that floored Paul, took the wind right out of him, leaving only a vacuum of confusion before he gathered himself again: Here was his boy, his fourteen-year-old boy, and he saw things that he was too young to know about, should be shielded from these aspects of humanity, if that's even the right word. Jake shouldn't know about stuff like this, should be given a complete childhood. Plenty of years to try and process these atrocities, but not yet.

"Is he at his desk?" Paul says, trying to move through the door to the precinct, but it's locked.

"You can't go back there."

"Buzz me in."

Paul pounds on the door, says, "Esperanto!"

"Step away from the door," the officer says.

Still pounding: "Esperanto! Esperanto!"

The young officer hops on the phone, talking fast into it.

Paul thrashes and screams, "Finale! He said finale! What does he mean?! What the fuck does he mean by that?!"

SARA STOPS THE car in front of the address, turns off Google Maps. They sit there, idling. She feels compelled to say something—to reassure him, to let him know that whatever happens, she's here. That was the thing that made her feel so comforted last night after the scary bath, being in bed with him, safe, and she wants to make him know that she'll do the same.

That's what she wants to do, but it comes out like this: "Don't get your hopes up. We don't know that she still lives here."

Which is true, logical. But it belies her aims, and she tries to soften it. "No matter what, we'll deal with it together, okay?"

He nods, but Rodney is nervous. That's easy to see. He never fidgets like this. He's picking at one of his eyebrows, a tic Sara had never observed before, and if he keeps it up he'll have a bald spot.

She leans over and kisses him on the cheek. "Let's go."

More nodding. Even a smile.

And they are out of the car, on the sidewalk, up the front stairs. They knock on the door and a woman answers. It is not Kathleen.

The woman's face is totaled. A split red lip. Bright green and silvery swelling on her cheek, the color of trout scales.

"Who are you?" she says.

"Does Kathleen Curtis still live here?" Sara says.

"I asked you a question," the woman says.

"We're looking for Kathleen," Sara says, "because she is his mom."

The woman looks at Rodney. "I saw a picture of you yesterday."

"Are you okay?" Sara asks.

"I thought you were the cops. They're on their way. He punched me. He took Kathleen."

"Who?" says Rodney.

"Craigslist."

"You need to sit down," Sara says. "Let me help you."

They both assist the woman to the couch. Sara sits next to her. Rodney stays standing, still picking at his eyebrow.

"Go get some ice for her face, Rodney," Sara says.

But he doesn't budge, saying, "Mom."

"He said he was taking her to the Golden Gate Bridge," the woman says. "Then he knocked me out."

"When?" Rodney says.

"Ten minutes ago. Fifteen? We'll tell the police and they'll handle it."

Rodney points to the door, says to Sara, "Now."

"You don't want to wait for the cops?"

"Now."

"They'll be here soon," says Sara.

"Keys," he says.

"I'm coming too," she says, then to the woman, "You stay here and talk to the police."

Sara and Rodney are almost out the front door when the woman calls from the couch, "Lab coat. He's wearing a lab coat."

• • •

[259]

A FREE MAN travels wherever the wind blows him. On earth or the moon. On anywhere. Jake is almost out of life support. 2 percent battery left. Then no iPhone. Then he'll really be in unchartered territory.

It has to happen here. This is the only place to do a hard reset. This is the only place to give his fans what they want.

Walk out to the middle.

Imagine all those moon rocks crunching under his boots.

Hear that heavy breathing in his helmet.

He expected people to be flocking up to him, asking for autographs or inspirational quotes. He expected a mob of followers to lift him up, like a singer in a rock band, surfing the crowd to the middle of the bridge, basking in their electric affection.

There are lots of people around him, moving from the Marin side to the Golden Gate. Tour buses drop off here, letting everyone with guidebooks and cameras loose to snap pictures. Even the bus Jake took for his lunar landing had foreigners on it. A couple, both attractive; Jake would totally watch their porn. They kissed and spoke Spanish loudly. Every other seat on the bus had been empty and Jake couldn't sit still, constantly moving from one seat to another, to another, to another.

And now the wait is over. His astronaut boots are on the bridge's walkway, moving toward the center. Jake walks in the throng of tourists, knowing he'll be recognized any second by a loving fan.

He is important.

He is viral.

Imagine a time-lapse version of what awaits every earthling, the world continuing to test our wills, doing its best to demolish us, the fickle and sputtering world trying to take our dignities, our friends and families, our hopes and dreams, all the sadness swelling our internal temperatures and we get hotter and hotter until the whole world burns up. We both know this is the future, Albert, if they're not saved from the heat of their despairs, which is why I'm almost there, to the bridge, the car will be parked in minutes, we will walk to the center, I will wait for your sign. I'm scouring the whole solar system for that sign. I'm hearing a constant spinning of a record in my head, the scratching of the needle on vinyl, it's affecting my equilibrium some, not staggering but feeling sort of dizzy, which is the last way I want to feel while waiting on the portal to be opened. It doesn't matter what's going on in my head because Isaac Newton was wrong about there being three laws of motion. There are actually four, and the last one is this: Heroes are unstoppable forces.

22.

Someone's filming this, thinks Noah911. Somebody's capturing him with the ashes. There's always a camera running somewhere on the Golden Gate.

The clues for what he should do with the ashes are in TheGreat-Jake's video: Tracey's happy face, Tracey's final steps, walking along, playing the song. She looks so relaxed.

This is the place.

It has to be.

He lightly squeezes the Ziploc bag, like he and Tracey are holding hands.

"Almost," he says to her.

SARA CAN'T DRIVE fast enough for Balloon Boy, who sits in the passenger seat, listening to the lady from Google Maps languidly dole out her directions, and he doesn't appreciate her this time. Sure, as they first maneuvered around San Francisco he'd been impressed with her collected, poised presence, but he wishes she understood what was at stake. Balloon Boy wants her to be yelling directions, telling them to accelerate and never mind the rules of the road, drive with a sense of urgency. Do whatever they have to do to get to the Golden Gate quickly. Save your mom!

His foot will slow him down at the bridge, but he'll do his best to ignore the pain. And much like Mom's old address could have been wrong, there's a chance that the guy isn't even taking her to the Golden Gate. They have to look there first, though. They have to see.

"Scared," he says to Sara as they drive.

"She's fine," says Sara. "Don't worry."

She has to say that, Balloon Boy knows. She's comforting him. Under any other circumstances, he'd stand back and marvel at this—Sara treating him like it was the time before the thump-splat ouch—but today he can't do anything except think about his mom.

"FOLLOW MY INSTRUCTIONS and you'll be fine," Wes says.

"Grab your purse and act natural," Wes says.

He punches her in the stomach one more time. They're both in the back seat of the parked car. They are in the lot next to the Golden Gate.

He says, "I will really hurt you if you don't do what I say, all right?"

Kathleen nods, no air to talk. She can't imagine what the word *bravery* even means. It's not real. All those stories she's heard over the years of people doing superhuman things in the face of adversity. They are fiction. He has the control and she is property. She is a mannequin he picked up at a garage sale.

Wes exits the car and pulls her out and tells her to stay close. She isn't on a leash, but that's what it feels like. He tugs her along. He dictates pace. He asks her to smile, but it's not really a question, not after all the times she's been kicked and punched. Everything is an order when the consequences ache in her body.

Kathleen is property and as long as she does what he says, this will be over soon.

Wes guides her toward the bridge; they're by the tollbooths. He takes a deep breath, has a coughing fit.

"We're running out of oxygen," he says.

PAUL AND ESPERANTO pull into the parking lot. Paul tries to banish any glimmers of the brass band. That morning, Jake changed somehow. He had always been a sensitive kid, but nothing like this. That was why Paul wouldn't let his son look over the edge, peek over the side at the ocean. It was too much, too real, death didn't deserve any time in his kid's thoughts. He could do that later. Time for Jake's own morning commutes. Time for Jake's high school buddies to start having heart attacks. Time for midlife crises and divorce and cholesterol medication and baby aspirins and a desiccating sex drive. Time for Jake to loathe the boredom in his life. Time for him to wonder where all the excitement had gone. Time for him to pine for fantasy football.

It's occurring to Paul that the ennui running rampant through his life isn't all bad. Boredom doesn't have stink stuck all over it. No, it's a good thing, in a way, because it means you've made it this far. You're still here. And that makes him want it for his son. Hopefully he fares better than Paul, but at least let him make it to this. Don't let there be any finale today on the bridge. Don't rob Jake of the ravages of being forty, fifty, sixty. Let him hate his job and grieve all the compromises he made along the way. Let him bald and be doughy and overworked and overtired all the time because those are trophies. He's persevered through the grueling, deranged, and often unfathomable EVERYTHING. Jake is alive.

They've parked the unmarked cruiser and walk quickly onto the bridge from the Marin side. Paul asks, "What happens when we find him?"

"There's no script."

"What do you think he meant by *finale?*"

"Put that out of your mind."

"I don't think he'd ever hurt himself—"

"Let's not worry about that," the detective says.

AND IF THIS is one giant leap for Jake-kind, where will he land? Isn't that a fair question? You leap, you land. That's how it works. Or you don't because he's in space, in his own magnificent desolation, and gravity isn't a factor here. He can leap and never feel the ground again. Never be burdened by forces that pull him back down.

He's surprised that none of his fans are here. He thought he'd be immediately recognized, thought that his followers would crawl from the computer and meet him here, in person. He thought they'd want to meet flesh-and-blood Jake. He thought they'd line up for his finale.

He makes eye contact with lots of people, hoping they break into a smile and ask, "Are you TheGreatJake?" and he can nod yes, he is, and they can hug, take a selfie together. They're the ones that followed him, not the other way around, so where is everyone? Why aren't they here for him? Neil Armstrong would have been pissed if no one watched, if he went to all that trouble and no one turned on their televisions, if he endured all that danger for nothing.

Jake knows that mothers will leave the country for any reason, just to be away from him. Knows that fathers can freeze up, like a program, staying stuck for the rest of their days. Jake knows that right now everything makes him mad and everything needs to be hit with his baseball bat and he knows he's carrying the brass band with him and followers should show up when they say they will.

He stops in the middle of the bridge and finally looks over the edge.

• • •

OR WHAT ABOUT a drone strike? Something unmanned, unpiloted, a weapon streaking into your life, poised to deliver its deadly cargo, no matter what gets ruined. Who gets ruined. Without even contemplating the legacies, the impossible detritus of trying to inhabit a smashed existence.

It's a drone strike, this blame explosion. Noah911 is engulfed in guilt.

This is the spot. He's watched the video so many times that he's sure this is the exact spot where the brass band jumped. He waits to feel close to Tracey, to feel her aura, her ghost, her kiss, but that's not happening. He's here alone with his Ziploc bag. He's here alone and there's only one way to feel close to her again.

Noah911 registers a kid standing nearby fiddling with his phone. Then Noah911 is right at the rail. In the middle of the bridge. Noah911 looks over the edge. Noah911 mutters more apologies, begs for mercy, clutches the Ziploc bag like it's a Bible.

THE CAR BARELY stops before Rodney jumps out, and Sara tries to keep up. They are in the parking lot next to the bridge, on the San Francisco side. Rodney tries to run, but he's limping really badly, slowing down with each stride. His foot must be broken.

"You . . . run," he says.

"What can I do?"

"Run!"

It's comical to Sara: She shouldn't be his proxy. She's too small to do anything. But if she sees them, at least she will be there. Try and get a couple beefy guys to help her. She'll figure it out. Whatever he wants. However she can assist. If Jumper Julie had the courage to walk this path and do what she did, then Sara can summon an unknown strength to help Rodney.

"I'll find her," she says.

NOAH911 PUSHES AGAINST the railing, at the edge, and he is crying. This is goodbye and he fingers the bag, traces its contours cautiously. He squeezes it, not with any anger but as a last way to show love. Noah911 ponders whether it was his mother or father who found his plate of leftovers in the kitchen after the funeral. Are they worried, wondering what he's doing, or are they lost in the arts and crafts studio, pretending not to remember?

He opens the Ziploc bag and shakes out the ashes. Her ashes. Tracey. He shakes her into the air, not seeing a drone strike but something with beauty to it. Tracey snakes from the Ziploc bag and for a moment the ashes circle and sit in the air like a swarm of bees.

Noah911 gets one second with all of the ashes frozen in the air. Face to face with them. Her. His sister. One last look in each other's eyes.

Then they flutter off in every direction; she flutters off in every direction.

Noah911 was wrong before about needing that YouTube clip. This is better. This is what he needs, the memory of watching her cremains drift in the sky. She's not that video. She doesn't come to life with the click of play. She doesn't die at the end. YouTube has nothing to do with his sister. She is a mosaic now, living in his heart, each tile a memory that if he stands back and examines their configuration, he sees Tracey.

He puts the Ziploc bag in his pocket and turns to walk away.

It's poetic, Albert, I'll give you that, it makes sense to trigger me with the scattering of ashes since our mission is to keep the world uncremated, and once I see the man throw the ashes up into the wind, I know I need to move to that precise spot. It's where the portal will open, this woman will move away from this world and once she's gone, you will materialize. I'm so curious to see what you'll look like. I'm excited to shake your hand. This woman doesn't seem to know what's coming, she moves next to me, clutching her purse. I steer her with a hand on her forearm, but she's not squawking or fighting me at all and the greenhouse gas of human sadness is almost over.

I'm so curious to see what you'll look like.

23.

There's the issue of Jake's bit rate. How many bits of his pathos can be processed per second. How it can be compressed to travel faster. How he is inflamed with anger and betrayal, how he feels so dumb for expecting to see a congregation of his followers. They said they'd be here. They told him that. They promised. But the only guy standing at the railing holds some dusty bag and he is crying and Jake wants his people, his friends. He hates being lied to and he's stupid for thinking his followers were real. They were like him, sitting in front of their computer or phone, and they never wanted to meet the real Jake. They don't care. He's alone and he's so tired of believing and being let down. He just wants one follower to show, one real breathing human to care.

All these compressed emotions and he needs to express them, needs to jettison some of the spam coursing through him, delete it, throw it away. How can he get rid of all the noise?

Jake needs a multimedia projection of his sadness, including audio and video, meaning motor control, meaning breathing, meaning facial expressions, meaning talking, meaning corresponding body language, then he needs to make sure his veins—those Ethernet cables under his skin—are capable of transferring all that data quickly enough.

Like how an HD DVD has 29.4 Mbit/s. That would be ideal.

Because now there is one follower standing in front of him: his dad. Jake needs to interact with his dad, seeing as how Paul screams at him, "What are you doing?"

Jake keeps near the edge.

"Will you step away from the railing?" a guy says, someone even fatter than his dad, someone in a cheap suit.

"Are you another therapist?" Jake says.

"I'm a police officer."

"Am I in trouble?"

"The opposite," Esperanto says.

Jake pauses, wondering what exactly is the opposite of trouble. Pleasure? Happiness? Peace? Siri would know.

"Stay away from me," says Jake. "I have to do something."

"LET'S STOP," SAYS Wes.

There are so many people around them that Kathleen can't figure out why she's not screaming. Someone would help. That's what happens. People help each other. Get out one syllable, one simple noise. Yell like Felix did over the phone. Talk like Rodney. Choke out any sound.

Instead, she does as she's told, stopping.

"Your hand," he says.

"Huh?"

Finally, she makes a noise. That wasn't so hard. Make another. Make the same. Do it louder. Save your life.

"Give me your hand," says Wes.

• • •

THIS IS WORSE than falling off the balloon because at least Rodney did that to himself. This is his mom. This is his mom who needs his help but his foot can't go more than a mile per hour and he's embarrassed and she needs him and he's letting her down and he's trying, Mom, he's trying his best, he trudges on with his broken foot, every now and again he tries to run but the pain is too much.

Balloon Boy is a bone, and a bone is a bomb, and its ignition in his foot blasts through him, up his leg like a chimney, ringing through his chest cavity, blazing in his guts.

THE TILE FROM his memory mosaic that speaks to Noah as he's walking away on the bridge, toward San Francisco, is this: Way back during her junior year in high school, Tracey sits in the driver's seat of her new car. Taking it out for the first time. By herself. She'd gone out with Noah and she'd gone around the block with their parents, but this was her first time navigating the streets alone. Responsible for herself. She has a huge smile on her face. Both hands on the wheel. The light blue polish on her nails is chipped, but she grips that wheel, ready to hit the open road.

There's his sister sitting in her car and smiling.

Noah and their parents watch her drive off.

SARA SPOTS KATHLEEN Curtis. There's a moment of second-guessing. But it's her. Sara's sure. Sara saw Kathleen every day for years, and Kathleen looks pretty much the same.

Sara spots Kathleen standing at the railing holding hands with the guy in the lab coat.

Looking like she's upset.

Distraught even.

A slithering panic.

• • •

PAUL IS FIVE or six feet away and doesn't know which impulse to trust: Should he bum-rush Jake, tackle him, throw himself at him?

Or should he talk to him, try and settle him down?

Or should he shut up and let Esperanto handle it?

Paul doesn't have much time to dwell on this decision because Jake says, "I have to do something."

"What?" Esperanto says.

"A hard reset."

"I don't understand what that means."

"Where are my followers?"

"Do you mind if I walk to you?" Esperanto says.

"Don't you come fucking near me!" Jake says.

"Okay, I won't, stay calm," the detective says.

"Can I walk to you?" Paul says.

Jake says nothing, only stares at him.

"Here I come," says his father.

I pick her up, Albert. I am holding her aloft.

24.

Sara sees the man lift Kathleen, and Sara looks back toward Rodney yelling his name. He's way back there. He's too far away. He won't be here in time.

Vibrating phone hands are nothing because now she's a whole cell tower. She's being inundated with signals, and her body ricocheting around. It's a fiasco, a frenzy. Sara shakes with all the incoming calls, all telling her what to do, ordering her around. Run away. Help Kathleen. A complete annihilation of her head, too many sounds and voices and motives and plans and agendas, so Sara just stands there.

THE VOLTAGE WRITHING in his body doesn't matter anymore, not after Balloon Boy hears Sara yelling his name. He's running. He's sprinting on the broken bone.

"I HAVE TO do something that you're not going to like," says Jake.

"What?" Paul asks.

EVERYTHING THAT HAD been stored inside Kathleen erupts. She's like a bottled beer that's been shaken, and the cap comes off, spraying everywhere, and thinking about a bottled beer reminds her that she still has one in her purse, and she can crack him with it. She reaches and retrieves the bottle for a second, but it slips from her hand. Clacks on the walkway but doesn't break.

She rakes Wes with her fingernails. She shrieks. She's getting higher and higher.

"WHAT THE FUCK?" Esperanto says, grabbing his walkie-talkie and talking to the other units stationed in the parking lot. Paul hears his voice describe the man hoisting the woman. Paul sees the detective walking toward the crime, only fifteen feet away. Paul sees Esperanto's hand on his holster.

"It's you and me," Paul says to his son.

NOAH HEARS A commotion coming from back toward the middle of the bridge. He sees a woman up in the air, being waved around by a man. He sees a woman being taken advantage of, sees another tragedy brewing here, and Noah takes off running. Tracey might be gone, but he can help this woman.

He passes Rodney, who limps along as best he can. They'll both be there soon.

BUT SARA IS already there. She is here. She is with Kathleen. She is with the man. Sara tries to think of what to do, and as she contemplates a man pushes past her—a guy whose face is beaten up—and he storms toward the man in the lab coat, and he punches him twice in the stomach and Kathleen is free, dropped on the walkway, and the man with the beaten-up face falls down and wraps himself around her, holds Kat in a hug, protects her.

But the man in the lab coat recovers quickly, keeps his gaze on them both. Sara knows he's gathering himself, another attempt brewing, and that's when she sees the beer bottle down at their feet.

That's when she leans down and grabs it.

That's when Sara swings her arm back.

ESPERANTO HAS HIS gun pointed at Wes, who is lying on the walkway, several men penning him in against the bridge's rail. Paul can see all this, and he understands, he guesses, why Esperanto had to get involved, but he can use some help with his son. There's still the issue of the finale. There's still what's going on inside his boy.

THE BOTTLE IS still in Sara's hands. She lets it fall, skittering on the walkway. She swung it at his face for all the rest of them. All the others who have harmed her, who have harmed anyone, all the monsters who think it's okay to prey on people. She falls close to the man holding Kathleen, nuzzling against them. She looks at his damaged and kind face. Her hands are buzzing again but in a different way.

KATHLEEN CAN'T DO anything. Except move on hands and knees. Back a few feet. Retreat from Wes. Get as far away from him as she can. Get away from the two people holding her. Finally, she is alone, lying in a heap, blinking her eyes like crazy.

"Kathleen," a young woman says, one of the people who were down next to her. "It's Sara. Sara Clancy."

Kathleen keeps blinking.

"Kathleen," Sara says.

"Sara?"

"Are you okay?"

"I don't know . . . " Kathleen's words trail off, stop off, pausing. She can't say anything else because it's her son. Her son! Limping up to her. Panting. Sweaty. Her son, Rodney, and Sara with her on the bridge.

Rodney leans down.

"Mom," he says.

JAKE DIDN'T FILM the fight. He was so close to the action. A few feet away. He could've posted this too, shepherded this disaster, but why, what's the point, it doesn't matter; he learned today that his followers are hoaxes. They are ghosts. They don't care about him.

There are other ghosts, too. The brass band. He captured them here and ever since that morning he's felt haunted, and he doesn't want that burden.

"They're in here," Jake says to his dad, shaking his iPhone. He presses the button to get that *boing-boing* noise and asks Siri, "Should I keep doing this?"

"Jake, I'm not sure what to say," Siri says.

It's when Siri uses Jake's name that he almost starts crying, but he's not going to. Astronauts do not weep during moonwalks. And he's not sure why when Siri says his name he feels comforted, and cared for, and when that lip-pursing therapist or his parents call his name he feels the opposite. He feels chastised, reprimanded, cornered. He feels violent.

Siri has reached out through that user interface and caressed his cheek and made him feel better, like doing this is possible, and Jake takes a step toward the railing and his dad says, "What are you doing?"

Both father and son are right at the bridge's railing.

The father's hand firmly bunches up Jake's shirt, pulling him, like a bully. Jake tries to fight free and turns his body toward the edge and then Jake throws his iPhone, throws it as far as he can, arcing down to the ocean.

Why?

Because he has no choice. Because it's become an urn full of digital ashes and it's the only way he can get rid of the ghosts, scattering them where they died. It's the only way he can separate them from himself.

IT'S BALLOON BOY and his mom and Sara, sitting on the walkway.

"Rodney?" Mom says.

"Mom," he says again.

"What are you doing here?"

It's hard to pick words to say, so Rodney smiles. It's been many years, and yet Balloon Boy and his mom are united again. Thanks to Sara. She made sure their lives went on. Made sure that every now and again you end up where you're supposed to.

"You," Balloon Boy says to his mom.

"Me?"

"You," he says, hugging her.

I'll flail one last time, one final flop to break out. All these men with angry faces and black eyes pen me in, saying to stay down, stay cool, you sick bastard, and not one of them realizes what they're doing, that they're jeopardizing the future. One final flail and I can go over the edge, which isn't ideal, Albert, which is the last thing we want, but a martyr has to do the unthinkable during emergencies and so I'll sacrifice myself for you, our savior. These men are trying to fight me back down, and the cop draws his gun and points it at me, and there's blood all over my face, not simply in my mouth, but spilling from my forehead. I'm woozy and cold and they use the bridge's railing as a back wall, but they don't know that's the direction I need to go to cool down our despairs. The cop has the gun trained on me but it's impossible to tell him how much sense this makes. I climb over the railing. All that's left to do is let go. My fingers relax, fingers open, fingers lose contact. I'll hit the water and open the portal and you'll save us, Albert, I'll be gone but everyone will experience a rebirth, a reboot. They'll all have lives pardoned from sadness and I'm thankful that the last thing anyone will see of me on my way down to the ocean is my lab coat fluttering behind me like a hero's cape.

25.

Despite her bruised face and an undiagnosed concussion, Deb is like a den mother the next day, ordering everyone around. She shuttles Rodney and Sara to the ER, to get a cast on his foot, and while they wait their turn to be helped, Deb makes sure Kathleen hits a meeting.

"I'm too mortified for a meeting," Kathleen had said when it was first brought up.

"Go get a chip," Deb had said. "That's all. You don't have to share, but you need your one-day coin."

True to her word, Deb didn't make Kathleen share during the meeting. It was hard enough finding the courage for Kathleen to stand up and walk to the front for the silver chip. Most people at this meeting knew Kathleen, so seeing her collecting a one-dayer told them all they needed to know. She took a deep breath and made her way to the front, but something strange happened: She didn't feel much embarrassment retrieving the chip. She had some shame, yet she also had her son. It was impossible for Kathleen to separate these beginnings.

She knew that going forward Deb would watch her closely, make Kat do ninety meetings in ninety days, rebuild that foundation. Kathleen doesn't want to come across as overconfident because nothing will conjure another relapse quicker than hubris, but it isn't an opulent confidence. It's having somebody to lose now that's tempering her reaction. She's not going to jeopardize anything with Rodney. This is the first day and her commitment radiates.

After the meeting, Kathleen and Deb walk in Dolores Park across from Kat's place, killing time until Rodney and Sara call saying they're done at the ER. It had rained overnight, but the skies are clear, blue. It's a little past nine, unusually hot, and they wend the path through the park, toward the playground. No parents or kids out there playing, at least none that Kathleen can see. The rain puddles heat from the sunshine, changing states, and steam makes the playground look like the set of a horror movie, dry ice concealing some lurking monster.

"Are they staying with you?" Deb says.

"I don't really know."

"You haven't asked?"

"I'm trying not to put on any pressure," Kathleen says, "but my inn does have a sudden vacancy."

"I'm so glad you're still with us," Deb says. "I'm trying to keep my mouth shut about what he tried to do, but I'm thankful you're still here."

Kathleen is wrong; there is a parent and child in the playground. She can hear voices and giggles but can't see them through the steam. "Don't make me cry."

"Okay, we'll talk about it later." Deb's phone chimes and she checks the text. "It's Sara. They're done."

"Let's go get them," Kathleen says.

"I want you to work today," says Deb. "I don't want any moping or awkwardness. Take them to work with you."

"Why?"

"You can't be idle after a relapse. Especially with Rodney around. Keep busy. I'll go, too. It will be fun."

"I trust you," Kathleen says.

BALLOON BOY IS getting the hang of this. The cast clicks in the hospital corridor, making a noise that reminds him of a cowboy's spur.

"How does it feel?" a nurse says.

"Great," he says, and he means it, clicking around the hall. This cast means that everyone is safe. It means that Sara is out of that motel's bathtub, and his mom is off the bridge. This cast means that a broken foot is the lowest price to pay for all he's received.

"I texted that we're done," Sara says. "They're on the way."

"Oh. Kay."

"Did you get any painkillers?"

Balloon Boy shakes his head hell no.

"I told you to give them to me!" Sara says.

"Sor . . . ree." But he doesn't mean it. The last thing Sara needs is painkillers.

"Let's wait outside."

They move out front of SF General, standing on Potrero Avenue. Traffic whizzes by. A bus hisses and kneels, lowering itself so a woman with a walker can get in. Rodney sits on the curb. Sara stands behind him. She doesn't want to see his eyes when she asks this next batch of questions. She can't imagine getting the wrong answer.

"Are you going to stay here?" she asks.

He shrugs.

"I don't have to go home," Sara says, thinking about her dead-end job that she might not have and her dead-end love life that she doesn't want and her dead-end brother who can't stand her anymore.

Why run back to a cinderblock life? "I mean, if you're going to stay here for a while, I can, if you want."

"Please. Stay." Only four seconds.

She relaxes and sits on the curb next to him, leans her head on his shoulder. "Have you called your dad?"

He shakes his head hell no again, then rests his on hers. Not exactly making out, though feeling the warmth of her head on his skin is wonderful. Balloon Boy wishes it were the old days, behind that 7-Eleven, kissing by the dumpster, but he'll take what he can get.

"They're probably fishing in the street anyway," says Sara.

THE FOUR OF them arrive at Kathleen's favorite spot in front of Pier 39. Balloon Boy helps his mom unload her art supplies, his cast still clicking like a spur. Sara and Deb trail behind them, making small talk, both avoiding anything about yesterday.

"There is a no moping ordinance," Deb says. "We're all going to have fun today. This is a mandatory fun zone." Deb pulls out a pair of binoculars. "I mean, how fun are these?"

"What are those for?" Kathleen says, setting up her easel.

"People-watching."

There really isn't anyone out here yet, the tourists trickling out of hotel rooms for designer coffee. By noon, the Embarcadero will be packed.

"We're people," Sara says. She has an urge to mention the sex tape, but she's not going to. She remembers seeing an old horror movie where a woman is being hunted in her dreams by a madman. The whole movie takes place in her head, really. She spends most of the film screaming, hiding, running away, fighting him off. But by the end, she won't do any of that anymore. She's had enough, decides to stand her ground and tell the madman that she takes it all back, every yelp, every stride, every bead of sweat, every tear. And once she stops empowering him by believing, he has no way to kill her.

He tries, swinging a metal claw at her face and chest, but it passes right through her like vapor. He is dematerializing. He is powerless without her fear. Sara will work on doing that to the sex tape.

"How about a picture?" Deb says. "Can you draw us all?"

"Let me finish setting up and I'll get on it," says Kat.

Deb points her binoculars at the Golden Gate Bridge. Balloon Boy senses that something catches her eye and asks, "What?"

She hands him the binoculars. Rodney puts them to his eyes and Deb guides him in the right direction with a pointer finger.

"Do you see that guy?" Deb says. There's a man working on a scaffold way up near one of the bridge's towers and Rodney nods. "He's painting the bridge," Deb says. "They have to do it all year, every year. The saltwater and fog strip off the paint pretty fast, and they're always touching it up. They call those spots scars."

"Let me see," says Sara, and Rodney hands her the binoculars. "Do they really call them scars?"

"Cross my heart," Deb says.

"The bridge is so pretty from here," Sara says. "You'd never know what happened yesterday."

Kathleen watches the three of them hand the binoculars back and forth, taking turns peering up as the man erases the scars with new paint. Sara's right: The bridge is beautiful from here. It is the site of her near-murder not even twenty-four hours ago, yet watching the sun hit its orange beams, the bridge shimmers, postcard perfect. Kathleen can't see any traffic from this angle, only the huge towers, the tangle of wires like a nest, the arch across the ocean. The sky is clear and the sun hits the ocean and bounces the brightness back up, making it almost too much light to bear.

Too bad that they can't point those binoculars and see into the future. Too bad they can't see Noah three weeks from now, sitting in a tapas restaurant in the Mission, at one of the new chic spots that Kathleen detests. He's on a first date, his inaugural social outing since Tracey died.

He had forgotten about his match.com profile until he got this notification email: "Swagga_gurl has winked at you!" He clicked on her page, read all about her, sent a note right back. Here was a woman who knew nothing about him, nothing about his sister, and that sounded fantastic.

They will go out a few more times, but nothing comes of it. It fizzles; they fizzle. Both will tell people that nothing was wrong with the other, there simply wasn't a connection. That word! Connection. To be connected. To be bridged across any divides. To be plugged into a network. To be alive.

It doesn't matter that they didn't connect. It only matters that Noah took the time to meet her, that he's trying, that the rate of vodka bottles being emptied in his apartment is slowing. There are no directions for putting the pieces together, like his dad assembling that chair in the new arts and crafts studio. No, Noah has to make it up as he goes along.

If the binoculars are pointed in a different direction, they can see Wes's body being immolated. Nobody claimed him, and six weeks after his death he was shipped to a county facility. To be cooked alone.

He is loaded into a cardboard casket and slid into the retort. A steel door lowers, the brick walls smeared with the film of thousands of deaths. Black smudges like signatures.

She was here.

He was here.

A few wands jet from the retort's ceiling, like stalactites. Fire wisps innocently at the ends of these until a worker throws the switch, and these wands are alive with fire. It engulfs the cardboard casket. The lid is the first to lose its solidity; slowly the sides slip away too. There's a moment when he lies there naked, completely whole. A flash before the fire does what fires do, and Wes starts disappearing. His skin bubbles and pops from the scorch. Skin smoldering. Hair burns and soon skin is torn, huge holes forming and showing his ribcage, see the matter and organs baking and burning, turning to ash. Watch his heart lose its codes of love, watch his heart cave in. The worker throws the switch again to turn off the fire, and he opens the oven's doors, collecting what remains.

Pity the binoculars can't spy Paul and Jake. They sit in the therapist's office, in the waiting room without any hanging meringue, the one with six chairs, a palm tree, a rickety Formica coffee table with old magazines.

Jake is dreading what will happen once he's ushered inside. What he'll find out. What he'll have to talk about. What he'll have to hear. Siri only answers questions that she's been asked. This doctor will pose anything he wants and sit there practicing his lip-pursing until Jake participates.

Paul is scared, too. What's going on in his psyche is a collision of extremes: He wants to know the doctor's diagnosis, and yet that information is the last thing he can bear hearing.

Finally, the doctor's door opens, and he wanders a few steps into the waiting room and asks Jake if he's ready.

The boy stands up but doesn't move toward the office, repulsed by the fact that the doc is already pursing his lips and he hasn't even asked any of his questions yet. Jake begins an entirely different walk on an entirely different moon.

"Go ahead," Paul says, ushering his boy with a supportive shove in the lower back.

Jake takes three steps and stops. He doesn't want to have his hard drive opened, doesn't want anybody running diagnostics and a debugger, doesn't want his head combed for malware. "Would you like to come in and talk?" the doctor asks.

Jake hasn't moved, looks back at his dad. Perhaps that first astronaut peered over his shoulder to the probe, to the others on his team, before striking out into the magnificent desolation. He's scared and maybe that's okay. Jake takes the next three steps, then crosses the threshold into the office before the doctor shuts the door.

There Paul sits. In the waiting room. In the dark. Trusting this man to help his child. He stares at the closed door, settling in, waiting for the hour to elapse, waiting an impossible amount of time to hear impossible news, hoping, tenderly hoping, that today turns out to be the best day of their lives.

"YOU ALL READY to be drawn?" Kathleen asks.

Deb, Sara, and Rodney huddle together, posing for their picture. They make silly faces. Sara, for some unknown reason, hums "Purple Haze."

"Remember that you have to draw yourself in this picture, too," Deb says. "We all have to be in it."

"Gotcha."

"We all have to be in it," Deb says.

Kat's sponsor knew she'd try to weasel out of putting herself in, and Kathleen is thankful for that. She wants to be accountable, and Deb is the perfect hard-ass to help her do that.

"Yes, fine," says Kathleen, "we're all going to be in it."

She starts this caricature, this family portrait of sorts, all the survivors. She puts the Golden Gate Bridge in the background, but doesn't paint it solid orange. No, she likes the idea of it showing its scars, and she leaves it mottled, gray patches all over it. She draws her boy first, her boy who has shown up at this surreal time, and she captures his face's likeness flawlessly, the only exaggerated detail is the cast on his leg, which is made of clouds in the picture, something to coddle his injury. Then she gets cracking on Sara, who once said that she was plenty scathed but in ways the naked eye couldn't see, so Kat evokes that by making Sara's skin solid gold;

there might be something severe swimming under the surface, but Kathleen wants to show Sara that no one cares. She has value. She's priceless. And it's easy to draw Deb because Kat wants to show her the same skyscraping respect that she heaps on the cancer survivors in her shop: Kathleen doesn't draw Deb's fat lip or swollen cheek or black eye, no, she draws lush vines snaking around her face, looking like a garden nymph.

There's only one person left to capture in this caricature, and there are so many ways to distort herself, so many ways to be acerbic and cruel. Take your pick. She's made so many mistakes. But she decides to take it easy on herself today. Why? She was almost thrown from a bridge, and if that doesn't buy you a morning of clemency, she's not sure what does.

Instead of being masochistic, Kathleen draws herself standing next to Rodney, her arm thrown over his shoulders, draws herself with one-day AA chips for eyes.

"How do we look?" Deb says.

"Yeah, are we gorgeous or what?" Sara says.

"Pret. Tee?" Rodney says.

Caricatures, avatars, usernames, however humans present themselves, whatever we are, there is one thing Kathleen knows: We are all scared. We are haunted by yesterday and terrified of tomorrow. It's this life, all this life, and we're frightened of it. There are addictions and relapses. There are weather balloons and wars, sociopaths and estrangements. There's climate change, mental illness, mood disorders. There are families assembling and dissembling. There are dubious genes dripping down. There are more strains of violence than the flu. The particulars of human misery are limitless, a rising ocean of humiliations and blues, too-low paychecks and pipe dreams. People cling so hard to so little, everything eroding a little more every day. It's enough to make you pour whiskey on an open wound or jump off a bridge. But that's what we have to endure.

Kathleen now knows that we need the scars on our skin before the tattoos envelop that ugly. We need those stakes stacked so high that we're lost in order to understand that it's okay to be lost. We will always be lost. We are the walking wounded and there's love in our hearts.

And then Kathleen turns her portrait around.

ACKNOWLEDGMENTS

First thing's first: Thanks to the indie booksellers! If it wasn't for your tireless and often thankless work, indie writers like me wouldn't have careers. From the bottom of my heart, you are so important. Keep fighting the good fight.

Thanks to Dan Kirschen and ICM. He endured several remixes of this book, none of which were very good, and he never lost patience with me, and if he did, he was gracious enough to only talk shit behind my back.

My editor, Dan Smetanka, challenged me in a way I'd never previously been tested. He called it a "tear down," said that he liked the characters and the plot of "All This Life," but wanted me to find a much more earnest tone to tell it, which meant writing the whole thing from scratch, basically. And that's what we did, from August through December 2014. It was brutal and insane and formidable and infuriating, and it's the best thing that ever happened to me. You are pure talent, Smetanka!

Cheers to all at Counterpoint/Soft Skull. Charlie Winton and Rolph Blythe. The publicity folks, Megan Fishmann, Sharon Wu, Claire Shalinsky, Corinne Kalasky, all held my hand. Kelly Winton put together a lovely artifact. I mean, this book in your hands is super pretty, right?

The San Francisco Writers' Grotto is a rad place to scribble and a much needed artistic sanctuary for me. My colleagues there continue to dazzle and inspire with their own projects.

The MFA program at the University of San Francisco still lets me teach there sometimes, despite all the weed I sell to the students. And Stanford's OWS is probably the best job I've ever had, except the summer I was a chimney sweeper.

Every author needs smart readers to help them along the way and huge thanks to the following for their wise eyeballs: Ron Currie, Sean Doyle, Andrew Ervin, Anisse Gross, Calder Lorenz, Tyler McMahon, and Lauren Saft.

Also, a certain unnamed novelist may or may not have needed someone to swoop in at the last minute and stop an avalanche of public embarrassment for a glaring error in the text, and that savior was Lori Hettler. She's a generous reader and the mastermind behind The Next Best Book Club. Go to your computer and check out her site right now.

Thanks to Diane and Sarah, Jess and Katy, Shany and Kerrie and Veronica, Eric and Eliza, Rob and Gina.

And finally, my girls, Lelo and Ava. It is a beautiful life.